The Moon.

Population: One hundred and fifty million humans, bioroids, bots, and xenos. There were rumors it was something like three times that in terms of population, but no one could really tell for sure because most of the place was underground. There were vast networks of interlocked tunnels, gravity manipulator stations, and hastily domed settlements cobbled together during the Second Space Race. That had occurred when humanity had been given cheap and easy space travel by the Lizards about a century ago. History, am I right?

The Moon was also the ass end of civilization. Human civilization at least. A place owned and operated by the transtellars that were mining the hell out of Sol's asteroid belts to produce the starships necessary to colonize planets that were amendable to humanoid inhabitation. Since any sane person would live on Earth or one of its luxury space stations instead of the Moon, it was a dumping ground for workers who were desperate for cash, grifters, low-rent criminals, and the descendants of refugees from Earth's Unification Wars.

It was, for all its majestic astral beauty, a dive. The place to send you when assigning you to Antarctica wasn't far enough for your angry bosses' satisfaction. Which I knew because I was being reassigned from the Antarctic PD to the Moon. It was, according to my contract, my home for the indefinite future unless I managed to pull off some sort of miracle that would allow me back to home sweet Terra.

MOON CITY VICE

Book Two of the Moon Cops Series

C. T. Phipps

CAST OF CHARACTERS

Lead
Neal S. Gordon: A former Atlas Security Marine turned Martian Detective. Neal stopped a conspiracy on Mars, but the consequences have gotten him reassigned to first Antarctica and now the Moon.

Supporting Cast
Priscilla Aim: Lead singer of the Knights and popular underground hyper-punk artist. Very little is known about the hard edged progressive rockstar.

Rashad Al-Fariq: A dataslicer and infonet journalist who goes by the handle of "Big Brother." He is, unfortunately, wanted by both authorities and his fellow criminals.

Farah "Cherry" Al-Fariq: Rashad's hostess sister that is in heavy debt to the Syndicate. She's not motivated by his love of justice.

Armstrong: A theatrical AI that is the secret master of all the Moon's functions and also the head of the Cyberlife Division of the Luna City Police Department.

Charles Barksley: A sentient toy Welsh corgi made for nannying children. Charles gained sentence due to a quirk in his programming and has since taken up work with the Moon's corporate police.

Nigel Blackwood: A Martian detective and Neal Gordon's former partner. He was a dirty cop and involved in a xeno-human trafficking plot. He also severely injured Neal despite their supposed friendship.

Ayanna Breeze: Star of a popular yet singularly awful series of trashy movies. Ayanna Breeze is the mother of Lucy and Shinobu. She is as immortal and ever beautiful as being super rich can achieve.

Tommy "The Razor" Calivari: A high-ranking independent crime boss with ties to both the food and narcotics trades.

Penny Cash: Second in command of the Church of Money and a famous television show commentator and political talking head.

Vitellius Cicero: A member of the Sons of Mithras terrorist organization and drug manufacturer.

Deep Thought: The central AI of Karma Corp and one of the most powerful on the Moon.

Dick Grayson: The deceased lover of Lucy and former holder of Neal's job. Dick was killed by dusting and his murder remains unsolved.

Shinobu Harris: The kooky daughter of Ayanna Breeze and sister of Lucy. Shinobu has a love of guns, quilting, and talking animals. She serves as the quartermaster, armorer, and avatar of the Cyberlife police department.

Zoe Hopewood: New Military Governor of the Moon and appointee of EarthGov. She is trying a softer touch with the unruly Lune populace.

Steve Rogers Hudson: A Lunar Ranger and ex of Lucy's. He has recently gotten some questionable company.

Kathleen "Kate" Roebuck: An Atlas Space Assault Warrior who has a past relationship with Neal.

Nena Romanova: One of the Knights hyper-punk band, and a former special operations team medic. Trans rights activist.

Gerard "Doctor Frankenstein" Saint Croix: A formerly famous cyberneticist who is presently hiding out on the Moon.

Aurelius Saxon: A cat psychologist and immigrant from Albion.

Mr. Smiles: A corrupt pimp and petty crime lord who runs a nightclub called the Hearts on Fire.

Lucy Westenra: The star of a vampire hunting infovision show who was bio-sculpted, enhanced, and then discarded. She proceeded to sign up for Atlas Security and received her information warfare degree before joining the LDPD.

Lady Zero: A mysterious vigilante with a mad on for killing slavers.

CHAPTER ONE

On a Stakeout with a Talking Dog

So, I was on a stakeout with a talking dog.

Charles Barksley was a bioroid Pembroke Welsh corgi with golden white fur and a pair of glasses that could turn into sunglasses on command. Tonight, he had them polarized and was wearing a ball cap that read POLICE, as well as a little square crystal badge hanging from his collar. The badge identified him as a member of Atlas Security's Cyberlife Division. We were corpo cops, not civi cops, but the distinction barely mattered on the Moon where the corporations had the contracts for providing security for their parent company's employees.

Which was just about everyone.

The Moon's civi police were a combination of corrupt, ignorant, and lazy so anything other than food smuggling was generally kicked up the chain to us. Cyberlife specialized in technology crimes but in the 23rd century, that pretty much could be anything. I'd dealt with robberies, homicides, insurance fraud, and even terrorism since coming to the Moon a year ago.

Cyberlife had been the dream of the Moon's mad computer god, Armstrong, and a last ditch "bailing water out of a sinking ship" plan to help with the lunar colony's all-encompassing crime problem. It was a department assembled from the best, albeit quirkiest, police officers in the solar system with a job to do real investigative work against dangerous criminals. I was using it to make war on criminals who were normally above the law and had money as well as power protecting them. It was a new experience having support against them.

Barksley and I were sitting in a ratty apartment building across the street from another equally ratty apartment building in the Deep. The Deep was the darkest depths of Luna's colony and made Crater Town look like Luna City. The windows of both apartment buildings were boarded over with cardboard lining them, and our room was empty except for a bedroll and a few hundred pieces of advanced surveillance equipment. Barksley and I were across from one another, fighting the boredom as we sat on our asses. It was significantly easier for my companion given he was, well, a dog.

We'd been here about three days, taking time off from our incredibly packed workloads to follow up on a tip given to me by my ex-partner turned suspiciously friendly archenemy, Nigel Blackwood. Nigel said this place was going to be the sight of an important meeting between some major players in the Slavers Guild (which I called the criminal conspiracy for lack of anything else to refer to it). Given we hadn't had any leads on the Guild in the past few months, I was willing to follow it up.

I wasn't exactly comfortable with this arrangement. Nigel was a Slavers Guild member himself and had shot off my leg and burned me alive. He'd also turned me into a posthuman cyborg without my consent. But comfort didn't mean a lot when you were up against criminals who were rich and powerful enough to avoid all consequences for their actions. I needed every advantage I could get, and if that meant dancing with the Devil then I guess I had to learn to waltz. Nigel had agreed to keep feeding me other members of the conspiracy, though, and so far, his information had panned out.

So far.

That wasn't what Barksley and I were talking about now, though, as the two of us ate from boxes of synthetic Chinese food delivered to us by a drone an hour ago. Well, I ate, and he watched. He could only eat specially designed food for bioroids (produced and sold by Ares Electronics of course). After three days, we'd mostly exhausted topics ranging from terrible movies we'd seen to the philosophy of whether the universe was a simulation or not. Barksley believed it was a giant hologram programmed by aliens and I didn't think it mattered whether life was an illusion or not. Neither of us followed sports. Which, unfortunately, only left relationships and other emotional stuff to discuss. Given he was an asexual toy dog, I did most of the talking. I was also getting *no* sympathy.

"So, let me get this straight, you and Lucy are still best friends," Barksley said before eating some of the noodles out of a paper box. He slurped them up and it was adorable.

"Partners," I said, pausing. "Which is a bit closer than friends."

"And having regular sex," Barksley said.

"We could have more," I replied, admitting our work schedules prevented us from hooking up more than once or twice a week. Which seemed an embarrassment of riches compared to some of my friends' social lives. But Lucy manifestly refused to stay the night or let me visit her apartment, so it depended on when she was near my place.

Well, Barksley's place. That was another odd element of my relationship with the talking dog. In the year or so that I'd been living on the Moon, I hadn't bothered to get my own place because Barksley offered me the opportunity to live in his apartment rent-free. Given the sky-high costs of real estate in the artificial atmospheres of the Moon's many domes, it seemed like a good deal at the time. Now I was starting to wonder as it was a real cramp in my style. Lucy had also made her feelings clear about moving in together: not a chance in Hell.

"But she doesn't want to move in, share bank accounts, and encourages you to sleep with other people," Barksley said.

"*See* other people," I replied, correcting him. It was a distinction without a difference since she'd offered to set me up with one of her old bandmates. I would have thought she was breaking up with me except for the fact we'd hooked up that very night. "Lucy says what we have is strictly friends with benefits. Casual hookups. A way to relieve stress."

"Despite the fact you've been dating a year," Barksley said.

"No, we just started sleeping together a year ago," I said. "We only started dating three months ago. At least, I thought we were dating. Now I'm not so sure. She keeps changing the parameters."

7

"Or you're looking for something she can't give. I remind you that," Barksley said, once more showing no sympathy. "Her last relationship ended badly."

That was an understatement. Lucy's last serious boyfriend was First Inspector Dick Grayson, my predecessor at Cyberlife, who had been dusted by parties unknown. That was a uniquely Moon-based method of execution where they dump a sack of the Moon's super-compact dirt over your head, which shreds your lungs.

"Yeah, I know," I said, admitting to myself that Lucy had never been anything but honest about our relationship. One of the first things you needed to learn in a relationship was to accept that your partner knew what they wanted and not try to change them.

"And your big issue is regular consequence-free sex with a beautiful woman?" Barksley asked, more than a hint of mockery in his tone.

I stared down at the dog before stabbing my General Tso's chicken with a fork. "Well, yeah."

Barksley rolled his eyes. "On the Moon—and most other human colonies for that matter—I think you'll find that qualifies you as *emotionally needy.*"

"I'm not going to be lectured on my sex life by a toy designed for toddlers," I replied, chewing down another mouthful of synthetic meat.

"Thank you, but I was designed for children four to twelve," Barksley corrected. "Also, you're the one who brought this up."

Swallowing, I said, "All I'm saying is that on Mars, we had a name for having sex with your best friend. It was called a *relationship.*"

"All I'm saying is you should respect Detective Westenra's boundaries," Barksley said, adjusting his glasses with his paw. I think they were built into him, so it was a purely an affectation. "If you're looking for more coitus in your life, you should know that I've actually set up a few profiles for you on various apps."

What was with everyone trying to set me up with hookups? "Oh, Christ, no."

Barksley lifted an infopad, which he apparently could do with a magnet or something on his paw, and held it in front of me. "It's called Finder and is very good at this. You already have three hundred hits."

"No, Barksley, no! Bad dog!" I said, grabbing the infopad from him.

"One of them claims she's an ex-girlfriend and has sent some very flattering pictures," Barksley said, cheerfully.

"Really?" I asked, sneaking a peek at the infopad.

"Ahem," a female voice filled the air. It was coming from the infopad's infocom feed and was a gentle reminder that we had a third officer participating in this stakeout: Lucy herself. I probably should have realized she'd left her connection open. She'd agreed to examine all the cameras and microphones we'd set up across the area and was probably on the roof.

"Thank you, God, I wasn't feeling your wrath enough this week," I muttered, closing my eyes. "Hi, Lucy! Did you hear any of that?"

"Would it help if I said no?" Lucy asked, sounding as embarrassed as I felt.

"Extremely," I replied.

"Too bad," Lucy said. "I heard everything. You *are* emotionally needy. Get a dog."

"Hey!" Barksley said, offended.

"I'm kidding," Lucy said. "Sort of. I don't understand your problem, but I hope we can work it out. I just hope it doesn't involve me changing my lifestyle or habits in the slightest. I'd hate for this to compromise our friendship. You're the third best lay in my life."

Lucy was just screwing with me now. "Thanks."

Barksley reached over and patted me on the knee. "There, there. Really, this is mostly a case of values dissonance. The early Moon settlers, or moonatics, had very cramped quarters, questionable gender ratios, and a massive hodge podge of cultures that caused reevaluation of existing taboos. Also, it was really barking boring, so they didn't have much to do but bark. Bark all the livelong day in every possible combination, position, and pairing. So, relationships are a lot more situational on the Moon."

I stared down at Barksley. "I see you have mastered word substitution."

"I don't know what you barking mean," Barksley said. "Bark off."

I rolled my eyes. "Well, if you're finished with humiliating me, do you have any updates, Lucy?"

"Oh, I'm never finished with humiliating you, Neal," Lucy said, jokingly. "It's my second favorite hobby after racquetball. However, I think it's time to call this stake out a bust. There's no sign of the big meeting your evil ex-partner said was going to happen soon and our other cases are piling up. We can leave surveillance equipment and hope that pans out."

I cursed. "Goddammit. I was really hoping this one would pan out."

"The Slavers Guild is your white whale," Barksley said, before pausing. "That's a reference to a book, by the way."

"I'm aware," I replied.

"It's called *Moby Dick*," Barksley said, continuing. "That's the whale's name, not anyone's genitalia."

"I *know*," I said, dryly. "I have read the occasional book over the years. Even ones without pictures of ladies."

"You see, it's about a captain who is obsessed with taking down the whale that cost him his leg and—" Barksley continued to explain the plot of the book, possibly because he knew he was annoying the hell out of me.

"I know!" I said, hoping to change topics. "I know the Slaving Guild is something I obsess over. Because they maimed me and *set me on fire*."

It had been on a mission against them that Nigel had done it at least. I'd gotten all of that replaced with posthuman nanotechnology, including a new leg, as well as a new face. That didn't get rid of the trauma, though. The only thing that would get rid of that would be taking them down and making sure that either their victims were recovered or avenged.

"Perhaps it is time to arrest Mr. Blackwood and close this case," Barksley said. "After all, he is perhaps the most direct object of your vengeance."

"He's given us names, evidence, and help against people we might not have otherwise been able to take down," I said, giving what even I knew to be an incredibly weak defense.

"A couple dozen," Lucy said, as if that wasn't worth it. "Given the number of people involved in the Slavers Guild were at least eleven thousand, it feels like he's just stringing us along. The highest ranking of the ones we'd gotten being a bunch of lawyers who were stupid enough to have themselves as clients. It's also interfering with our other work against equally nasty people of other criminal persuasions."

I hated to admit she was right, but she was right. I had dreams of taking down the Slavers Guild, but even if I knew the names of (most) everyone involved, proving their complicity in a court of law was almost impossible. There was also the fact that it was tough to choose who to go after hardest. There were thousands of little fish doing the actual kidnapping, murder, and transportation of the people sold to the alien crime syndicates. Was it worth it to let them off if it could build an iron clad case against the organizers who moved the money around behind the scenes and made the deals? Which, if any, was the better option?

"I'm not giving up on this," I replied, determined that I could at least make something resembling justice come from this turd sandwich. We'd managed to take down some big players in all of this, including the governor of the Moon, but that hadn't been enough. I wasn't sure anything could be except finding all the victims and returning them safe and sound. But the chances of that were between nonexistent and slightly less than me developing magical powers.

"Nor do I want you to," Lucy said, reassuring me that she didn't want to stop investigating. "I just think we should cut our losses with Nigel and open up our own separate investigation. We've been letting Nigel dictate who we go after and when. Well, I say we take him in and shake him down for everything he knows. Maybe he'll be more talkative with a set of cuffs on as well as ten thousand life sentences."

That was extremely tempting. I didn't know if it would work given he was the newly promoted Chief Security Officer (CSO) of Karma Corp, but I was the only man in the solar system who knew his real identity. To the public, Nigel Blackwood was John Black, the hero of the Knights concert terrorist attack. He would only have to kill or discredit me to—

"Holy milk bones," Barksley said, distracting me from my thoughts. "They're actually here."

"You're shitting me," Lucy said, showing she had the face of an angel but the mouth of a space port worker.

"Nope," Barksley said, going to a nearby camera and interfacing with its holographic display.

The holographic display showed no less than three Caliburn-9000 luxury flying cars descending from the sky to the rooftop of the building beside us. Furthermore, some old-fashioned ground transports were pulling up in front of the place as well. Given both buildings were abandoned due to being scheduled for demolition, it was an impressive display of muscle. I also recognized each of the vehicles' respective gangs by their tags: Fleur de Lis, Cyberpunk, and Golden Tigers. Three of the largest gangs on the Moon.

"We need facial identification on these guys," I said.

"Yes, because I am an idiot and didn't think of that," Barksley muttered. "I'm running a scan now."

"Lucy, do you have eyes on the Caliburns' passengers?" I asked. "I have a feeling they're not the usual scum."

"I'm the rooftop now," Lucy said. "Holy shit."

"I never understood that phrase," Barksley said, tapping the holographic display with his paws and nose, sitting on his hindquarters. "I understand holy milk bones but why excrement?"

I walked over to the equipment and tried to set up the microphones and DNA recording as best I could. This was all very high-tech stuff from EarthGov's security division and shouldn't be detectable to your typical gangster's anti-surveillance equipment, but I didn't want them picking up on our presence. There was a reason the windows were all boarded over with cardboard covering them. It kept people from looking in and people throwing rocks at the windows if nothing else.

"What is it?" I asked, getting an answer on the holographic feed as Lucy tagged each of the people getting out of the Caliburn-9000s.

It was, in simple terms, a mother lode of scum. There was Karma Corp's for-profit prison company's (Fiddler's Green) president, Johan Johansen; Logan Olafsson, the executive director of Xeno Affairs for the Colonial Council; Margaret Orleans, the Karma Corp R&D Specialist who had several outstanding warrants on Earth for illegal human testing; and Rodan Yadav of the Syndicate's Inner Council. There were a few more people the computer didn't recognize, and you have no idea how rare that is.

"This is basically the opening of *Thunderball*," Barksley said. "The boardroom of SPECTRE part, not the part with James Bond and a jet pack."

"I take it that's a movie?" I asked.

Barksley glared at me.

"If it wasn't made in the 1980s or 2180s, I don't know it," I said, raising my hands.

"Have you got any names on the gang members below?" Lucy asked, finishing her surveillance.

In fact, we had. I was surprised at the names there too. Quite a few of these guys were lieutenants in their respective gangs, and a couple of bosses, too. The others were blooded gang members with multiple suspected murders or warrants out for them. "It's SlaverCon and we have a bunch of special guests."

Nigel's tip had paid off and this was a collection of the major movers and shakers in the Slavers Guild. If we managed to implicate them in something criminal—and I suspected this gathering wasn't going to be about cupcakes and doilies—then we could potentially deliver a major blow to the organization.

"Can we get some sound here?" I asked, turning to Barksley.

"Aren't you in charge of sound?" Barksley asked.

"Yes, but I'm terrible at this," I said.

"Fine," Barksley said, staring at the equipment before it all leaped to life, functioning perfectly.

"Really?" I asked, turning to Barksley.

"I'm magic," Barksley replied.

I rolled my eyes. "Okay, let's see what these guys are saying."

"That would be the idea," Lucy muttered. "Okay, they're tagged, and I have audio feed. You should be receiving it now."

The holographic display focused on the big boys meeting on the roof over the gang members below. As I'd once said to a partner, the guys on Wallstreet steal a billion dollars and kill thousands of people by taking away their homes and ability to pay for medicine while the guys on the street kill one guy to steal a few hundred bucks. As hypocritical as it was to be a corporate stooge—bought and paid for— and hold these views, the prospect of going after these guys was much more enticing than their henchmen. If I didn't miss my guess, though, all these guys were guilty of crimes against humanity (or sapience since we'd discovered aliens and built AI).

Johan Johansen, a Norwegian man with a thick accent, spoke first, "Must we meet in this appalling hellhole?"

"It's off the grid from Armstrong's network," Margaret Orleans replied, a black woman in her mid-fifties. "Deep Thought's protections from our efforts do not apparently extend to crossing its brother AI. We've lost several high-profile agents in the past year and it's important that we get our ducks in a row before Project: Jenner."

Great, codenames. What was it with white collar criminals and codenames? In the military, you used codenames because you didn't want anyone figuring out what you were up to. Among criminals, they tended to choose names that were as closely tied to the project as possible like Operation: Kingkiller when trying to take down someone important or Operation: Chickenroost when they're, I dunno, stealing chickens. I didn't really think this metaphor through. Still, finding out what they were up to after a year of inactivity was important.

"We should kill Gordon and Westenra," Rodan Yadav said, immediately escalating things. The Syndicate boss was not someone to mince words and was powerful enough that being recorded saying these things didn't really threaten his freedom. Sadly, the march of technology meant that most of these things were inadmissible as evidence. Anything could be faked given enough time, but at least I knew who was plotting against me. In a way, it was flattering to know I'd made it onto his radar.

"They're peons," Johan said, immediately deflating my ego. "Just a pair of corporate goons marching at the order of Armstrong. Eliminating them will be like killing Grayson."

Wait, what?

"There're still questions on that elimination," Rodan replied. "Ones I want answered."

"Shit," Lucy said, hearing the name of her boyfriend before me.

"Someone is feeding them information," Johan said. "We need to cover up that leak and find out what they know."

"Nigel should be here," Logan Olafson said, speaking with a deep Martian drawl.

"I don't trust that Nigel isn't the leak," Yadav said.

Crap. They suspected. That, of course, was when the top of the building on which the gangsters were gathered exploded. The drones attacked seconds later.

CHAPTER TWO

I Hate Shootouts

Hollywood has a lot to answer for as does the new studio system they built on the remains of it when Los Angeles was paved over to build the New Angeles arcology. One of these things it must answer for is the depiction of explosions. For one, if you're anywhere near one, you're likely to get thrown down and deafened because they're explosions. Explosions are bad for you. You can't just power walk away from them without losing your hearing or catching shrapnel.

In our case, the explosion of the neighboring building's roof ended up causing our boarded-up windows to blow in as well as throwing me to the ground. If they hadn't been boarded up, I imagined it would have been even worse. I had no idea what they did to Lucy above us but it sure as hell wasn't good. Barksley, who had super strong hearing, ended up throwing his paws over his ears a little too late. All our equipment was ruined, and a fire broke out as our portable generator failed.

"What the hell!" I shouted, the ringing in my ears drowning out everything else.

INTERFACE ACTIVATED, a voice sounding like a dull monotone version of my own spoke. ATTACK AI APPROACHING. RECOMMEND DEFENSIVE MEASURES.

Interface was the computer program that managed my nanotech enhancements. The ones I'd neither asked for nor wanted. He was semi-sentient, which was a nice way of saying that he was more like a split personality of mine than an actual AI. Unfortunately, he was usually right and about the only way I could use any of my special tools.

No kidding! I thought back. *Do what you got to do to get us through this.*

ACKNOWLEDGED, Interface replied.

I felt immediately better as the tiny machines in my blood, stuff that human beings flat out had no equivalent technology for, prepared my body for combat. Posthumans were humans enhanced by Galactic Community technology—alien science—and it was far superior to bog standard cybernetics. Most posthumans were veterans of the Unification Wars, sponsored by the Galactic Community against the Neo-Militarists, but I'd received my enhancements from parties unknown. Maybe Nigel had done it to make up for burning me alive, I didn't know. However, at that moment I was just glad I wasn't dead.

"Barksley, you okay?" I shouted, drawing my Herakles-7 pistol before loading a very illegal clip of explosive ammunition. Herakles-7 pistols came with a stun setting and a separate cartridge for "icer" rounds that paralyzed most humans without permanent damage. I preferred to take my suspects alive, but I had a feeling that wasn't necessarily going to be possible right now.

"I am functional!" Barksley shouted, perhaps assuming I couldn't hear him through the rapidly fading ringing in my ears.

It occurred to me that our shouting might have tipped the surviving criminals on the ground to our presence, but that was less of a concern than the fact I heard the buzzing noise of drone turbines. Seconds later, our windows had three separate Assassin-class combat drones. They were about two feet long each and the same in height, with a mounted fusion rifle and a pair of machine guns. They had a single red line across their front which glowed back and forth, probably because it looked cool.

As their name implied, Assassin-drones had only one purpose and that was to identify individual targets and eliminate them. They'd been used extensively during the Unification Wars and had flooded the market afterward. One fact was true, though: if they managed to scan your face, you would have been dead.

Facing these things with normal human reflexes was suicide but, as we've established, that didn't exactly describe me anymore. Time seemed to slow down as little green squares appeared in my vision around their weak points. I brought the Herakles-7 pistol around and fired three times, the machines detonating one after the other before falling to the ground. That was when time resumed around me.

"I always love it when you do your superspeed thing," Barksley said, looking up at me in awe. "Is it like an old Hong Kong action movie effect from your perspective? I have superior scanning abilities to any organic and you still look like a blur."

I could hear fusion blasts, gunfire, and shouts coming from outside. It was a sign that there were more drones active, and they were actively carrying out a massacre. I normally would be playing the world's smallest violin—why yes, I do speak in nothing but cliches—but these assholes were my only links to the higher-ups in the Slavers Guild. I needed them alive if there was a chance to bring down the whole thing. Oh, and I was pretty sure whoever was doing this wasn't going to be keen on leaving behind any witnesses.

"Barksley move!" I shouted, not wanting to endanger my second favorite police partner.

Sorry, doggie, but Lucy has a few things over you.

Barksley responded by jumping into my arms as the two of us bolted from the room and headed down the empty concrete halls of the ruined building, making a break for the stairs since the elevator had long since ceased functioning.

It was ironic that I'd served two tours in the Atlas Security Marines but had never fired my weapon outside of practice, but since joining Cyberlife, I'd been in over a dozen gunfights. Right now, it sounded like an outright war was going on outside and I was torn between getting to safety versus trying to salvage something from this nightmare.

Lucy! I mentally shouted, attempting to contact her through our posthuman infocoms. In simple terms, this meant some asshole installed a cellphone in our brains. Which, I'm fine carrying it around in my pocket, guys.

Why are you shouting? Lucy responded, clearly more comfortable with this means of talking.

Because someone is shooting at me while I'm running! I said, slightly exaggerating the situation. *That seems like an Occam's Razor answer there. Where are you?*

Moving out of the line of fire, Lucy replied. *This is a bust.*

It is the exact opposite of a bust as a bust implies arrests and not corpses! I snapped. I immediately regretted it, but I doubted she'd hold any shouting done under gunfire against me.

Lucy was having none of it, anyway. *We'll worry about that when we're alive. Backup is too far away, and we can't deal with the number of drones out there. There's also a ninja.*

I stopped at the top of the eighth-floor stairwell. *A what now?*

I didn't get a good look at her but there's a ninja down there directing the drones and tearing through the crooks, Lucy kept talking as if this was not a conversation stopper by itself.

A ninja? I repeated, not sure I'd heard her correctly.

You know, wearing all black, katana, jumping around killing everything. A ninja. Lucy continued to talk like this was perfectly normal and maybe on the Moon it was. We'd dealt with some weird people in our cases together.

Welcome to the Moon, I muttered. *I don't suppose you got any pictures of her?*

I'm not your personal porn hustler, Neal, Lucy said.

For evidence! I said, starting to run down the stairs again. *Wait, is she hot?*

That was me being an ass, I admit.

That's not relevant, Lucy said, confirming she was. Which was strange since Lucy said she hadn't gotten a good look at her. *You need to evacuate the area now. That's an order.*

Lucy had significant seniority on me as a member of Cyberlife, but I was higher ranking than her as First Inspector versus her, well, Second Inspector. Neither of those really mattered in our partnership, though, as I could tell the real source of her words was concern. It was one of the rare occasions that Lucy let her emotional walls drop. It was also utterly ridiculous that I was focused on this rather than the fact there were a bunch of killer robots rampaging outside.

"You got it," I said, deciding to slip out of the back and hope I could get to our hidden vehicles.

Unfortunately, I was at the top of the third floor when I saw a group of Fleur De Lis gang members racing up the stairs with their weapons drawn. They were dressed in purple plexi-plastic jackets, black leather pants, purple trimmed neon night vision shades, and their symbol emblazoned on just about everything they owned. Two were holding Arc-9 handheld automatic machine guns while another had a gold-plated Herakles-7. As generally was the case with the Fleur de Lis, they were all of French Algerian descent.

Much to my surprise, I recognized one of them as Pierre Al-Hassan. He was a member of the Fleur de Lis who was heavily involved in the accounting for the organization and part of the group's lieutenants who had sold the gang out to the Syndicate. I brought him in a couple of times to interrogate him, hoping for insight into the Slavers Guild, only for him to slip out without any charges. I really hoped he didn't recognize me.

"Holy crap! It's the Duck Detective!" Pierre shouted, pointing at me. "He must be behind this! Dust him!"

Well, that wasn't good. I had my gun drawn but Barksley in my arms also prevented me from aiming it properly and "superhero" mode didn't exactly activate automatically. I wasn't going to be able to aim my weapon in time.

That was when Barksley opened his mouth and proceeded to fire an energy blast that sent me flying back up the stairs and slamming against the back of the stairwell wall. It was like being hit by a car. The blast was his all-purpose stun beam we'd nicknamed, "The Tenderizer", and had a recoil that was not designed for humans. It did, however, take down all three of the Fleur de Lis members and leave them twitching on the ground helplessly.

"Next time, warn me!" I snapped at Barksley.

"I did!" Barksley said, jumping out of my arms.

"You did not!" I said, slowly bringing myself up.

BEGINNING REPAIRS, Interface said. TISSUE AND BONE DAMAGE. YOU WILL REQUIRE SUSTENANCE.

No kidding, I thought back. That was one of the flaws of being a posthuman in that you had to eat a crap ton of food to use even the weakest of the abilities and on the Moon, that tended to be mushroom flavored everything (due to darkness as well as shit being readily available because it was a growing location) or high nutrient goop tubes of various flavors. The restrictions on food importations had been relaxed since the overthrow of Governor Barnum, but a cup of real coffee still cost twenty credits.

I jogged down the stairs and disarmed everyone just in case they were chromed up enough that they might be able to resist Barksley's attack. I took each gun and popped out their clips and the bullets in their firing chambers before dumping them over the side of the stairs. Not exactly perfect gun safety but I didn't intend to be here very long. I didn't want to abandon these guys, possible members of the Slaving Guild or not, but I wasn't sure how to get them to safety either.

I was about to drag them to one of the abandoned apartments and hope the drones outside missed them when Pierre moved, showing he was resistant to stun fire due to his artificial organs that I vaguely remembered from his police report.

"Help me, man," Pierre said, looking up. "I know you know Farid. I'll tell you everything. I'll tell you about Maelstrom. It'll happen soon."

Farid Al-Fariq AKA Big Brother was a former Fleur De Lis gang member who'd switched to a full-time career as an infonet journalist as well as hacktivist. He was a good guy and someone I had a decent relationship with when he wasn't saying how much he thought the police should be abolished. He also was still in hiding from people like Pierre who had put a standing hit on him. For him to invoke Farid's name, I had to assume that Pierre was desperate.

"Sure, absolutely," I said, grabbing him by the collar and starting to drag him up the stairs. "Tell me what Project: Jenner is and I'll get you out of this alive."

I would have helped him anyway—I wasn't that kind of cop—but there was no need to let him know that.

"A big score," he said. "Lots and lots of bodies. The bosses at Karma Corp have spaceships all ready and buyers."

Unfortunately, anything more he was going to tell me was interrupted by an Assassin-drone zipping up from the bottom of the stairwell to open up its machine guns on Pierre's body, showering me in the guy's blood. It also took advantage of the distraction long enough to run a red light over my face, scanning my identity.

"Dammit!" I said, grabbing for my gun to shoot it, only for the drone to spin around and fly away. I could hear gunfire further down the stairs and saw that the other two Fleur de Lis had also been executed by other drones. These didn't stay to go after me but joined their fellow in departing back down the way they came. "Huh. Well, that was strange."

Barksley, who was unharmed as well, looked up at me. "Maybe you weren't the target."

"I don't care!" I shouted, running down the remaining stairs with my gun drawn.

Eventually, I reached the first floor and saw the doors had been blown clean open. On the other side of it, I saw that the entirety of the gang members had been massacred by at least a dozen flying assassin drones as well as, well, a ninja. She had her back turned to me and was surveying the carnage like it was a work progress.

The ninja was most definitely female with a painted-on black stealth suit that was, um, very attention getting. It was particularly noticeable around the hind area and, okay, I'm moving on. The ninja had black hair sticking out of the top of her suit which had been pulled into a topknot.

She had some sort of belt device that seemed like it was projecting a barrier around her, and she was surrounded by spent bullets on the ground, as if it had somehow sucked out the velocity from all of them. The most noticeable quality, though, was the fact she had two thermal katanas in her hand. Well, technically, a katana and a wakizashi. Well, technically, katana just means sword so two katanas.

Okay, I'll stop now.

I was too late to save any of the gang members and not all of them had been killed by the drones. Instead, a lot of them had been cut up by thermal katanas that were sort of a novelty weapon over something that people used in day-to-day combat. Specifically, people used them as intimidation devices since having someone cut through like a slice of cheese had an intimidation effect that guns only marginally approached.

So, she had an army of drones, and had a magical shield protecting her from any attacks, effectively making her bulletproof. It meant there was only one thing to do: the absolute stupidest thing possible.

I lifted my (useless) gun and aimed it at her head. "You're under arrest!"

The woman turned around and I saw only her lower jawline was visible. Her eyes were covered with a stylized mask that showed them as milky white. Noticeably, and I kid you not, she had a symbol on her chest piece with a big zero. I mean, a *big* zero since she was a buxom—okay, moving on. Sorry. You could tell it was a zero and not an O, too, because it had a slash through it.

Anyway, the sight of her full costume was enough to shock me into silence because I'd seen a lot of things in my profession, especially since coming to the Moon. However, in my entire career, I'd never seen one of these.

A goddamn superhero.

"Hey, Neal," the woman said in a modulated voice.

I blinked. "Do we know each other lady?"

I admit, there was something familiar about her. Unfortunately, before I could respond, she aimed one of her katanas at me.

"Stun settings only," the ninja—who I mentally named Lady Zero because I was a fourteen-year-old mentally—said, "Target and fire."

That was when all her drones surrounded me and began unloading with icer rounds.

Fuck.

CHAPTER THREE

Where the Chief Chews Us Out

"**Y**ou complete *borking* morons," Chief Deckard said, staring at us as if we were something unpleasant he'd stepped into on his way to work. Which, given Luna City's Uptown was immaculately maintained by machines so the rich never had to so much as smell something unpleasant, was a rare occasion indeed.

Richard—pronounced "Rich-ARD" like he was French or something—Deckard had been blessed and cursed with two things that made him unique. One, he happened to share the same name with Harrison Ford's seminal character in the 1982 classic sci-fi movie, *Blade Runner*. Two, he was a man who fit every possible stereotype of a bad cop movie's police captain. Which was funny because while he wasn't even our department's head let alone Cyberlife's captain.

The two-meter-tall black man was probably in his mid-sixties but appeared to be about twenty years younger thanks to longevity drugs. However, he looked like those had been a hard forty-five years with cracks in his face and the signs of intense stress that made it look like he was about to pop a vein in his forehead. He was wearing a white button-down shirt, black linen pants, and a pair of suspenders that were distinctly unfashionable with most Lune's sensibility and all but advertised he was a transfer from Earth.

Lucy and I just sat there, staring across the man's overcrowded desk full of plexi-paper and other permanent pieces of documentation that would survive long after humanity had gone extinct. Barksley

24

wasn't present but that was because the Chief seemingly had the mistaken impression that so many Earthers did that AI qualified as equipment rather than employees. It might be the only thing that saved Barksley's job, though, as I was pretty sure this yelling was a prelude to our termination as employees.

Lucy was a lovely woman with long blonde hair and a diamond tattoo over her right eye. She was wearing the somewhat sexist dress-uniform of a Cyberlife policewoman with its short skirt and hose, even as her hands were balled at her side. She was the picture of a proper policewoman, but I could tell when she was suppressing her rage. Usually, she just displayed it when talking to or about her mother, famous action and sexploitation actress, Ayanna Breeze.

"To our credit, none of this is our fault," I said, attempting to offer what even I knew to be a completely unconvincing excuse.

"*Thirty* dead," Chief Deckard said, his voice emphasizing the point with the kind of disgust that the casualty figures deserved. "Thirty dead including not just a bunch of lowlifes no one would miss but also extremely important suits and gangsters whose deaths will cause a power vacuum throughout their organizations."

"I think the lowlifes are actually the ones that were the biggest loss of the group to humanity," I said, not knowing when to keep my mouth shut. No, wait, that wasn't correct. I didn't care about keeping my mouth shut. Big difference. "The others are really a net positive."

Lucy stared at me as if I was insane. Which, to be fair, she was far from the first person to look at me as being. "Really, Neal?"

"I'm not saying all rich people are bad," I said, pausing as Lucy was one of the one percent herself. "I'm just saying we should eat them. The ones that aren't all plastic and fat, at least."

If I was going to go down, I might as well go down in flames. Seriously, I knew how this was going to end.

Lucy facepalmed.

"All dead while you watched on and did *nothing*," Richard said, slamming his fist on the edge of the desk before pouring himself a glass of water and putting a pair of dissolving "stress relief" pills in it.

"Not nothing," I replied. "We were kind of busy trying to survive."

"On an *illegal* surveillance mission for a *ridiculous* conspiracy theory," Richard said, clenching his left hand into a fist while emphasizing words like he was rolling over rocks in his mouth.

"Illegal is stretching it," I said, knowing that we were screwed here. "*Unauthorized* is more accurate."

"This isn't helping, Neal," Lucy said, finally interjecting.

"Is *anything* going to help?" I asked, turning my head to her.

Lucy didn't respond.

She knew the answer. So did I.

"It's my job to clean up this department and I'm glad you've given me the excuse to do so," Richard said, interlocking his fingers and staring at us like we were pieces of meat waved before a hungry stray dog.

"You don't believe they were involved in a trafficking ring, do you?" I asked.

"I believe you have turned ordinary crime into pure and utter fiction," Richard said, dryly.

"Truth is stranger than fiction," I replied.

The Slavers Guild wasn't something that most people believed in. Forced labor was as old as anything else in human history, but with the advent of robotics, you needed to really want to cheap out in order to use your fellow humans that way. Besides, we had so many wonderful euphemisms and exceptions for it like "prison labor" or "subsistence wages" to handle it. The Slavers Guild's old fashioned "kidnap people and sell them to aliens in exchange for super-advanced tech" was the kind of thing that got shared as a conspiracy theory on social media. Usually with the caveat that Jews or lizard men were involved.

Neither of which were, I should point out.

"Not in my opinion," Richard said. "My opinion is also the only one that matters right now. Not yours. Not your AI friend's. EarthGov has placed me in charge to put an end to the constant and never-ending abuses of power by the Moon's corporate police."

Dammit. Armstrong, the AI that ran everything on the Moon, had tolerated my obsession with trying to bring down the Guild, but the AI and primary stockholder of Atlas Security wasn't quite as influential as it used to be. In what had to be the worst timing ever for a good idea,

EarthGov had started dramatically rolling back corporate immunity and privileges. Civilian oversight was the new byword of the day and that meant putting a civi cop in charge of Cyberlife's Internal Affairs/Human Resources.

AKA Richard here.

Now according to the liberal touchy-feely hippie Reformist politicians of Earth—who I generally preferred to the asshole Neo-Militarists—this was because us dirty mercenary private security types were inherently corrupt. Fair. However, the previous guy who held the position of civilian oversight had been a literal member of the Slavers Guild and honest-to-God fucking *terrorist*. While Rick wasn't as bad as the late Reggie "Iceman" Reynolds, the practical effects were that the civi cops were in charge and thus cheaper to bribe as well as half as trained.

Lucy took a deep breath. "Sir, we have evidence that there was a massive criminal conspiracy that—"

"The job of the police is not to solve crimes," Richard said, speaking with the conviction of someone who had just discovered conspiracy videos about vaccines causing autism on the infonet.

"What?" Lucy, clearly thrown by this line of argument. Any possible last-minute defense she had planned crumbled to dust.

"This is a new line of argument," I said, leaning back in my chair. "Probably more honest, though."

"The police exist to preserve the public order," Richard said, showing exactly where his priorities lay. "To make sure society continues to function by preserving the—"

"Can we skip the speech about you being a shitty cop?" I asked, deciding I was done with this bullshit.

All humor left Richard's face and he just stared at me like I was a cockroach he wanted to step on. It was notably the same look that I had received from multiple superiors over the year. "I can't fire you—"

"Oh, you can't?" I asked, standing up. "Right. I forgot, we work for Atlas Security and are contracted to Luna City. Great talk then. I'll just go back to my office—"

Lucy pulled me back down to my chair, which annoyed me. She really had way too much respect for the system. Mind you, that usually came with being a cop, but I'd long since realized the system was a series of compromises between the people and the rich. Guess who Richard had decided he was on the side of?

"You'll have to forgive, Neal," Lucy said, disappointing me before revealing I was wrong to doubt her with her next words. "He still believes the lie the job of a police officer is to protect the innocent and punish the guilty. Something you clearly have no interest in."

"I can't fire you," Richard said, enunciating each word and looking like he was going to have a stroke. There was pissed off and then there was whatever I'd managed to invoke inside him. Some sort of Buddhist meditative state of rage. Madvana. "But I can suspend you, both, without pay, pending a review I can assure you is never going to come. Turn over your badges and firearms. Clean out your offices. You have an hour before I'll have you escorted out. Now get out of my office."

"Thank you very much, Chief," Lucy said, standing up politely and walking out the door. I got up, put on my antique fedora (a gift from Barksley), and followed her.

I paused at the door and said, "By the way, you really should yell more when firing someone. This isn't remotely as bad as some of my—"

"GET THE HELL OUT OF MY OFFICE!" Richard shouted.

"There! Perfect!" I said, cheerfully before catching up to Lucy.

"You couldn't put away your childishness for an hour?" Lucy asked, clearly pissed off with me as well.

Damn.

"He was going to fire us anyway," I said, sticking my hands in my pockets. "You know it, I know it. He knew it."

"Yes," Lucy said, pausing. "But you turned a potential fight into a certain one. The important thing to remember when playing office politics is that you should never let your enemies know that they're your enemies. That way they don't know when you're coming for them."

I blinked, unsure I'd heard that correctly. "Yeah, I wasn't aware working at Cyberlife was like living in Westeros."

"Wester-what?" Lucy asked, blinking.

I gave a dismissive wave. "Barksley is on a fantasy kick. Kings, queens, dragons, incest."

"Uh huh," Lucy said. "What I'm saying is we might have been able to maneuver around this. Now that's impossible. Not even Armstrong can go against EarthGov."

I wasn't so sure about that. The Reformers talked a good game but transtellar corporate power was the proverbial six-hundred-pound gorilla crossed with the elephant in the corner. Lots of big talk about reigning them in, but the laws instituted—what few there were—were all easily subverted. If Armstrong wanted to help us—and the AI owed us big for saving its digital ass—then it certainly could.

"Do you think being suspended from the force makes us less dangerous or more dangerous to the bad guys?" I asked, doing my best impression of a movie cop.

"Less," Lucy said, not falling for it in the slightest. "We don't have authority to investigate the Slavers Guild or their allies anymore, nor do we have backup. Even if we exposed their crimes, like Rashad, all we'd be is one more voice on the infonet. That's not including the fact the Slavers Guild has already consumed way more of our time than it should have."

I stared at her, uncomprehending. "You've got to be kidding me."

Lucy stared back, realizing I was serious. "Taking them down has become an obsession with you."

"Yeah," I said, not denying it. "They took my leg. They've kidnapped tens of thousands of citizens. Worse, they're getting away it."

"Murderers and kidnappers get away with it all the time," Lucy said, sounding distinctly like Richard in that moment. "They're getting away with it right now because we're not going out there to deal with them. You've been focused on the Guild so hard that you've begun ignoring other cases, easier to solve ones at that. Cases whose victims' families also deserve justice."

I wasn't comfortable having this argument in the middle of the hallway and was pretty sure that by tomorrow, the entire station would be discussing it. The only things that traveled faster than light were jump drive engines and gossip. Fortunately, I'd just been *de facto* fired and wouldn't have to deal with it.

"I'm not happy about this, Lucy," I said, trying to figure out a way to salvage this conversation.

"Aren't you?" Lucy asked. "Because you always play by your own rules and expect things to work themselves out when it's actually your friends picking up the pieces."

"Is that what we are? Friends?" I asked.

Okay, that was a low blow. This was not the time to bring up the fact I was looking for more between us.

"I would normally ignore that," Lucy said, unfortunately finding a new target for her anger. "However, maybe we spend a little too much time together. It's probably better that we don't anymore."

Ouch. Well, I hadn't intended to make this a breakup but clearly I'd pushed things in that direction. Then again, could you really break up if you'd never been together in the first place? Either way, I felt like shit. "Sorry."

"You don't know what this job meant to me, Neal," Lucy said, shaking her head. "It was the one thing in my life where I was doing really good. I thought you understood that. It was why I tried to help as much with your crusade as I did. But there's no helping some people."

My natural inclination when someone went on the attack was to attack right back. I could have said that as the "poor little rich girl", Lucy had a lot less to lose than I did in sheer financial terms. She could afford to lose her job and live off her residuals from her still syndicated TV show or the money from her mother's vast holdings. I could have pointed out no one had twisted her arm into going after the Slavers Guild. I also could have pointed out that we'd made plenty of "regular" arrests but getting away from the pointless over-policing of vice to focus on violent crime was exactly what the Cyberlife division existed for in the first place.

But I didn't.

Because I wasn't an asshole.

Okay, I was still thinking it but that only made me somewhat of an asshole. Which could be the title of my biography when I finally wrote it. I was presently imagining it as a three-volume set with *Naked and Screaming* for my early years, *An Asshole With A Gun* for my Martian years, and rounding it out with *I Got Shot in the Face* for my Moon years. Mind you, I hadn't been shot in the face yet but getting shot in the leg was just inherently less dramatic.

Lucy surprised me by adding something to her breakup speech. "Plus, it seems like they're cleaning up their own mess."

"Excuse me?" I asked.

Lucy stared at me. "The stripper ninja murdered most of the people involved. Unless she was there for our benefit, we can assume whoever was behind her is getting rid of the Slavers Guild and doesn't care how high up they are in the food chain."

"Stripper ninja? Really?" I asked, wondering if people were paying attention now.

"What would you call her?" Lucy asked.

"Uhm," I paused. "Lady Zero? Because of the zero."

"Oh god, you gave her a superhero name," Lucy said, shaking her head. "You are fourteen years old."

"Yes, because calling her the stripper ninja is..." I started to throw back a rejoinder but stopped myself. "If they're targeting the members of the Slavers Guild, we should move more quickly."

"Why?" Lucy asked.

I paused. "What?"

"Let them finish it up," Lucy said, surprising me. "You want them dead as much as anyone else. The ones we have managed to arrest aren't spending life in prison unless they're poor. Isn't this better than struggling to bring them down through a system that doesn't want to?"

I was speechless. When the hell did, I become the good cop in this? "This is about Dick, your boyfriend."

I felt the need to add the qualifier at the end because our new boss was also a Richard and absolutely a dick.

Lucy closed her eyes and counted to ten. "Yes, it's about Dick. It's about your boyfriend too."

"Excuse me?" I asked.

"Doesn't it occur to you the person most likely to be behind killing all these rich assholes is probably Nigel? The Chief Security Officer of

Karma Corp with access to a bunch of cyborg super soldiers? Including ones who look like they got their bodies at WhoreMart?"

I blinked. "That's not a real place. Believe me, I'd know. I'd do all my shopping there. Uh, I know because I do a lot of vice work. Yeah, I didn't really think that rejoinder through."

Lucy looked ready to explode then calmed down. "He's the worst one of them all and we've been running around doing his dirty work. He's probably the guy who killed Dick in the first place and we should be focused on him."

I didn't have a response for that. Probably because she was right. It wouldn't surprise me in the slightest to find out that Nigel was responsible for killing her boyfriend. The man had done unimaginable evil things and had been willing to do the same to me, his supposed best friend. I didn't believe Lucy was right about Lady Zero and Nigel, though, because there was one quality that Nigel did not possess and that was being theatrical. If he was going to kill all his former associates—which he absolutely could do since he'd been willing to narc on them—then he would have done it without telling me.

No, wait, that wasn't right.

He absolutely would have told me to come down there and witness the massacre, but he would have made sure I'd died too. That would have wrapped up the whole thing rather neatly. Cops killed in criminal conspiracy slaughter. Unfortunately, I didn't think that would be an argument that would fly with Lucy. No, I don't believe our informant—a charming psychopath I used to think as my best friend—is involved in this because if he was then he'd have killed us both.

In fact, that was the most confusing part of all this. Most assassins who would be willing to kill thirty-fucking people in a single sitting weren't going to sweat killing a couple of extra witnesses. I knew some special operators in my time who'd *done things* in the war. The people capable of doing this kind of stuff would not have left Lucy and me (or Barksley) alive unless they had a reason to. Forget what movies suggested, once you were willing to drop more bodies than existed in a small building, you didn't sweat collateral.

"Right," Lucy said, looking up. "Goodbye, Neal. You can keep the dog in the divorce."

Dammit. I'd clearly zoned out there for a second or two. "Lucy, I—
"

"Neal! Officer Westenra!" A voice called to me from down the hall. "I'm so glad to catch you! I was afraid I'd miss you."

I blinked.

"What the hell is my wife doing here?" I muttered, doing a double take.

Lucy did a double take.

CHAPTER FOUR

New Flame, Meet the Old Flame

Just like that, I was back on the jungle Moon of Helios XIII. Which wasn't completely jungle but certainly felt like it at that time. We were among the humans farthest from the planet Earth and visiting alien biomes that had been terraformed millennia ago by ancient species beyond our comprehension.

So, of course, I was getting drunk at a dive bar that suspiciously resembled the tacky Tiki places that were somehow still a fad centuries after their heyday. The only difference from the ones I'd visited on Earth was that this bartender was a lizard man in a Hawaiian shirt versus a middle-aged white guy with a mustache.

"We should get married," Lieutenant Kathleen "Kate" Roebuck responded.

Kate was one of those special operator psychopaths (but in a good way) that I'd mentioned earlier. She had short strawberry blonde hair and a perpetually bored expression that barely changed when getting plastered on whatever fermented beverage they were serving here that I was pretty sure was only mildly toxic to humans.

Kate wasn't built like a special operations officer for Atlas' Space Assault Warrior (or SAW) troopers. She was not precisely thin, exactly, but not someone you'd assume could rip the head off a man three times her size as I'd literally seen her do when dealing with a guy having a Loop freakout with a grenade. She was more "firm" like you would expect a professional swimmer or volleyball player to be. She did, however, fill out nicely the tank top she was wearing with her army fatigues. That was new.

I think it said everything you needed to know about our relationship that not only was I violating centuries-old taboo of being a Marine dating an Army officer but seeing her literally decapitate a man had just resulted in me asking her out that evening. She'd said no. Then took me behind the supply tent for a quick bork.

"Are we even dating?" I asked, leaning back on the table as something very distinctly like Jimmy Buffett was playing on the jukebox. It was just being sung in something I called "Space French."

That was another thing I'd found out while journeying through space as part of Atlas' Colonial Militia—there were already humans out here. Alien abduction or whatever had resulted in there already being human "colony" worlds out there. Generally, worlds more advanced and utterly uninterested in Earth the same way I was uninterested in my 85% Scottish, 10% Mexican, 5% Nigerian ancestry according to the DNA swab of my mouth they took at enlistment.

"Who cares about dating?" Kate asked. "We're friends, we fuck, and there's a ten percent pay bonus to married couples off-planet as well as a shit-ton of other benefits."

"Ah, the plot thins," I said, taking a drink of something that was supposed to be beer but hit like vodka. Chum, I think it was called, and I really hoped it wasn't made from fish. "You don't want me for romantic reasons. It's all about financial benefits."

"All marriage is about financial benefits," Kate said, staring despite being more than a little drunk. "It exists so men have to pony up when they put women through the horrors of pregnancy. Christ, how did you become such a romantic? You're on first name bases with every whore in the corporate brothel."

"Candy, Thumper, and Bambi are all studying to be nurse practitioners," I said, knowing their real names but not wanting to admit it. "Also, that was before I met you. I have to take vitamins to keep up."

"That's the nanites," Kate said, pausing. "They've pumped us full of alien shit as part of our tour of duty. It makes you super-strong and horny."

I narrowed my eyes. "Aluminum makes you horny."

Kate nodded. "It is the sexiest metal. Anyway, I thought you'd be more practical growing up in the *favelas* of New Angeles."

"The Refugee Zones are surprisingly uncynical places," I replied, defending my neighborhood. "It's not like, say, the Moon where it's every man or woman for themselves. The bonds of community run deep there. Besides, I was raised by the Gordon Foundation."

"I know," Kate said, rolling her eyes. "You sound like all of them."

"All of them?" I asked, surprised.

"I knew a couple of Foundation kids from the spooks that make up our missions," Kate said, probably revealing more than she should have. "They all act like you do."

Atlas Security was officially neutral in the latest Unification War between the Neo-Militarists and all the countries in revolt against their rule, but it was an open secret they were supporting the latter. They were arming and training the revolutionaries while serving as a go-between for the Community to do the same. Still, it was probably against the rules to admit Atlas' special operations were outright carrying out wetworks against the fascists.

"Charming and erudite?" I asked, smirking.

"*Chatty*," Kate explained. "You're also all raised on television from like two centuries ago. I don't know what a *Star Trek* or a *Star Wars* is, and I certainly don't care who was a lethal weapon fighting an exterminator from the future."

"Terminator," I replied.

"Don't," Kate said, softly. "Don't or you will never see me naked again."

"That would be a tragedy," I replied. "Especially with recent adjustments."

"I don't tell you how to spend your money, you don't tell me how to spend mine," Kate said, chuckling as she looked down at her top. "So, are we getting hitched or not?"

I paused, thinking about it. "Sure, why not?"

We'd found ourselves a base chaplain whose only god was drink and signed the paperwork for what ended up being an eight-month long marriage that hadn't sufficiently changed much of our existing relationship. Then the Unification Wars had ended while she'd been off on a mission to blow up some Neo-Militarist shipyards and the next time I'd heard from her had been when she was sending divorce papers.

That had been twelve years ago and the last of my tour before becoming a corporate investigator.

A lifetime ago.

Yesterday.

Now she was standing across the hall from me, and I was unsure how to react after over a decade of being apart. The fact I'd been able to recognize her voice as she was waving over at me while Barksley was at her feet was something that took me a second to process as real.

Kate didn't look any different from the way she had twelve years ago and had aged gracefully. There were also a few more "improvements" she'd made to herself that were noticeable but didn't detract from the fact she still looked like an athlete everywhere else. She was also sharply dressed in a white business suit that made her look more like a lawyer or executive than the soldier I remembered. She even had a briefcase.

"Your what now?" Lucy asked, doing a double take.

"Oh, right," I said, doing a double take. "I was married for a while during the war."

"And this never came up in a year of a relationship?" Lucy asked, more than a little offended judging by her tone.

A good man would have let that go. "Oh, I'm sorry, I wasn't aware we were in a relationship. I thought we were just friends."

Yeah, I was just okay.

Barksley came up to me with a smile on his face and got up on his hindquarters to shake my hand. "You should have introduced us much earlier! She's a delightful human being. It turns out she's a fan of a lot of the music I like."

"You like eight thousand songs," I replied.

"And she likes at least thirty of those!" Barksley said. "We just discussed 'Harlem Nocturne'! So how did your meeting with Chief Dullard go?"

That was as close as Barksley got to swearing. "Not well."

I met Kate's gaze and struggled with what I felt. I'd expected after twelve years that there wouldn't be any feelings leftover. There had been other women—hell, Lucy was right beside me—but the surge of feelings that washed over me was a lot stronger than I expected. Being a grunt who guarded ammo dumps and military bases was not a part of my life I had much to remember fondly about—but she was one exception. Kate had been tough, take-no-prisoners, and crass. She'd helped teach me to be the same way. Also, a fantastic lover. I wondered if this was how Rick had felt in *Casablanca* when he saw Elsa again.

"We were indefinitely suspended without pay," Lucy said. "The only reason we weren't fired was because he can't fire employees of Atlas Security. He can, however, remove all our ability to operate as police officers. I've known actual murderers that haven't been suspended indefinitely."

"Perhaps that says more about the system than you," I said, not looking at Lucy but taking in Kate's face. Which was rude as hell, but Lucy had just dumped me, and I was a petty, petty human being.

They said the eyes were the window to the soul and you could find out everything about a person just by looking at them. Like most things "they" said, that was complete horseshit, but there were clues in the face of someone you knew intimately. Despite how fancy she was now, the past twelve years had not been good for her and there was a mask she'd put over her scars. It was a look that many veterans had that had chosen the appearance of normality overachieving it. Some cops had it too. There was something else, though. An urgency. Like she was putting on a face while privately panicking. The Kate I knew didn't panic.

Something big was going down.

"Ah," Barksley said, talking to Lucy. "Did you throw your badge dramatically and embed it in the wall like a shuriken?"

"No," Lucy said. "I did not imitate my mother in *Fair Cop 2.*"

"Wait, you're Ayanna Breeze's daughter?" Kate asked, notably turning from me. "I love those movies. God, they are such trashy fun. Your mother is so hot."

Lucy's smile looked pained. "Oh yeah, she's great."

"Oh sorry," Kate said, smiling. "My name is Kate Roebuck-Gordon."

"You still go by your married name?" Lucy asked.

Kate paused. "We're not going to be friends, are we?"

Lucy blanched. "I see no reason why we shouldn't be. Neal and I just broke up."

Barksley gasped in horror. "No!"

"Apparently, we were never together in the first place," I replied, dryly.

"He wanted more than I can give," Lucy said, dryly.

"Ah, he does that a lot," Kate replied, suddenly making me feel like the odd man out here.

"So, what have you been doing for the past... decade and change?" I asked, pausing as I felt quite a bit older.

"We need to have this conversation in private," Kate gestured down the hallway. "Your office would be good."

"We no longer have an office," Lucy said, bitterer than I expected. Being a cop had meant everything to her. It was a way to honor her late father, Alex Breeze, and also provide a structure for herself after failed acting and musical careers. In a very real way, Lucy had lived the kind of life that people made holo shows about. If I'd been more attentive, I would have realized this sooner and offered her comfort rather than flipping Deckard off on my way out.

Which I should have done.

Dammit.

"You'll have more than an office," Kate said, surprising me. "I've already spoken with Armstrong and recruited your sister. We don't have much time, but this isn't something that can be rushed past either. However, you should be prepared to gather your things and relocate."

Lucy and I exchanged glances, confused.

"Excuse me?" I asked, hoping for clarification.

"Not in the hall," Kate said, quickening her pace.

All of us headed down the hallway to our office where someone had already helpfully provided plexi-boxes for us to put our stuff in outside the door.

Dicks.

Picking one of them up, I followed Kate in and started packing up what few knick-knacks that I'd kept there like old books and holo photos. I hadn't assembled much in the way of material possessions over the years. Capitalism, even when you were a corpo cop—especially when you were a corpo cop—was like *Through the Looking Glass*: you ran as fast as you could just to stay in place. I wasn't a communist, don't get me wrong, or even a Reformer—my politics were "don't fuck with me and I won't fuck with you"—but I understood society existed to put the squeeze on you.

Once the door was shut, Kate locked it and pulled out a small pocket-light that she activated. "There, now no one can hear what we're discussing."

I blinked, having suddenly entered a spy movie. "Is it that important?"

"Yes," Kate said. "I should clarify that I am *Special Agent* Kate Roebuck-Gordon. I'm an operative working for Special Homeworld Interstellar Defense."

"SHID?" I asked. "You couldn't add a couple of letters and be SHIELD?"

"I've heard they're restructuring the various intelligence agencies into multiple united departments," Lucy said. "The Reformist government feels like starting a newer, sleeker, singular agency to deal with threats to Sol safety would be welcomed by a public sick of STRIKE and other groups' abuses."

"In practice, it's to bring us in line with the security standards of the Galactic Community," Kate said. "SHID would be Department Four, supervising catastrophic natural and nonnatural disasters."

Okay, it felt like Kate was burying the lead here. "By that you mean—"

"Meteor strikes, volcano eruptions, asteroid strikes, horrific plague..." Kate said, pausing. There was a pained expression on her face as if this wasn't something that they were preparing for a possibility in the future. No, it was the expression of someone who was about to inform us that it was stage four cancer and somehow developed sentience. Which was another Ayanna Breeze movie's premise and still involved a lot of nudity.

Lucy and I exchanged a look.

Oh crap.

This was going to suck.

"So, which of these are about to happen?" I asked, really hoping she'd say she was only speaking in the hypothetical and knowing she wasn't.

"The latter," Kate said, dryly. "We have reason to believe the Moon is about to be subject to a massive pandemic."

A moment passed with no one saying anything.

"Define massive," I replied.

Lucy elbowed me in the side.

Kate put her briefcase on the table and opened it up, revealing a laptop and several pieces of equipment I didn't recognize. It also contained a new set of holographic badges in crystal cases that she handed to both of us. "It's not common knowledge but there are other human colonies outside of the Sol system than the ones made by Earth. Ones with millions, sometimes billions, of inhabitants."

"I've heard rumors, but I thought it would be national news," Lucy said, taking her badge.

I wasn't about to point out that I'd known about the extra-solar human colonies for about a decade. Indeed, the fact it wasn't more commonly known about was more that people just flat out didn't believe aliens had been abducting humans for real over the past few millennia.

"Space is big and our diplomatic efforts toward our 'wayward children' have been inconsistent in their success," Kate said, emphasizing wayward children as if she'd identified why our attitude had pissed them off. It was the same condescending attitude Earthers had to the Moon, Mars, and Cylinder Colonies. "They're almost all members of the Community and resistant to bringing Earth in. Even more so than most aliens."

"Why is that?" I asked, taking the badge, and looking at it. It had a holographic Phoenix on it. Underneath the mythological bird of resurrection was written, *Cinis Ex Surgite*. My Latin was a bit rusty, but I was pretty sure that translated to, "Rise from the ashes." It was a little on the nose, to be honest. Then again, branding was 90% of successful government endeavors. "I mean, aside from us calling them our children and ignoring they were in outer space while the rest of Earth was killing each other with swords."

The few off-world humans I'd met aside from our colonists had generally had the same attitude toward us primitives as Han Solo would have meeting Indiana Jones. It's not that they were trying to be dismissive, but the general assumption was that they were better travelled and educated even when they weren't. On the plus side, the parts still lined up and I'd met a couple of genuine green- and blue-skinned space babes. Not sure how evolution had brought that about, but I wasn't complaining. Then again, Kate said they were just micro-tattooed for cash, but I preferred the illusion.

What were we talking about? Oh right, plague.

Better pay attention.

"The extra-solar humans are afraid of Earth's instability jeopardizing their own chances at becoming major players in the galaxy," Kate said. "Almost all of them were colonized in the last thousand years and since the Community is about ten thousand years old, plenty of them are still waiting for economic development to reach galaxy standard."

"Well, that's depressing," I said, realizing we were poor cousins to the galaxy's poor cousins. "What does this have to do with a plague?"

"We have reason to believe that a group of Albionese political extremists have decided to use biological weapons against Earth as well as her colonies. These so-called Sons of Mithras believe using the kind of diseases that have evolved and mutated on their worlds for centuries against us is a way to utterly cripple Earth before it becomes a competitor."

I stared at her. "You think they're going to attack the Moon."

"I think they already have," Kate replied, her tone grave. "Which is why I'm drafting all three of you along with other Cyberlife operatives to help with this matter. We don't want to start a panic before things go completely tits up, but the fact that you're both posthumans means that you're immune to disease. Barksley is a bioroid and thus the same. This will make you all useful in any area that might be infected."

I blinked. "How did you know I was a—"

"Right," Lucy said. "Of course, we will help. Especially if Armstrong has agreed."

"He has," Kate said, "We need to set up quarantines and mass testing to understand how far the virus could have spread, but all of this is still in the early stages. It may be nothing, it may be everything. I'm transferring the address of our field office to you."

"You have my word," I paused. "Man, it is awkward meeting up under these circumstances."

Kate gave a sad smile. "You wouldn't believe what I've been up to all this time. We should catch up. Have dinner sometime."

"Sure," I said.

Lucy and Barksley looked at me strangely.

Kate closed her briefcase. "I've got fifteen other places to be and a hundred holocalls to make. I'm sorry I can't stay longer. With any luck, we may be going crazy over nothing. Goodbye."

She turned around and walked out the door, me watching her leave with intense focus on her backside. Which wasn't just me being a pig. There was a strong sense of missing something, but my detective brain just wasn't putting the pieces together yet.

"So, you know your ex-wife was Lady Zero, right?" Lucy asked, suddenly breaking the mood.

"Yeah, that was totally her in that outfit," Barksley said. "You can tell by the hindquarters."

Holy shit, you could.

CHAPTER FIVE

Martian Law is Wild and Untamed

Lucy was driving the Purple Rain, a ridiculous flying car that looked like it had come out of someone's Seventies-inspired, drug-induced fever dream, as the song, "Good Cop, Bad Cop" by Ice Cube played in the background. It had been totaled after Reggie Reynold's attempt to cover up his terrorism, but Barksley had done some accounting kung fu to get the thing repaired on Cyberlife's dime. The thing looked like it belonged to a pimp and smelled like a stash house, but I'd become used to it as my civilian transport. Barksley was sitting in the back while I sat on the passenger's side, Luna City passing us by outside the windows.

Luna City was one of the two parts of the Moon that wasn't a horrifying underground slum, industrialized nightmare, or prison plantation for growing the planet's food. The Moon hadn't been colonized by human hands until after the aliens had done the grunt work of establishing a massive base for their long-term project of repairing Earth's crumbling environment.

Luna City had been designed for the rich and powerful to live over the plebs who toiled down below. It was the part advertised in the brochure with its artificial sea, soaring Flash Gordon-esque towers, and beautiful parks that were justified for oxygen production even though we had atmosphere processors everywhere. It was a grossly impractical city like Vegas or Dubai and consumed about thirty percent of the Moon's resources to keep afloat. I'd never gotten comfortable with the place and much preferred the underground despite its crime ridden hellhole nature—probably because it reminded me of my childhood. The skyways were particularly packed on our way from the Cyberlife building and I couldn't help but imagine the bug silently moving around us. We hadn't been briefed on its nature yet, but it was already preying on the back of my mind.

Which was why I'd spent the entire trip skimming the SHID handbook. I'd been reading rather than taking in the sights. Kate had helpfully provided an upload of it while we drove to our rendezvous point.

"From what I can tell this is basically FEMA with guns," I said, referring to the defunct American agency from before the Eruption. It was still popular in holos set around that time as the anger over its failures was now a cultural memory among people from North America. "Lots of very dubious authority, broad extrajudicial powers, and uncertain wording. If I didn't know better, I'd say it was written by Neo-Militarists, but they aren't nearly smart enough to put in so many exploitable loopholes."

"They can declare Martian law!" Barksley said, cheerfully. "It'll be like the wild-wild Red Planet! Everyone carrying guns and having shoot outs at high noon."

I blinked. "If you mean *martial law*, then that would be the exact opposite. Also, it's on the Moon that everyone keeps shooting each other. On Mars, I had to deal with about two-gun crimes in my entire ten years stationed there. You must be ex-law enforcement or military to get a permit and they're all bio-locked to you."

Barksley looked disgusted. "Such an impediment to freedom. It ruins Mars' frontier ambiance."

Yeah, I wasn't getting into that. *The Moon is a Harsh Mistress* was a Robert E. Heinlein book from the 1960s which envisioned the people from Luna being incredibly freedom obsessed, sexually open, and violent. He hadn't exactly gotten all the details right but there were some striking parallels. Lunes were, in simple terms, a bunch of lunatics. Lovable ones but lunatics, nonetheless.

"You know Wyatt Earp and the shootout at the OK Corral actually happened because they'd imposed a law against carrying handguns in Tombstone—"

"That monster!" Barksley said, shocked.

"I generally favor being the only person to carry a gun in any situation," I replied. amused. "Not as a political statement but because I like having the upper hand in a conversation."

"Well, I am a gun, so I'm biased," Barksley said. "Everyone should have one of me."

"AHEM," Lucy said, making a coughing noise.

"I take it you have something to say," I said. "Either that or have come down with the horrifying virus that is going to kill us all."

"She can't be the latter," Barksley said. "Both of you are posthumans."

THE BIO-CONSTRUCT IS CORRECT, Interface said. I HAVE ALREADY HACKED INTO THE SHID DATABASE AND EXAMINED THE STRAIN OF DISEASE. YOU AND LUCY ARE INCAPABLE OF CONTRACTING IT.

Yeah, that's what Kate said, I replied, not at all reassured. Nor was it reassuring that Interface could just break into the SHID system. It meant that, with the number of data slicers on the Moon, it was only a matter of time before this all got out.

"Yes," Lucy said. "I was trying to get your attention because I've been expecting you to freak out for this entire trip."

"I don't freak out," I replied. "Except that one time I won twenty grand in a craps game and blew it all in one night. I wish I knew what I spent it on, though."

Lucy growled. "Your wife—your *ex*-wife—killing thirty people in front of us. We're not going to discuss that?"

"No, because it's not true," I said, not looking up at her.

"Seriously?" Lucy asked, looking at me skeptically.

I turned to her. "You think my wife—*ex*-wife—returned from a twelve-year absence to become a, and I quote, stripper ninja, who kills thirty people in front of me. Then shows up the next day to offer me a job at the Department of We're Already Fucked?"

"The WAF would have been a better name than SHID," Barksley commented as "No Vaseline" started playing. "Ooo, I love this song."

"You love all of them," I replied.

"It explains a great deal of why you're still alive as well," Lucy said. "It also fits with the evidence. Only a posthuman special operations officer could have pulled all of that off. Maybe she's offering us these jobs with Department Four as a way to make up for costing you your job."

"What evidence?" I asked, staring. "Also, clearly you don't know Kate as the only time she's ever felt guilty for anything she did to me was when she stuck me with the bill at the Wages of Sin after going home with one of the strippers."

Lucy stared.

"Too much information, sorry," I muttered. I wanted to blame jealousy for Lucy's theory, but I admitted that I was deliberately avoiding analyzing the question.

"The fact Lady Zero looks exactly like your ex-wife in a skintight bodysuit," Lucy said. "This isn't that guy who wears glasses, and no one can recognize him."

"Clark Kent?" I asked, confused.

"Yeah, Batman," Lucy said, smirking.

"Okay, you're doing that deliberately," I said. "As for her secret identity, it was dark, chaos was ensuing, and I didn't get a good look at her. Neither did you or Barksley."

AN EXAMINATION OF HER BODY TYPE AND FACIAL FEATURES INDICATES A NINETY-EIGHT-POINT-TWO CHANCE OF BEING THE SAME PERSON, Interface responded.

No one asked you! I replied.

HER PENCHANT FOR WELL TAILORED SUITS THAT FLATTER HER FIGURE PROVED TO BE HER DOWNFALL, Interface said, displaying something shockingly close to humor.

"So, it's her," I replied, putting down my infopad. "She technically hasn't done anything illegal."

Lucy blinked then looked at me before turning back to the car's controls. "Are you fucking serious?"

"He's not wrong," Barksley said, speaking up. "I processed the SHID charter in a few seconds and cross-referenced the executive orders related to it. If there really is a pandemic and order 432 has been invoked, then extrajudicial executions are within her authority."

"Who knew the Reformists had it in them," I muttered.

"Anyone who has grown up in a Leftist dictatorship rather than a Right one, I'd imagine," Lucy muttered. "So, what you're saying is that just because you used to sleep with the murderer of those individuals, you don't care anymore?"

Finding out Kate was the person responsible for killing all those people was a helluva game changer for my opinions on the situation. Was it completely biased that it being someone I knew made me inclined to think she had a good reason for it, leaving me uninterested in pursuing the matter? Abso-frigging-lutely. It was also 100% true.

"Not care is a bit much," I said. "More like... okay, I got nothing."

Sometimes you lost an argument simply because you couldn't come up with the right words to explain how you felt.

"You do realize she killed a bunch of people like they were animals," Lucy said.

"I knew Kate was a killer long before I became one myself," I muttered, thinking back to the incident that lost me my leg. "However, Kate is someone I once considered my best friend. I owe her that much to give her the benefit of the doubt."

Ah, there we go. Benefit of the doubt! That was nice and neutral.

Lucy crossed a line with her next words. "Not to point out the obvious, but you don't have a good track record with best friends. Nigel used to be your best friend and Nigel is a monster."

"No shit," I muttered, now pissed off. I decided to deflect. "Barksley, do you have any horrifying secrets I should know about?"

"Take this seriously," Lucy said, under her breath.

"I am," I said, looking back. "Seriously, now's the time to confess it."

Barksley looked up. "I have an online business that imports maple syrup—something that functions like high grade Moonshine with Sorkanan lizard men—and I have been smuggling it on transports leading to the extra-solar colonies. This avoids both the tariffs and laws circumventing food regulation."

"Barksley, you dog," I said, smiling. "You're a drug dealer. Cut me in."

"It's a cash business and I need someone to carry the money," Barksley said. "You better carry a weapon, though, because the syrup cartels are not to be barked with."

"We all need our side hustles," I replied. "Just understand I know people in the pound if you squeal on me."

Yeah, we were terrible cops and I 100% believed Barksley wasn't joking. There really were a bunch of armed crooks willing to kill over cookies and steaks. But I wasn't a cop to enforce the law, I was a cop to... Christ, I just realized Lucy had me pegged at Deckard's office. Now I felt bad for hassling her.

Sort of.

"It's the politics of contraband," Barksley sang some song's lyrics I dimly recognized. "It's the 'Smuggler's Blues'."

Lucy shook her head. "Fine, you're going to have to sleep with her."

I did another double take, my second of the day. "Excuse me?"

"I mean, I know you're going to do it anyway," Lucy said, as if it was *fait accompli*, "but this is an excellent opportunity for you to get in with a possible member of the Slavers Guild other than Nigel."

"She's not a slaver," I said, coldly. "Also, you seem very determined to push me onto other women. If this is a fetish of yours, I wish you'd just told me—"

"I need to know who killed Dick," Lucy said, cutting me off. "Just because I'm pissed that you got us fired doesn't mean that I'm not committed to the end to seeing these bastards taken down."

That shut me up. "You don't think we should be worrying about this upcoming apocalypse?"

Lucy didn't initially respond. "We better hope that she's able to get a hold of this quickly. If there is a risk of disease, the Moon will be screwed."

"Because it's an enclosed environment?" I asked.

"Because lunes are naturally belligerent, resistant to authority, and prone to conspiracy theories," Lucy said, finally admitting to some of the cultural flaws of her homeworld. "There have been disease outbreaks before on the Moon and they have a history of going very badly. People deliberately flout whatever rules the government sets up and resist treatment."

"Yeah, it's hard to trust the government after knowing it was deliberately selling your poorest into slavery," I muttered.

That was the thing about conspiracy theories, just because you were paranoid didn't mean they weren't out to get you. The corporations, Neo-Militarists, New Neo-Militarists—which was a stupid name if I'd ever heard one—and Syndicate were always plotting against the public. The thing was that every time you mentioned that to your average lune, they ended up somehow believing the real enemy was the Reformers, aliens, or immigrants. Which, granted, aliens could be up to anything, but I doubted they were poisoning our water with fluoride. Frankly, the fluoride was the only thing drinkable about the Moon's recycled piss.

"Same with the police," Lucy muttered, sounding depressed rather than angry. "How can we do our job if the public doesn't believe we have their best interests at heart."

"When the police don't," I muttered, remembering the pride in which Deckard had said they weren't here to solve crimes. The mask was officially off, it seemed. "Why did you want to be a cop, Lucy?"

"My dad believed that if you didn't have someone pushing back from the inside, no one would," Lucy said. "It got him killed in the end."

"I know," I paused. "Hey, Barksley, did the documents Kate sent over include anything about these terrorists and why they want us killed?"

"You could ask your cybernetic link up," Barksley said. "He's already deep into the SHID files."

I turned to Barksley. "Wait, you talk to my cybernetics without talking to me?"

"It's an AI thing," Barksley said, looking guilty.

THE SONS OF MITHRAS ARE A NATIVIST EXTREMIST IDEOLOGY GROUP FROM THE PLANET OF ALBION, Interface explained. ALBION IS THE LARGEST HUMAN DIASPORA WORLD. IT WAS SETTLED BY HUMANS KIDNAPPED FROM THE BRITISH ISLES MILLENNIA AGO. THE ORGANIZATION, NAMED AFTER A ROMAN WARRIOR GOD, ARE VIOLENTLY OPPOSED TO EARTH ENTERING THE GREATER GALACTIC COMMUNITY.

Why is that? I asked Interface. *I mean, Earthlings suck but I can't imagine they're much different even if they were settled by the Lost Legion and a bunch of Celts.*

If you had no idea who either of those groups were, look 'em up. Fascinating history.

THE GALACTIC COMMUNITY HAD SET ASIDE 100 TERRAFORMED PLANETS TO BE SETTLED BY ALBION AS PART OF ITS LARGER EXPANSION PROGRAM. THIS NUMBER HAS BEEN CUT IN HALF WITH THE REST GIVEN TO EARTH TO COLONIZE. THE LOSS OF PERSONAL PROPERTY AND WEALTH IS IN THE QUADRILLIONS.

Ah, I thought back. *That will do it.*

THEY'RE ALSO XENOPHOBIC SCUM THAT LOOK DOWN ON ALL NON-ALBION HUMANS AND ALIENS, Interface added, not losing his computer monotone. A MODERN BRITISH PERSON WOULD SEND A TYPICAL MEMBER OF THE GROUP INTO APOLEXY.

Lyndon Johnson had said the root of racism in America was that if you could convince a man that he was better than another, then he wouldn't notice you riffling through his pockets. Call it a hunch, but given this involved a lot of money, I suspected whoever stood to lose a fortune was the one who had outfitted the Sons of Mithras with the tools necessary to attack the Sol System and stoked their fears about us dirty homeworlders.

What do you think, Inferface? I asked, knowing he knew everything I knew and thought. I was effectively talking to myself whenever I had a conversation with the AI but that was the least strange thing about arrangement.

A NOT UNREASONABLE HYPOTHESIS BUT LACKING EVIDENCE, Interface said. BUT LACKING EVIDENCE AS WELL AS RELEVANCE AT THIS TIME.

"Anything noteworthy?" Lucy asked, clearly able to tell when I was talking to my inner computer or not.

"They hate our freedom, blah-blah-blah," I said. "Unfortunately, not enough to provide a lead. I've been a cop awhile. I know the difference between the victims of society, the bent but not broken, the poseurs, and the genuinely evil. The people carrying a grudge and wanting to do it for politics are the hardest to figure out. Self-interest is easy to follow up on. True believers are another matter entirely."

"We could start by asking actual Albionese humans about them," Barksley said.

"Do you know any?" I asked, sarcastically. I didn't know how many extra-solar humans had made their way back to Earth given, apparently, we were the ass end of the universe.

"Oh yes!" Barksley said, surprising me. "Ms. Breeze's cat therapist, Aurelius Saxon, is one."

"Her... what now?" I asked.

Lucy put the car on auto pilot as we began descending to Crater Two. It was a massive tunnel leading through the surface of the Moon to the giant cavern city below. "He's a live-in pet psychologist. He cares for Chairman Meow's needs."

"Chairman... Meow?" I asked, unsure I'd heard that right.

"He's a Siamese," Barksley explained.

Which just made it more racist.

"Is he a talking robot cat?" I asked.

"No," Lucy said, annoyed.

"Is there anything that would make a live-in pet therapist make sense?" I asked, confused.

"Aurelius is twenty-six and addicted to fitness," Lucy said, suggesting Ayanna's relationship with her employee was not strictly professional.

Shock.

"Ah," I replied. "Say no more."

I don't suppose you know much about this plague, do you? I asked Interface. *How bad is it?*

A GREAT DEAL OF HUMAN DISEASE OUTBREAKS ARE MADE WORSE BY PARALLEL EVOLUTION, Interface said. THE BLACK DEATH DEVASTATED EUROPE BECAUSE IT CAME FROM MONGOLIA VIA TRAVELERS. THE DEVASTATION OF THE NEW WORLD CAME BECAUSE NATIVE PEOPLES HAD NO NATURAL RESISTANCE TO SMALLPOX.

"*Yeah, well I'm glad we wiped out the latter,*" I thought back.

NOT ANYMORE, Interface replied.

My blood went cold. *"What*?"

THE SHID FORCES ARE FEARFUL OF A PARICULARLY VIRULENT VERSION OF WHAT THE ALBIONESE CALL RED FEVER, WHICH IS A DESCENDANT OF SMALLPOX HYBRIDIZED WITH THE COMMON COLD. THE ALBIONESE HAVE A NATURAL IMMUNITY AND TREAMENTS SO THE CHOICE OF INFECTING EARTH WITH IT IS DESIGNED FOR BOTH SYMBOLIC AS WELL AS PRACTICAL REASONS.

"Well shit," I said, aloud.

IT ALSO GETS WORSE. THERE ARE NO DOMESTICATED ANIMALS ON THE MOON OUTSIDE OF A FEW PETS AND ANIMALS FOR EXOTIC MEALS VERSUS VAT GROWN MEAT, Interface said. EXPOSURE TO A VARIETY OF MICROBES TO CREATE STRONGER IMMUNE SYSTEMS ISN'T HAPPENING IN A SPACE COLONY LIKE THIS. THOUGH THE SHEER INFLUX OF—

"Yeah, yeah, I get it, we're screwed," I said aloud.

YES.

"I take it that wasn't good news," Lucy said.

"Nope," I replied. "Maybe we should turn everyone into a posthuman."

EXTREMELY IMPRACTICAL, Interface said. ALBEIT EVEN MY KNOWLEDGE OF THEIR SYSTEMS IS LIMITED AND YOU SHOULD... DANGER ALERT.

"What now?" I asked, looking up.

We had entered Crater Town, which was certainly a place that you had to be there to appreciate. It was kind of a mixed underground city, giant slum, and post-apocalypse junk town all in one. It had been constructed out of just about everything handy when humans had moved into the base the Community had abandoned. The Community's technology had created artificial gravity, atmosphere, and hollowed out a state-sized location here, but it had been for housing equipment rather than people. It wasn't the only underground habitat on the Moon, but as it was underneath Luna City, it was the most important.

The place was a mixture of hastily put together brutalist architecture, prefabricated habitats, and the genuinely well-constructed buildings that had cost four or five times what they should have because getting the materials down here had been a nightmare. There were a lot fewer buildings made from Community shipping crates and hovels now that the Reformers had appointed Governor Hopwood, but it was still a long way until the place stopped being something of a science fiction dystopia.

I didn't immediately see anything wrong when the flying car started to descend, heading to a part of the city I was unfamiliar with. I wasn't too concerned and even relieved that nothing was happening until I saw Lucy was struggling with the controls.

"We've been hacked," Lucy said, growling. "I can't get control back."

"I don't suppose this could be the SHID folk showing off their cool tech," I said, before trying to encourage Interface to do something. *Make something happen!*

THAT'S NOT HOW I WORK, Interface corrected. THIS TECHNOLOGY IS MORE ADVANCED THAN MINE.

Oh crap.

"No," Lucy said, looking down at the building we were about to land on. "I don't think so."

"Why?" I asked.

"There's a bunch of armed men down here, looking like they're going to kill us," Lucy said.

Barksley frowned. "I just got the car painted."

Well shit.

CHAPTER SIX

More People Trying to Kill Us

"So, who do you think is trying to kill us today?" I asked, looking outside of the window to the rooftop that was covered in trash. It was one of the many failed factories that had been condemned by the new governor. She'd promised the social safety net would be expanded but, moonatics being who they were, had been pissed off by the prospect of being given anything rather than "earning" it. I swear, they were the only people in the solar system pissed off by the prospect of free stuff.

Probably best to focus on the armed gunmen I spotted a few seconds later. There were at least eight of them in flexible plastisteel armor and carrying automatic weapons. It was all locally sourced equipment, which told me we were dealing with either Moon-based criminals or foreigners who'd equipped themselves here. Which was a good thing because if they had fusion weapons or Community-based equipment like what had apparently hacked our onboard computer, we'd be utterly screwed.

"The fact there are so many suspects to that question is both flattering as well as depressing," Lucy said, staring down. "Out of curiosity, did you actually turn over your gun?"

"Hell no," I responded. "I even kept my badge. Did you?"

"Of course," Lucy said, off handedly. "I, thankfully had my spare as well as a half-dozen extra weapons in my tote bag."

Yeah, that was being a lune in a nutshell. They used to say a well-armed society was a polite society, which was bullshit because lunes were all jackasses. However, for once, I was going to be grateful for it.

The Purple Rain hit the ground of the roof with a slam. I tried to call for backup with my cybernetic link but, of course, they'd turned on some kind of jammer and I couldn't even contact Interface. Which was impressive given that the cyber linkup insisted it was nothing more than a manifestation of my unconscious, not to mention how often it talked about things I didn't know.

"Do you think they'll ask us to surrender?" I asked Lucy, pulling out my Herakles-7 pistol before Lucy went for her weapons in the back.

That was when the eight heavily armored figures proceeded to unload with their repeating rifles, the bullets smashing up against the heavily reinforced armor that had been installed by Barksley as part of the "improvements" to his car. Unfortunately, the ammunition was a pretty high caliber, and I didn't think the armor would last very long under their onslaught. Especially if they had anything heavier, like fusion weapons or grenades.

"It doesn't seem so," Lucy muttered, holding a handheld Ninja-12 submachine gun, shaped like a box with a handle. "Did you pack any other surprises in the vehicle there, Barks?"

"Yes," Barksley said. "But, sadly, they're in the trunk."

"Great!" I said, already seeing cracks begin to appear in the windows as I slouched down in the vain hope of defense.

"Ah dah ha dis," Barksley said, speaking with something in his mouth. It took a second to register it was a smoke grenade.

"Fuck yes," I said, grabbing it. "This may be our only chance with these assholes."

"Bad news, Neal," Lucy said, pointing. "They're bringing out a fusion cannon."

I could see that Lucy was right as two of the armored troopers had put aside their assault rifles and were now setting up a tripod with a fusion weapon. They were a lot slower than typical machine gun fire, but fusion weapons were how aliens preferred to do things as they were precision devices that would utterly tear through ordinary armor like an anti-material rifle. This one seemed like it would blow the car up in one blast.

"Mother pus bucket," I snapped, loading a clip of explosive rounds into my Herakles-7. Which I always kept on hand because, you know, murderous cyborgs and armored thugs. "Out the side!"

"I know!" Lucy shouted.

One thing I appreciated about these assholes was the fact they were clearly not skilled tacticians, or they would have surrounded us rather than firing all from one side. If they'd been smart, they would have crashed the car or used harder ordnance from the beginning. They clearly were planning on making it look like a local hit but were improvising since Barksley getting his ride pimped—or was it pimp ride pimped? —had thrown a wrench in those plans.

Lucy and Barksley headed out the driver's side doors as I dropped the smoke grenade while throwing myself out behind Lucy. The windows had already collapsed on the passenger's side and the smoke poured out, creating a brief cover for us. The sound system was playing "Smuggler's Blues" by Glenn Fry at full blast. Weirdly, despite the fact people were trying to kill me, I noted that was the song Barksley had quoted earlier.

"I swear if I owned real estate in this town and Hell, I'd choose to rent here and live in Hell," I muttered.

That was when I heard the telltale sound of the tripod mounted fusion cannon powering up and I knew we had to move even further away from the car, exposing ourselves to further attack with only the smoke cloud around us protecting us. Still, Lucy and I got up and bolted with our heads kept down.

That was when Lucy scooped Barksley up off the ground and proceeded to plant herself against the ground before blasting with our dog gun, shooting out a continuous beam of stun fire that led to several shouts from the other side. That was my cue, and I used the shouts to deliver shots with my Herakles-7's explosive rounds.

If I had performed a miracle and every single shot counted—something maybe possible with my enhanced posthuman senses, that I didn't currently have access to—then all the stunned attackers had been killed. We would be safe and just must explain eight new bodies to the local authorities that we no longer had behind us. The sound of the fusion cannon going off followed by the car exploding disabused me of that notion.

The destruction of the Purple Rain sent us both flying backwards and showered us with flaming wreckage. If both of us hadn't been posthumans, involuntarily or not, we would have probably died or at least been deafened. Actually, given I couldn't hear anything, I was pretty sure we both had been deafened. My entire body also felt on fire, and I started patting my arm before throwing off my coat when I realized I was. Worse, my fedora was burning as well.

Fortunately, my skewed priorities were immediately distracted from my hat by the sight of Lucy lying on the ground with her arms wrapped around Barksley. She'd shielded the dog with herself and looked like she'd taken a piece of shrapnel to the back. I tried to get up, failed, and crawled over to her side before hearing our attackers' stomping plastisteel boots against the ground.

I managed to reach Lucy but couldn't see where my gun was. My head was also ringing as Interface had reactivated and was flashing a damage report across my eyes. Except, it was fricking French, and I couldn't read French.

The numbers didn't look good, though.

DOMMAGES GRAVES DÉTECTÉS

TOTALE CAPACITÉ 58%
RÉPARATION 23%
PHYSIQUE 74%
MENTALE 93%

SERVICE D'URGENCE À PROXIMITÉ

The numbers turned into code even as I saw three of the attackers coming towards us, one of them with a massive crack in his armor from where I'd shot him. They stood over us and raised their weapons. I tried looking for my gun, but it was pointless as it had been knocked out of my hands and was across the roof. This was it; I was about to be executed by a bunch of people I had no idea the identity of or for what reasons. I tried to think of a badass one-liner to go out on, but I was struck by the unfairness of it all.

I dimly heard some sort of shouting from above, but the big surprise of mine was the three attackers raising their weapons to fire were speaking in something vaguely like Latin. Of course, most European languages were pretty like Latin too, so that didn't really help me identify matters. What followed was a very short and one-sided fire fight as the attackers were gunned down above us, fusion rounds tearing through their armor and leaving them dead beside us.

Gradually, my vision cleared as I saw there was a black gunship hovering above the rooftop, its side open and armored soldiers rappelling out. Either Interface had sent out a distress signal before everything had been jammed or Armstrong, being the omniscient machine that it was, had picked up us being hacked. Either way, I didn't particularly care as a medic was by Lucy's side first, followed by two familiar figures standing over me.

The first was Priscilla "Priss" Aim, former pop star and mercenary, who was wearing a STRIKE uniform with its khakis and red beret, a plastisteel vest, and knee pads contrasting to the attacking soldier's full armor. There was also an energy barrier belt—which was basically shields from *Star Trek*—but that was cutting edge technology even in the Community. She was holding a fusion rifle and was presumably the person who'd gunned down our attackers.

Priss was a brown-skinned woman who had features so sharp you cut yourself on them. She was also built like an Amazon goddess and looked like the kind of person who could throw someone like Kate around like a ragdoll, but I put the odds of any fight between them at about even. Like many servicemen after the war, she'd been disillusioned and become something of an anarchist. Why she was wearing the uniform of the most hated and derided public agencies was anyone's guess. I'd heard her career as a singer had ended dramatically so there was an A to C correlation missing a B here.

The other person was Nigel Blackwood. A person that invoked all sorts of feelings inside me ranging from loathing to fear to regret for

59

our lost friendship. He was a good-looking man, even by the standards of modern genetically engineered super beings. He had pale skin, long black hair kept in a ponytail, and a beard that made him look like he could have done a decent Dracula. Something I always thought was an interesting comparison to make given Lucy's role as an ex-vampire hunter on TV.

Nigel wore a business suit that cost more than I made in a year and had a presence that seemed to suck the light out of the room, but maybe that was my just my feelings toward him affecting my perception. He hadn't always looked like a vampire, but the past years hadn't been kind to him and had enhanced his worst qualities while erasing his best. Weirdly, he seemed to think of me as his best friend still and I didn't know how to parse that.

"You okay, Neal?" Nigel offered his hand down.

I ignored it and slowly climbed to my feet. "Given I was just blown up, no. I've been better. Thanks, Priss."

Priss was already checking on Lucy as another one of the former Knights hyperpunk band was treating her. It was Nina Asimov, a pink-haired true crime fan that I'd understood had been a medic during the Unification Wars. She was also dressed in a STRIKE uniform.

"How is she?" I asked Nina.

"If she was human, she'd be dead," Nina said. "Thankfully, she's a posthuman and she'll recover with a half-dozen food tubes. It's going to hurt like hell, though, for the next few hours."

Lucy managed to raise her right hand in the air and flip Nina off. That was the first sign to me that she was going to be alright. It was further supplemented by Barksley crawling out from under her and shaking himself off with only a bit of singed fur to show for it. An immense relief flooded me, and I let loose a breath I hadn't even been aware I'd been holding in. If this were a movie, I would have some sudden overwhelming revelation about how I'd almost lost Lucy and it would convince me to reaffirm my love.

That didn't happen.

I'd wanted that kind of relationship with Lucy, and it had helped push us apart rather than bring us together. Maybe she was still in mourning over Dick or maybe she simply didn't care as deeply for me.

Instead, I was more worried about the loss of the two closest people I had on the Moon. Anywhere really. That wasn't the same as love but maybe it was a kind of it.

"Are you alright, Officer Barksley?" Nigel asked, looking down at the bio-mechanical dog.

Barksley looked up to Nigel. "Mr. Blackwood, are you familiar with the songs of the 21st century artist, Cee Lo Green?"

"I can't say that I am," Nigel said.

"He has a two-word song title for you," Barksley said, walking past him. That was about as close to swearing as Barksley was ever likely to get and probably still was violating the spirit of his programming.

"Wow, the dog hates you," I muttered, watching Barksley jump on the gunship's side as it hovered at the rooftop's edge to let off more soldiers. "He loves everybody."

"It senses evil," Priss muttered, showing she had a pretty good idea of who Nigel was.

"Congratulations," Nigel said. "You managed to take down three of the Sons of Mithras cells. We took down four more and the eighth was incapacitated. We're going to take that last one in for interrogation."

My head was gradually clearing as I saw the information display switch from French to English again. The numbers were also going up, slightly, which told me that I was gradually repairing myself. However, it was also something that made me ravenously hungry.

GRAVE DAMAGE DETECTED

TOTAL CAPACITY 63%
REPAIR 28%
PHYSICAL 75%
MENTAL 95%

I saw the other STRIKE soldiers securing one of our attackers on the ground as they checked the other bodies for life signs. They didn't seem to have any, which I had about as much sympathy for as a dead slaver, which was to say none. I didn't recognize any of the others and was almost disappointed not to see any more of the Knights band having joined up. It would have added to the surrealness of the experience.

"Why the hell would the Sons of Mithras be here? Why the hell would they target us? How the hell did you guys find us in time? Were we bait?" I looked at Priss. "Also, when the hell did you join STRIKE? You hate the government. Plus, since I'm asking ridiculous question because I have a concussion, what are the next winning lotto numbers."

"You know the lottery is rigged," Nigel said. "I know because it's one of my jobs to rig it. I could give you the winning numbers—"

"I don't want your dirty money," I said, hating myself for saying it but flat out unwilling to accept anything that might have been bought with human freedom. I noted he didn't answer any of my questions, though, and I had a lot for him after the way his last tip went down.

"Those are all good questions," a voice came from the gunship. It was Kate. She was still wearing her white business suit but had managed to put on a barrier belt and had a fusion rifle in her hands as well, which made her look like she'd been doing an advertisement for Atlas Security's "Businesswomen With Guns" spread. Which was a real article I'd read in *Fortunato*, I swear.

"Am I going to get any answers?" I asked, looking at Lucy and Nina.

Nina provided Lucy a tube of goop, who rapidly squeezed the contents down her mouth before reaching for another. I didn't ask for one since my injuries were less severe. The fact goop looked appetizing right now was a sign of just how hungry I was. The stuff was a nutrient rich paste that had been created primarily to keep people from starving during the Long Winter. It had worked too.

Much to my surprise, I could see the injuries on Lucy's face and back healing before my very eyes. It reminded me of just how powerful the Community's technology really was. It was a relief to see she was getting better. I noticed she didn't even look at Nigel but was staring directly at Kate.

"Not right this moment," Kate said, gesturing. "Everything will be made clear, though, when we get to base. Unfortunately, the fact the Sons of Mithras have a cell operating here is a sign that things are much worse off than we could have imagined. We've also got more information that the infection has already begun to spread. We may have to quarantine the Moon."

I wasn't sure if quarantining the Moon would do any bit of good since if these guys really were terrorists trying to spread a plague, the fact was that they looked like everybody else. There wasn't much space travel between Earth and the rest of the galaxy but enough that its fellow humans could disappear in as well as out. As usual, while humanity's bigots had been worried about the lizards and slugs, the real enemy had been us.

"We'll get going," Lucy said, standing up and heading to the gunship. She pushed aside Nina when the medic tried to help. "I need a change of clothes, though."

I nodded. "Be right with you."

Priss surprised me by speaking. "Yeah, I called the CEO of Karma Corp a literal child rapist and got sued. All my songs' proceeds were put in a charitable trust so they couldn't be touched but I'm pretty much forbidden from ever making music again. STRIKE's healthcare plan is surprisingly good. There's not really a story there."

I looked at her, skeptically. "That's not a story?"

Well, it wasn't a story I believed but it was a story.

"I mean, I call a lot of suits child rapists," Priss said. "Mostly because they are."

Nina muttered something under her breath and got up to head to the gunship.

I wasn't about to talk to Nigel here, but I did see a look exchanged between him and Kate. Much to my surprise, the expression on Kate's face was cold-blooded disdain while the one on Nigel's was unease bordering on fear.

What the hell had happened to my ex?

And what kind of pull did she have that Nigel feared her?

CHAPTER SEVEN

It's Worse Than We Thought

SHID has set up shop in Crater Town in an old apartment building that had been scheduled for demolition. It was a strange decision but was apparently made in the hope that a lid could be kept on things for the next few days before those things really went to shit. Given the speech that Kate was delivering, that hope was probably in vain.

I was sitting in a room with a couple of dozen people in folding chairs as Kate stood in front of us, giving us a lecture. We all had a seat between us and some of us were wearing masks even though we were all immune to normal diseases as part of our recruitment. That meant the group was top heavy with posthumans, bioroids in the shape of human beings, or people with heavy cybernetics. Barksley was to my left while Lucy was behind me in a STRIKE uniform. To my right was a guy I didn't recognize who looked like he'd been made in a factory for action movie stars. Action Dan would have been envious of his jawline.

Kate was standing in front of a holographic projector and holding an old-style pointer that seemed to add to the weird post-apocalypse ambiance of the decaying duracrete building around us. A lunar cockroach skidded across the floor for emphasis. What was the difference between a lunar cockroach and an Earth one? An Earth cockroach would survive a nuclear war. Lunar ones would eat them for breakfast.

"As some of you already know the details, Division Four or SHID has been activated for the purposes of dealing with the potential outbreak of a virulently dangerous disease on the Moon," Kate replied. "Cross-species diseases are almost impossible, so it was considered a low-level risk to deal with the Community initially. However, that was before we discovered that there were numerous human settlements out there. They were created by forces unknown for reasons unknown, but this means that our biology is compatible."

That was burying the lead and obscuring the fact that both the government and transtellars had been aware of the extra-solar human colonies for decades. The only reason it wasn't more commonly known was because it was a fucking huge journey to the Community with Earth's existing jump drives—almost a year—and the nature of rumor and conspiracy meant that no one really trusted what was coming from the extra-solar colonies that were only a few months to six months away. Sailor stories had regained their reputation for insane exaggeration. I mean, I'd heard everything from the idea the center of the galaxy had a bunch of billion-year-old AI living there and that the Community's politicians were actually nice.

Nonsense.

"That the Sons of Mithras is the terrorist organization behind this is still being investigated, but it is generally assumed that they would be using infected carriers passively spreading this disease," Kate said. "However, due to the efforts of Agents Gordon and Westenra, we've discovered that there are already terrorist cells within the populace of the Moon. We've managed to take one prisoner alive but genetic testing shows the dead were all born off-world and these ones have been here six months."

Well, that was going to cause massive paranoia when it came out. It also told me these guys were true believers. It was one thing to kill someone in a fight or, hell, bomb them from orbit. I knew a drone strike operator who had a kill count in four figures but never lost any sleep over it and wasn't a psychopath as near as I could tell. However, it was another when you were living among people, eating their food, and speaking their language. It took a special kind of evil to decide, "Yeah, I'm going to infect all of these people with a horrifying disease."

Lucy surprised me by interrupting. "How many off-world humans are living on the Moon presently?"

"Close to a hundred thousand," Kate said, causing me to straighten up in my chair. "It turns out a large chunk of the workers the Community brought to set up the equipment on the Moon for Earth's environmental repair and uplift were humans. They were all enhanced through their brain implants to be able speak Earth languages as well as to be familiar with Earth customs. Quite a few of them chose to stay after the Community ended most of its relief programs."

The description of the Community's efforts as "relief programs" was the easiest way to identify everyone who had been born on the Moon versus the people who had come from Earth, Mars, or a space station colony. Every lune here, save maybe Barksley, had an instinctual revulsion to the concept of accepting charity. The Moon had been settled by refugees, radical libertarians, and a bunch of religious ideologues who considered the concept shameful. This had been encouraged by their corporate masters who instilled the ideology through state media that the only people who deserved to live were hard working drones. It was better to rob someone than receive a handout.

The Community, by contrast, got its kicks from condescending compassion. In the opposite of *Star Trek*'s Federation, the Community loved finding less developed worlds and showering them with gifts while showing off how righteous they were. Earth had been on its last legs when they'd repaired the environment and helped construct all the orbital colonies necessary to address serious inequity. They'd even started work on Mars and getting us into space when the Neo-Militarists had kicked them out. Well, asked them to leave. Apparently, that had been less of a complete withdrawal than I expected.

"How the hell do they leave behind a hundred thousand people, and no one knows?" Priss complained, reacting as much as everyone else with disgust. Which was ironic since she was as close as the Moon had to a radical leader with her own charities.

"People knew," Kate explained. "Just not the number or extent of their presence. They were valuable assets during the Unification Wars."

Wow, that was all but admitting they'd helped overthrow the Neo-Militarists. Also, that the government was involved in covering all this up—something that would have been impossible if not for the fact that AI like Armstrong controlled the infonet and other communications.

"One thing puzzles me," I said.

"One thing?" Barksley asked, looking at me.

"If we've got a hundred thousand Albionese among us, then we should have been riddled with diseases already," I replied. "Assuming we don't have any resistance to their disease or vice versa, a pandemic should have happened early on."

"That's your question?" Barksley asked.

I was really annoyed by that dog sometimes, but I just crossed my arms and stared at Kate.

"Interplanetary travel requires stringent disease control. The people of Albion have been properly vaccinated with their own protections and treatments, things far beyond our present ability to utilize."

There was an obvious response there but one that I knew Kate had almost certainly thought of and would go over like a ton of bricks with this audience. However, being as I was all out of fucks to give—and I'd never had that many to begin with—I said my peace anyway. "So, if the Community has all this incredibly advanced healing tech, why not ask them for help? They keep a battle cruiser in-system for a reason, after all."

If there had been popcorn in the crowd, I was sure I would have been pelted with it. If there was one subject more sensitive than accepting charity on the Moon, then it was asking the Community for help—which was either apropos or ironic depending on how you thought of the fact this colony wouldn't exist if not for the Community setting it up as a resupply base before all of the current residents had rushed in.

The Neo-Militarists had come into power playing on a combination of human pride and xenophobia, staying in power longer than the rest of Earth on the Moon, albeit that was mostly because the lunes were too busy fighting each other to mount an effective resistance. The Community hadn't exactly helped their reputation, though. A year ago, the Community's local admiral had threatened to reduce the Moon and its entire population to atoms in retaliation for a terrorist attack that had killed the local ambassador.

I was pretty sure it was just a negotiating tactic to force local authorities (i.e. me) to find the parties responsible, but it had left a powerful impression on the Moon's inhabitants. Among other things it had also ruined the Moon's relationship with Earth since EarthGov had barely muttered an objection over the whole thing. A year ago, independence talk was a fringe idea— because it was stupid given the Moon was utterly dependent on Earth goods—but now support was hovering around 30%.

"Attempts have been made to reach out to the Community battle cruiser, *Heart of Sorka*, in the asteroid belt," Kate said, looking embarrassed at having to admit to this.

"Let me guess, they've said no," Lucy said.

"They've said that they've passed the request to render assistance up to the Community proper," Kate said. "Which is universal for covering their asses with layers of bureaucracy. We could get an answer in three weeks, or we could get in a year. Either way, it wouldn't necessarily help as this virus is unique. Doctor Frankenstein?"

A good looking but aging black man stood up, a joint hanging out of his mouth as he wore a pair of sunglasses even though we were in the basement of an apartment building with bad lighting. He was wearing a Hawaiian shirt and khaki shorts with flip flops, making me wonder if he'd come from the beach. Dude was over a hundred years old but looked about mid-to-late fifties due to being mostly cybernetics.

I recognized the guy as Doctor Gerard Saint Croix AKA Doctor Frankenstein, not his real name in case you were wondering given the Moon's odd naming habits. He was a doctor as well as occasional medical examiner, which was rarer than you might think. The guy's nickname came from the fact he was one of the last old school street cyberneticists. Before everything had been handled by robots, he'd set up criminals and Runners with their equipment.

Somehow, he'd gotten a pardon by the governor and a cushy government job working with the police. I'd never worked with the guy, avoiding civi police like the plague, but he was one of the few people to turn down a job with Cyberlife after being headhunted by them.

Doctor Frankenstein turned on the holo-projector and showed a bunch of horrifying images of people covered in sores, lying dead with foam in their mouth, and being eaten alive by alien wildlife. "Okay, short version, because I don't want to be here, and I just want to impress upon you screwheads that this is some bad shit. These images are from the Nergal colony in the Tiamat system. It had a population of 27,320 and now has a population of zero."

"It killed everyone?" I asked, horrified. I really should have kept my mouth shut and paid attention, but the images were horrifying.

"No, dipshit, it did not," Doctor Frankenstein said. "The Red fever has a fatality rate of just above fifty percent, twenty percent more than smallpox used to have. Which is shocking given advancements in science. The geneticists who modified this virus lowered the initial fatality ratio because the goal was to spread it as much as possible. The rest of the population is currently in quarantine off-world. We can speculate a good ten percent of humans are immune and an additional five percent are asymptomatic carriers that will fuck up our attempts to quarantine this if we don't do a lot of testing quick."

"We believe this was the attempt at testing the virus," Kate explained. "Nergal is one of the disputed worlds between Albion and Earth that the Community terraformed for human settlement. The other colonies have been isolated and we believe that resulted in them planning to infect the Sol system as a whole."

Doctor Frankenstein wasn't done yet, though. "There's something funny about mixing smallpox with a rhinovirus, given they have different modes of spreading, but the mode of spreading also controls how they do damage. Rhinoviruses spready through the air, and so express themselves in the lungs, causing congestion and so forth. Smallpox spreads by physical contact, and so has pustules all over the body to cover the victim in viral fluids. Making a smallpox virus spread by air makes it... something that isn't recognizably smallpox at all. Kind of weird, eh?"

Was he drunk?

"Uh huh," Kate said, looking at him. "Anyway, the first cases of Red fever started appearing on the Moon thirty-nine hours ago. We've managed to identify the vectors for this outbreak, keep the area its manifested under lockdown, and it's now on you to determine if there are any other potential sources while implementing whatever measures necessary to contain this. I've transferred the information to your infopads."

"How long have you known?" I asked, looking up to Kate.

"Excuse me?" Kate asked.

"You just said that one of the first human colonies in outer space was wiped out by these guys, which is fucking huge news to me by the way," I said, blinking. I'd served as a guard on places like Nergal. "Now you're telling me you were looking for a potential viral attack that you only recently found out has already occurred. Which was before you found out there's actual fucking agents of this Sons of Mithras group here already. Have I got that right?"

I didn't mean to come off as accusatory, but, well, this reeked of a cover up. We weren't being brought in to head off a potential disaster in the making, we were being brought in because the government had already fucked up, tried to sweep it under the rug, and now that was unraveling.

"Three months," Kate said, causing everyone in the audience to become deathly silent. If you knew anything about lunes, that meant everyone had gone from being annoyed at me to being quietly furious.

You could have heard a pin drop.

"What was the vector used to deliver the virus?" Lucy asked, keeping her calm and focusing on the disaster at hand.

"Loop," Kate answered automatically, seemingly grateful for the interruption.

"Loop," Lucy said, pausing. "They're using *narcotics* to kill the population?"

There was one exception to the fact that the moonatics believed in maximum freedom with a minimum of government oversight and that was the Food and Drug administration. Most drugs weren't *illegal* on the Moon, quite the contrary, but they were intensely *regulated* because one of the Moon's two major megacorporations was a pharmaceutical firm.

Karma Corp, in its desire to squeeze every credit out of its customers pockets, made sure that manufactured drugs were incredibly expensive as well as subject to constant inspections and oversight. If you didn't have one of Karma Corp's licenses to produce happy pills or pep pills or sex pills, you might as well be a mass-murderer.

Of course, when there's a huge demand for something that people can't afford, the black market finds its way of providing. Loop was an all-purpose designer stimulant used extensively as a combat drug and a "work performance enhancer" for laborers, allowing them to pull 72-hour shifts at once. As Sergeant Barnes had discovered when Kate had pulled his head off, it was also prone to driving you fucking nuts.

"Yes," Kate replied, continuing a conversation I'd briefly checked out of. "The Albionese government is deeply conservative with a strong taboo against chemical enhancement or recreation. Thus, using Loop is a way for them to strike at us through our decadent degenerate culture."

I had no idea what that meant.

Kate continued. "We believe the Sons of Mithras sent their operatives to set up shop here on the Moon, manufacture narcotics, and then sprayed the results. Given the invisible nature of the work, the disease will be able to move through the city via a network of people that isn't aware they're digesting poison before naturally spreading the disease."

Well, we were fucked before but now we were royally fucked. Tracking the free movement of who used Loop was not so much looking for a needle in a haystack but looking for a needle in a bunch of other needles. Everyone from executives to students to crazy homeless guys used Loop. The differences were the quality and cost, not whether they used it at all.

"Do we have any leads?" Lucy said.

"Yes," Kate said. "Unfortunately, our initial strategy was following the spread of the infection and trying to find our patients zero. Now we have a prisoner who might be able to give us another avenue to tackle this. I want you and Detective Gordon to interrogate him."

"Why us?" Lucy asked, not realizing this was a dictatorship.

Kate clearly hadn't spent much time on the Moon because she was exasperated by the constant interruptions and questions. The thing was that this is how lunatics preferred to conduct things and were a planetoid defined by leaders trying to herd cats. Like all stereotypes, this was mostly perception versus reality but there was enough of a grain of truth in it— especially as lunes liked to think of *themselves* as freedom obsessed rugged individualists—to make it more than just other planets' ignorance.

Kate decided to abandon professionalism and adopt the sarcasm I knew her for. "Not to put too fine a point on it, but the Moon's cops have a history of just beating whatever they want out of prisoners. Which rarely yields actionable intel."

"This guy wants to kill me and everyone I know," Lucy said, staring. "I'm not sure I'm not going to beat him within an inch of his life."

"Then it's a good thing Neal will be there," Kate said, dryly.

I looked up, confused. "When did I become the good cop?"

"Good cop, versus bad cop is a matter of degrees. I mean, compared to me, you don't have much in the way of hair," Barksley said.

Nigel, unfortunately, chose that moment to join the conversation. He was just sitting here among the others with a big smile on his face like a wolf among sheep. "You're more the tricky cop. You could sell ice machines to Eskimos."

"That was one time and Antarctica had plenty of them. Repairing global warming was something I figured they could use at the North Pole too," I replied, only half lying. I really had made some peculiar less-than-legal deals while down there.

"Either way, we have to chase down every possible avenue and organize mass testing to hold this pandemic off," Kate said. "With any luck, we can prevent it from reaching the populace as a whole."

"Yeah, that's not gonna happen," Doctor Frankenstein said.

Kate closed her eyes and counted to three. "But if we locate the infected Loop and destroy it, we can minimize the spread and maybe keep casualties low until a vaccine can be created. EarthGov's Spacefleet and Karma Corp has been working on it for three months."

I looked at Nigel, who didn't look back at me. That explained why the survivors of Nergal had been quarantined well past the expiration date for the disease, they were being used as human guinea pigs. It also meant as Chief Security Officer of Karma Corp, he'd known about this as well. I couldn't even object too much as this might end up being the salvation of the people on the Moon.

Of course, that thought immediately left my brain once I remembered that Karma Corp was one of the big sponsors of the Slavers Guild. It was possible the very people I'd been trying to rescue for a year were even now getting infected with this virus. In which case, I was now party, however distantly, to some real mad scientist garbage. Which made me wonder if Operation: Jenner was related to this. Another reason to shut this shit down quickly.

"Obviously, I don't have to tell you that this is all classified," Kate said.

The response from the audience was silence.

Yeah, this was going to be a disaster.

CHAPTER EIGHT

The Lost Art of Interrogation

"So, that went well," I said, taking my most sarcastic tone possible while looking at Lucy and Barksley.

The three of us were outside a basement janitor's office that had been converted into an interrogation chamber. We'd been shuffled off here against our will to wait until the prisoner was prepped for speaking. Thankfully, that didn't appear to be a euphemism for torture, but we'd still been out here far longer than I'd expected. About the only consolation to each of us was I'd finally gotten some goop tubes to eat as well as three bottles of water. Thus, I no longer felt like my body was starving to death as it repaired all the damage.

YOU WON'T BE ALLOWED TO DO DAMAGE TO YOURSELF BY HEALING PAST YOUR STARVATION LIMIT, Interface corrected. WE ARE NOT PROGRAMMED TO BE STUPID THAT WAY. YOU WILL, HOWEVER, STALL REPAIRS WHEN YOU DON'T HAVE BIOMATTER TO FUEL OUR WORK.

That was one benefit of being a posthuman, you could eat like a spacer and never gain any weight. Mind you, food was prohibitively expensive on the Moon anyway. It was why goop existed in the first place and so much of it was mushroom based. Hint: humans produce a lot of crap that needs to be used for something.

"It was a disaster, but I know you're being sarcastic," Lucy said, adjusting her STRIKE uniform. It was a button-down brown khaki shirt, neckerchief, and green shorts that made her look like she was a scoutmaster. The little skull pins and patches with guns on them lent it a decidedly different tone if you looked closely, though. Lucy looked uncomfortable with it, but it was the only change of clothes they had. "God, I hate this outfit. I look like Fascist Barbie."

"I think impersonating a STRIKE officer is a federal crime," I muttered.

"Not actually," Barksley said. "Despite the fact STRIKE works as a federal agency, they're technically a corporation of independent contractors the same way Cyberlife is. However, the use of STRIKE uniforms is meant to help cover up this massive threat to the public this Red fever is. Which is a stopgap measure to begin with."

"I thought they were phasing out STRIKE," I said, looking at the dog.

"What better time to let them take the blame for everything?" Barksley said. "I'm annoyed, though. I wanted to go undercover. Maybe I could get an eyepatch or a scar to be an EVIL dog."

"Corgis can't be evil," Lucy said, leaning down and scratching behind his ears.

"I can try!" Barksley said, smashing his paw on a lunar cockroach and killing it. "You know the reason these things are so huge is because they grow them to make up the protein for Red Goop."

I paused slurping down a red tube of goop like I was drinking toothpaste.

"That's a lie," Lucy reassured me. "The red comes from vats. The cockroaches are in entirely different meals."

"You're both evil. "I finished off my tube despite myself. "I'm glad you're looking better, though, Lucy."

"It's not the closest I've ever come to death, but it was pretty close," Lucy said. "The fact they knew where we were and had the technology take us down is worrying. I wouldn't be surprised if your ex was covering her bases. Just because she let us go last night doesn't mean that she didn't decide it was a bad idea."

I stared at her. "Really? That's your theory?"

Lucy grimaced, perhaps knowing she was making a wild accusation. "This is where you point out that hiring us in the first place is a strange choice when—"

"Actually, I'd point out they saved us so setting us up in the first place is a dumb decision," I replied. "Next, I'd point out that this guy we're interrogating does seem to be a member of the Sons of Mithras since sending us in there is otherwise incredibly stupid. Third, we could also just ask him how they knew."

Lucy blinked. "Okay, my theory has some holes—"

"You think?" I asked.

"But there could be a leak in the Department," Lucy said. "I don't need to point out that the other most likely suspect is Nigel, whose presence here I find to be revolting."

"No kidding," I replied.

"He could be allied with the terrorists," Lucy said.

Wow, she was just on a wild conspiracy roll right now. "I think that is extremely unlikely."

"Because you think your former friend isn't capable of it?" she asked.

"I think my former friend is fully capable of anything," I replied. "Once you're kidnapping people to sell into slavery—"

I paused as a pair of guards passed by. This really wasn't the place to be having this sort of conversation. Then again, most of the conversations were every bit as wild and conspiracy filled. Most people were talking about the plague, obviously, and what measures they could possibly take to avert it. Lucy's was hardly the only idea about its origins and what the government was doing (or not doing). More sensible but equally dangerous people were discussing how they could get their relatives or other loved ones to safety or even if that was possible.

"—Well, there's nothing you won't do," I continued. "However, Nigel's not an irrational actor. He allied with the guild to cure his wife's condition as well as move up from being a lowly corporate detective to being an executive. He's also been helping us, to an extent, so I don't see reason for him to suddenly want us dead."

"I do," Barksley said. "Again, we're loose ends. I believe he's only using you to handle his business partners. I think that means any brotherly affection you once shared is nonexistent."

"Preaching to the choir, doggie," I said. "I have plenty of questions about what's going on here. However, now's not the time to be debating all this if the Moon really is on the verge of a massive outbreak of Red fever."

"I think we have to act as if it's real even if we're chasing shadows and keeping eyes in the back of our heads," Lucy said.

"I knew a guy who had one of those cybernetically inserted," I replied. "It ended up causing brain damage that killed him in a year."

Lucy rolled her eyes. "In any case, we have other people we have to watch. Priss and Nina are definitely going to be a problem."

"You don't buy her story about taking a job with the government after losing her fortune?" I asked, willing to trust Lucy's judgement here.

Lucy stared at me skeptically. "If Priscilla has joined STRIKE or is pretending to do so, it's only so she can burn the place down from the inside. She's lived in squalor in the Depths just fine and has plenty of fans who would be willing to put her up. And the other band members are missing. The Knights are kind of a murder sex-cult as much as a sisterhood. They wouldn't abandon her."

I stared at her.

"You're contemplating the fact I was part of the band and just described it as a murder sex cult," Lucy said, reading my expression.

I blinked. "I make no apologies."

Priss, Nina, and Lucy were the most conventionally attractive of the Knights, but I wouldn't have kicked any of them out of my bed for eating crackers. Which had to be the weirdest old timey saying in the world. Who gave up sex for crumbs?

"I'm afraid she's going to try to do something insane like expose everything," Lucy said, pensive. "It's why this can't be let out to Rashad either. Big Brother is exactly the kind of site that would see something sinister in EarthGov's actions here."

"Probably because there is something sinister in covering up ten thousand people dying on one of our 'hope for the survival of the species' colonies?" I pointed out. "Not to mention that this Red fever should be announced to the heavens so people can be properly warned. The people have a right to know."

"You really think that?" Lucy asked.

"Hell no," I said, tossing my discarded tubes in a nearby rubbish bin. It was already filled with creatures even more unsettling than the Moon roaches. "People are stupid animals and will inevitably make any situation they get involved in a whole lot worse. I just believe the government and so-called experts aren't any better."

"We should put the dogs in charge," Barksley said. "Then the world would have you serve us! Oh wait, that's already the case."

"That's cats, Barks," I replied. "You really think Priss is a mole?"

"I think it was utterly insane to hire her," Lucy said. "Someone had to rubber stamp her through a dozen security warnings or hack the system or both. Her presence along with Nigel's makes me think your ex-wife must be..."

Lucy trailed off.

"What?" I asked.

"She's behind me, isn't she?" Lucy asked.

I smirked at her joke then looked up to see that, in fact, Kate was standing behind Lucy next to Lucy's half-sister, Shinobu. Shinobu was a small, beautiful Eurasian woman who looked like everybody's ideal kid sister (if you were heavily into Japanese animation). She was also majorly into explosions and heavy ordnance. Her eyes were an eerie set of blue and I meant that in the *Dune* sense, not the she just has blue irises way.

Shinobu had merged with Armstrong and become the Cognition AI's avatar when dealing with threats to the Moon and Ares Electronics, of which he was a primary stockholder. It had resulted in her personality subtly shifting and becoming more ethereal while Armstrong had, well, started to develop the habits of an oddball gunsmith girl.

Shinobu was wearing her Cyberlife uniform still and it made me wonder if we hadn't been fired whether we would still be members of the corpo police when attached to Department Four.

"Yes," I said. "Also, the Oracle of Delphi."

"Armstrong not Delphi," Shinobu said. "Delphi is an entirely different AI attached to Department One."

"I was hoping to get you to sign some paperwork," Kate said, handing over an infopad. "Your verbal consent or thumbprint will be fine."

"What's it for?" I said, taking it and starting to read.

"It prevents you from discussing anything you hear here upon penalty of twenty years to life in prison," Kate replied. "Plus, other issues. We'll have you take the SHID oath later."

"I'm not comfortable with this without consulting a lawyer," Lucy said.

"You don't get paid unless you sign," Kate said. "As specialists, you get full coverage and pay equivalent to your Cyberlife jobs as well as additional overtime and danger bonuses, the latter of which will be applied retroactively to today."

"I consent," I said to the infopad then tapped my thumb on it. "Done and done."

"Really, Neal?" Lucy asked, turning to me. "There are more important things than money."

"A phrase invented by either the very rich or the very poor," I replied. "Can I get a replacement trench coat and hat? My shirt is a bit singed as well. I'm not a big fan of Gestapo chic, though."

"You'll have to do your own clothes shopping, Neal, but I can get a voucher for your expenses. Paperwork is the meat and drink of government. Which you'd know if you ever bothered to do yours," Kate gestured to me as she watched Lucy sign. "How have you put up with this guy?"

"We're not going to be friends," Lucy replied. "Ms.?"

"*Agent*," Kate clarified. "And you will be too once you sign up. With all the due responsibilities and expectations of a government employee. Earth is a little stickier about the whole rules thing than the Land Upover. Which is Australia's nickname for the Moon."

I shrugged. "Yeah, I got that."

"You can trust these people, Lucy," Shinobu said, smiling. "They're an unscrupulous ruthless government paramilitary organization that is already breaking dozens of laws in the pursuit of stopping this plague. However, their primary desire is to stop the plague instead of just covering up for EarthGov. They're just going to try to do both until they can't anymore."

Shinobu had an interesting argument style.

Effective but interesting.

"EarthGov will always do the right thing," I replied. "After they have exhausted every other possible option."

Lucy grabbed the infopad from me. "Fine, I'll sign."

"Good," Kate said, looking up. "In any case, I've acquired the best possible assets from this land of thieves and whores. Really, it's my kind of place but Armstrong and the other AI have determined that our selection of agents for this crisis was always going to come with people of immense personal *quirks*. If you want to know, I don't trust either Priss or Nigel, but they're needed to solve this."

"Can this be solved?" I asked.

"I dunno," Kate said, surprising me with her honesty. "But we're sure as hell gonna try."

"Armstrong says that we have a 33% chance of keeping the casualties under three million!" Shinobu said, pausing. "Mind you, those statistics are completely made up and basically just amount to a good feeling about it since predicting the future via statistics is crazy Moon science. Pun intended."

"Just three million," I said, horrified.

"Versus a fifty to a hundred million if we do nothing, yeah," Shinobu said. "That's also not including the organized breakdown of society, looting, civil war, destruction of vital infrastructure, potential disruption of necessary supplies, life support systems collapsing—"

"Stop," I said, raising my hand. "You've made your point."

"It was fifteen percent without you and Lucy," Shinobu said. "Ten without Nigel and Priss."

"You just said that your statistics were made up," I replied, dryly.

"Yeah, but we know we're screwed without all of you," Shinobu said, waving her hand. "Accept our genius computer's wisdom. These aren't the droids you're looking for."

I decided to change the subject. "I don't suppose you have any information on this Sons of Mithras guy I'm supposed to interrogate. Name, likes, dislikes, or so on."

"We have almost nothing on him prior to his arrival in-system a year ago," Shinobu said. "However, we have identified his cover identity. He has been living in a single large communal apartment with the rest of his cell. We've gone over that with a fine-tooth comb and cross-referenced the resulting information to learn what little there is to know about him."

"Boyfriend, girlfriend, dog?" I asked.

"Hey!" Barksley said.

"I mean as a pet instead of a romantic partner," I said. "Unless—"

"No," Shinobu said, dryly. "He doesn't have any particular attachments to the locals, and he's seemingly associated almost exclusively with his fellow cell members. We found a drug lab and bio-manufacturing setup on the roof of their apartment building. We're dealing with a very austere sort of fanatics."

I nodded. "That gives me an idea."

"Interesting," Kate said. "It's always nice to see you work. What's your plan?"

"Do you have any Loop?" I asked.

"Ooo, I know, you're going to infect him and force him to reveal where the cure is," Barksley said.

"No, Barksley," I said, looking down. "Also, that's from *Fair Cop 3*."

"Those are *fantastic* movies," Barksley said.

"They're really not," Lucy said. "People only see them because of my mother's tits."

"I know it's why I saw them," Kate said.

Shinobu and Lucy looked at her.

"Kill me now," I muttered.

"You know she's my mom too, right?" Shinobu asked.

"I did not!" Kate said, grimacing. "Probably not a thing to mention here. Or the fact Neal and I once had sex in a theatre during a showing of *Fair Cop 2*."

Lucy and Shinobu stared, the awkwardness of the joke having gone from one to a hundred in Kate's attempt to brush it off with another, equally inappropriate, bit of humor.

"Fuck. I'm terrible at this command stuff," Kate muttered, sighing. "It's why I always said anyone over a lieutenant was a horse's ass."

"That was because you were a lieutenant," I replied.

"Exactly," Kate said.

"What do you even hope to get out of this guy?" Lucy asked.

"We need to find out where he and his fellows sent their Loop." Kate said. "These guys aren't distributing it themselves, so we need to know who they sold it too. From there, we can figure out what has been distributed and what not. There could be thousands of pills sitting in a warehouse somewhere or they could all be with dealers waiting to sell their wares."

"Got it," I said, looking at Lucy. "I have an angle here but I'm open to suggestions."

"No," Lucy said, raising a hand. "You take it from here. If I go in there, I'll probably strangle them to death."

"I have ways of making him talk," Barksley said, low and growling.

"No, Barksley," I said. "For many, many reasons."

"Aww," Barksley said.

"Such a cute doggie," Kate said. "Anyway, Steve is almost finished up."

"Steve?" Lucy asked, looking uncomfortable.

That was when the fantastically handsome male model meets action hero guy I'd been next to in the briefing walked out of the impromptu interrogation room. He was dirty with a little stubble and just this side of rugged without losing any of that chiseled beauty. It was the rare fellow that made me self-conscious about my looks, but this guy pulled it off. He was wearing a Lunar Rangers uniform, which basically was desert gear in grays. Don't ask me why they did it that way when they had to wear spacesuits, but it was a look.

"Uh, hi," I said, looking at the guy.

"Oh, hello, Steve!" Barksley said. "Long time no see. What a coincidence, this is Lucy's other longtime boyfriend and serious relationship."

"You're kidding," I said, looking down at Barksley.

"No, he's not," Lucy muttered, feeling her face. "Hi, Steve!"

"Oh hey, Lucy," Steve said, smiling at her with a big broad grin. He then turned to me. "You must be Neal Gordon. I'm Steve Rogers."

Okay, the universe was just clearly fucking with me now. Dick Grayson, Steve Rogers, and Rick Deckard? Hell, the Knights' stage names were apparently all influenced by an old anime and science fiction authors. Did the people on the Moon just have no creativity when it came to names? Was I going to be running into Bruce Wayne? Probably best not to jinx it.

"Huh," I said.

He offered his hand. "Steve Rogers Hudson."

I shook it. "So, you're Lucy's other ex, huh?"

"Unfortunately," Steve said. "I'm familiar with Albion customs and the language. I also used to do underwear modelling and was the Moon's entry into men's distance swimming at the 2210 Olympics. I only got silver, though."

One look at the guy told me that was entirely believable. "Okay. Super."

"Apparently, someone is just assembling the most awkward collection of people possible," Lucy said, dryly, casting a withering look at Kate. "Possibly because they're going to make a reality television show out of this pandemic."

"Believe me this is a happy accident," Kate said, amused at everyone's discomfort. "It seems people qualified to be Division Four personnel is a very small number that knows each other. A bit like Special Operations."

"I hope this won't be awkward," Steve said, smiling. "Lucy has told me all about you. I invited her to join my line marriage with my husband, but she decided to keep things casual. I think Dick was the only one to ever get her to say yes."

I almost explained to the total stranger that Lucy and I had broken up this morning. Instead, I just shook my head and pointed to the door. "The terrorist dude is in there, right?"

"You still haven't explained your plan or why you need the Loop," Kate said.

"I'll be fine," I said, walking past the cologne ad before me.

CHAPTER NINE

Too Dumb to Fool

I don't suppose you know whatever the hell language that these Albionese speak, I said, stopping at the interrogation room—a janitor's closet—door.

YOU REALIZE, AGAIN, I AM JUST AN INCARNATION OF YOUR OWN SUBCONSCIOUS AND METHOD OF ACCESSING YOUR CYBERNETICS, CORRECT? Interface asked. I KNOW NOTHING THAT YOU DONT KNOW. EVEN IF YOU DON'T REALIZE IT.

Uh huh, I said, not believing it in the slightest. *So, that's a no, right?*

I SWEAR, Interface sighed in frustration. I CAN DOWNLOAD THE LANGUAGE MATRIX FOR ALBIONESE FROM THE COMMUNITY JUMPNET.

So, that's a yes? I asked, wondering how exactly Interface had access to the alien internet from across the galaxy.

YES, Interface said, sounding disgusted. JUST DON'T EXPECT TO SOUND LIKE A NATIVE.

Sure, I said, walking through the door. *How long will it take?*

DONE, Interface replied.

You're kidding, I said, trying to think something in Albionese. Much to my surprise, I suddenly knew the meaning of a bunch of words.

Huh.

The interior of the room was a large concrete box with a single plastisteel table in the center with a drain below it. There were no windows in the room and a fluorescent light of the kind that had existed for centuries that was equally unpleasant to everyone who had to be under their glare. There was a single STRIKE soldier standing in the back of the room supervising the prisoner who, just a few hours ago, had tried to kill me as well as Lucy. The prisoner was sitting behind the table, handcuffed to it with wrist manacles as if he might suddenly leap up and go for someone's throat. There was also a pitcher of water and a set of glasses. The room was swelteringly hot from the furnace currently running in it, probably as a deliberate interrogation tool.

He was wearing a pair of gray overalls like prisoners on the Moon wore and was, to put it simply, one ugly mothersucker. It was difficult to put into words, but he had a kind of pug look to his face with an upturned nose, big lips, and platinum blonde hair done in a crew cut. It reminded me of someone who had too much plastic surgery done and somehow had forgotten what ordinary people looked like.

Seeking out the words, I tried to speak with him in his native language. "Howdy, I'm here to talk with you. I don't have much information about you, so why don't we—"

"Silence your defilement of the holy Albionese tongue, primitive!" The man said in an accent I'd never heard before but was closest to a high-pitched German that almost sounded like someone making a bad version of the accent for a comedy skit. Later, I'd figure out he was speaking something derived from Old English that had gone in an entirely different direction linguistically. "You are a Goth! A Vandal! A creature from beyond the pale who seeks to defile our holy civilization with your boundless trash of savage barbarians."

Jackpot.

Now, you may think from the guy's reaction that this was a bad thing. Quite the contrary. There were two ways an interrogation could go for it to yield useful intelligence. The first way was befriending the subject, to build a bond of trust that would eventually result in them believing they were helping themselves by cooperating. Sometimes you could even get a criminal to realize they'd done wrong, but that was always iffy. I didn't much care for this method because one of the dangers in all of this was false confessions and if you convinced a guy that it was better to admit to a crime than stay locked up being asked repeatedly the same questions, well, that was going to be a real pain in the ass.

No, the second successful interrogation technique was one that was very effective when dealing with fanatics but almost useless with professional criminals or spies. They knew the smartest thing to say was nothing. No, for this second successful technique, you needed someone who was a stupid *and* arrogant sort of criminal. Either a rich kid or guy who thought doing time would give him street cred.

I was hoping this guy was exactly that. We could only be so lucky. "Please, sir, I don't know what you—"

"Ha!" the man said. "You do not know who you address. I am Vitellius Cicero, last of four generations of Albionese soldiers meant to fight and die for the preservation of our glorious race against the alien filth and lesser breeds of humanity. Do not think for a second that because you thwarted our assassination attempt against the Apostate and his whore that you have won anything. Your corrupt and decadent society of degenerates will be cleansed from the face of the Earth with Mithras' holy fire."

Okay, I was getting plenty of information out of this guy without having to even try and my opinion of him as a stupid criminal was being cemented. He'd already informed me of his name, that the Albionese genuinely worshiped this Mithras guy, that they had issues with "degenerates", and had been going for me rather than Lucy. At least, I was assuming I was the Apostate and Lucy was the whore because I felt a bunch of Space Romans would not be the most gender-enlightened people in the universe. Perhaps I was mistaken and should double check this. A lot could change about cultural values in a millennium or two.

"By the Apostate, you mean—" I didn't even have time to finish my sentence before Vitellius went onto another rant.

"Neal, Son of Gordon!" Vitellius said, also demonstrating he had no idea who I was. He probably didn't even recognize me as the guy he'd taken a bunch of shots at on the rooftop without my shirt or hat. "The foul blasphemer who is the chief assassin of the sinister cabal of Earth-based bankers that seek to outlaw Mithras' true brotherhood of warriors and replace us with weak feminized Xianity and atheism! He assassinated the Pontifex of Londonium ten years ago and was behind the mass poisoning of the Hightown commune!"

Okay, I had no idea what the fuck this guy was talking about as you might guess. *Interface? Do you have like a version of Googleplex or Encyclotron for searching alien databases? Can you tell me what he's talking about?*

FAMOUS CONTROVERSIAL EVENTS ON THE PLANET ALBION, Interface said. THE RELIGIOUS LEADER OF ALBION WAS KILLED BY A FANATIC WHO BELIEVED HE WAS SELLING OUT TO THE COMMUNITY BUT WAS LATER CAST AS A MARTYR KILLED BY A FALSE FLAG OPERATION VIA RUMORMONGERING. THE HIGHTOWN COMMUNE MASS SUICIDE WAS OF A RELIGIOUS COMMUNITY OF FUNDAMENTALIST MITHRAS-ITES WHO WERE KILLED BY THEIR LEADER WHEN ALBIONESE AUTHORITIES ATTEMPTED TO ARREST HIM FOR CHILD MOLESTATION. THE SONS OF MITHRAS MARKS THAT AS AN EXAMPLE OF GOVERNMENT OVERREACH. SOMEHOW, YOU'VE BEEN CAST AS THE ARCHITECT BEHIND BOTH.

You'll have to find out more, I told my internal computer.

I'M LIMITED BY HOW MUCH BANDWITTH I CAN STEAL FROM THE *HEART OF SORKA'S* COMPUTERS WITHOUT BEING NOTICED, Interface said. THERE WOULD BE SIGNIFICANT LAG IF NOT FOR THE FACT I'M PIGGYBACKING ON THEIR EMBASSY'S FASTER-THAN-LIGHT COMMUNICATION.

That was one of those answers that generated a shit-ton more questions. Not only could Interface interact with the Community's version of the infonet, but he was doing so by hacking into their space cruiser's computers. I wasn't sure if that qualified as an act of war, espionage, stealing someone's infonet bandwidth or some combination of the above. It was certainly something I couldn't do and made me wonder just how powerful my cybernetic enhancements really were.

NOT VERY, Interface said. ALL COMMUNITY-BASED TECHNOLOGY IN THE SYSTEM IS LINKED TO THE JUMPNET TRANCEIVERS ONBOARD THE *HEART OF SORKA*, AT LEAST UNTIL THEY CAN OFFICIALLY BUILD AN INDEPENDENT ONE

IN THE SYSTEM. THEN HUMANKIND WILL BECOME LINKED TO THE REST OF THE GALAXY AND UNDOUBTEDLY BE ABSORBED BY THE SUPERIOR TECHNOLOGY AS WELL AS CULTURAL HEGEMONY OF THE COMMUNITY.

I poured myself a glass of water and one for Vitellius as well since he looked like he was sweating profusely. I slipped a Loop pill in my glass and swished it around a bit as it dissolved while fizzling. You may be wondering why I'm carrying some of that around, or why I asked anyone if they had some of their own and expect some excuse about it being for a case or something. No, it's because a friend of mine gave me a bag of forty and it had been in my desk drawer when I'd cleaned out my office. It was the incredibly weak 20% pure cheap brand but allowed me to work twenty-hour days or have hours-long sex depending on the pill.

And you know what horrifying consequences I suffered from this? Not a goddamn one.

It was just the polluted amateur made stuff that was dangerous and that was much because of the outlawing of the stuff. Yeah, it could be addictive or maddening but that was only if you took it 80-100% pure versus Loop cut with sugar. I'd have to explain why I had some in my pocket to my employers, but I suspected they wouldn't care too much since my broad powers of authority as a Department Four agent included killing people, let alone drugging them.

Of course, it could be that my bag of Loop was one of the poisoned ones and I was unwittingly carrying a ticking timebomb, but the bag was over a year old—my friend had ended up getting busted for twenty years for steak smuggling—and I was down to eight Loop candies. They were damn stale, but I didn't exactly take them for the taste. Since I hadn't developed so much as a fever, posthuman physiology or not, I was gambling on them being safe. It was also why I wanted someone else to have Loop, so I didn't have to use my own supply. There's not really a story there.

"So, who exactly told you the Apostate was going to be there?" I asked, almost saying the word "me" and breaking my ruse.

Vitellius hissed and backed away, stopped only by his handcuff chain and leg shackles. He managed to pull the table along with him a bit, which wasn't a good sign as it should have been bolted down. "Degenerate drug addicted filth! You think I am a fool! You hope to get me to reveal the spy in your ranks!"

I did, indeed. For example, I didn't even know for sure there was a spy in our ranks until he mentioned it. It was possible, of course, that Vitellius was just an incredibly talented actor feeding me false information, but it was also possible we were all trapped in a gigantic simulation where some jerkass was typing out my adventures to get his jollies off to hot police and military girls. Possible, but unlikely.

"I just want to know how you managed to distribute the virus," I said, speaking softly and coming off as weak as possible, switching the waters while his eyes were focused on me.

Vitellius grabbed "my" drink and threw it in my face, splashing me with water before drinking down "his" drink. "Fool! Imbecile! I have killed you! Me and my brothers have turned your foul and sexually depraved society of castrati and catamites into a graveyard. You just do not know it! The water carries the Red fever, passed along by your drugs, and in forty-eight hours you will begin coughing blood, and in a week you will be dead!"

"You don't know my dealer, pal," I said, smugly. I'd intended to drug the guy to put him in a more manic and overconfident frame of mind because Loop users tended to be that way. Apparently, that was wholly unnecessary because the guy was already acting like he was tweaked out of his head.

Ah crap.

He *was* tweaked out of his mind. I hadn't given that much thought, but if the guy had been running a drug lab, it was possible the guy had been exposed to a shit-ton of the chemicals that were used in the creation Loop. Enough that the guy might be high at all times and only alive because of a built-in tolerance.

And I'd just given him more.

Dammit.

Vitellius pointed at me, his eyes bloodshot. He was clearly entering a "red" high that shouldn't have been possible on the diluted Loop, but my shot had clearly pushed him over the edge into. "You don't get it do you! We've been producing massive tons of this poison and selling it at rock bottom prices to the Five. They took it in bulk, and we didn't even poison the first few loads, so they'd trust us. Calivari, Calivari, Calivari..."

That was when Vitellius started to OD before my eyes. He began foaming from his mouth and I called for the guard to get a medic. He fell out of his chair, his arm hanging up against the side of the table while he went into convulsions. It was probably a good thing that his high didn't result in him believing he could rip his hand free of the cuffs and take off his wrist.

Instead, Doctor Frankenstein came into the place and spent the next few minutes stabilizing the guy before he passed into a deliberately induced coma. It would be a couple of days before he could be safely revived.

Lucy and Kate were both in the room at that point, staring at me. It felt uniquely like I was being judged by upset parents, which was a weird and upsetting feeling given that I'd slept with both women.

"I may have made a few errors," I said, pausing.

"You think?" Lucy asked, dryly. "I think we would have been better off having me beat answers out of the anyxhole."

Yes, anyxhole not asshole. Moon people had a weird accent sometimes. Lucy seemed to shift between their space-y swearing and more typical Earth profanity at will. It was one of the things I admired about her. I only knew English, French, and Spanish curse words, mostly because they were almost all the same.

Kate, surprisingly, came to my rescue. "Let's not judge him on his methods. He got what he needed from the prisoner."

I was very much judging me on my methods. I was also wondering if Lucy had taken something herself since this bloodthirsty side was not going to help matters. Sure, shoot the guy in the head when he was trying to shoot us, but beating him wasn't going to save more lives. Besides, I was a cruel man and believed that when you died, your pain ended, and it was much better to toss someone in a jail cell for the rest of their life if they genuinely deserved it. Which was restricted to about five crimes of which I am not going to inform you of. Okay, it's anything that hurt kids, rape, Neo-Militarism, and murder. Also, playing music too loud at 3:00 AM. Those latter guys may deserve death, though.

"Are you kidding?" Lucy asked, staring at Kate.

"He mentioned the Five and Calivari," Kate replied. "You know who those are better than I do."

She was right. The Five were the Syndicate narcotics bosses of the Moon and extremely rich, and low priority for most of us in Cyberlife. They were even less of a priority for Black Briar and the civi police as they could afford the best legal protection possible: bribes.

Drugs weren't nearly the hot button issue that food smuggling was, so most people ignored their efforts anyway. Tommy "The Razor" Calivari was a mixed Thai-Italian narcotics baron that partied like the 2090s with his garish lifestyle and was known for his excessive use of violence to keep his street cred.

"They've been flooding the market," Lucy said. "After all, why not take advantage of a bunch of idiots selling Loop in bulk on the cheap? What could be more moonatic than that? We're screwed."

"If they've been distributing the poisoned stuff everywhere, there would already be a massive spike," Kate said. "We need to hit their warehouses and get every possible drop of the stuff out immediately. Whatever it takes."

Lucy stared. "The chances of us hitting them and them not being forewarned about it are slim and zero. Especially if you're choosing to keep this all a secret and—"

I cleared my throat.

"I'm really not in the mood for your suggestions right now, Neal," Lucy said, still pissed off at me for poisoning our witness.

Which, hey, fair.

"We should tell them," I replied.

"What?" Kate and Lucy asked, simultaneously before glaring at one another.

"Tell them the Loop is poisoned. Offer to buy it," Neal said. "Make use of those billions of EarthGov bucks."

Kate stared. "Offer to buy millions in illegal drugs from drug lords. *That's* your plan?"

"Yes," I replied. "It can't be more expensive than a couple of atmosphere fighters and it's a helluva lot more practical for resolving this gigantic death plague that's looming over our heads than trying to fight an impractical war against people who don't want to die of plague themselves."

"Then why not simply warn them?" Kate asked, sounding like she wasn't entirely opposed to my plan.

"Because money talks on the Moon," Lucy said, pausing. "Is there any chance of actually doing this?"

"If I asked permission from EarthGov? Absolutely not," Kate said, sighing. "The Social Reformers are of the opinion that the Moon's social habits are a reason for the fact its violent crime rate rivals your typical Action Dan movie."

Action Dan was my favorite movie series. It had virtually no plot, gratuitous nudity, and a body count that rivaled the population of small countries. They were in many ways the spear counterpart to the Fair Cop films.

"But—" I asked, hoping there was a but.

"I may be able to black budget it," Kate said. "They don't necessarily need to know how we acquired it if it works. They'll pay millions for bribing a warlord to tell them where a Black Lotus field is to burn but not to offer an alternative."

"Bureaucracy," I muttered.

"Go," Kate said.

"What?" I asked, confused.

"I'll assemble teams to visit each of the Five," Kate replied. "You and Lucy should head to Calivari and try to arrange a deal."

I blinked. "You want me and Lucy to go to a guy called The Razor and ask to buy all of his drugs."

"Without mentioning the plague, if possible," Kate said.

Lucy pinched the bridge of her nose, looking like she was having a migraine.

I nodded. "I love this plan!"

That was when Doctor Frankenstein revived Vitellius, much to my surprise.

"Death to the Gordon!" Vitellius shouted.

"What the..." Kate asked.

"I have no idea."

CHAPTER TEN

Talking with Monsters

"Great job, Neal," Lucy said, dryly. "Now we have to make a plan that is almost certainly going to fail."

The two of us were walking to the parking lot of the temporary headquarters for SHID after having been given an activation key to a replacement vehicle for the late, great Purple Rain. I was fully expecting either an old clunker or another STRIKE vehicle that would just make us a target for everyone who hated having their shoes checked at the airport despite the fact we had censors for that now.

"I don't see you giving any ideas," I muttered, following her down the old hallways of the apartment building. Along the way we'd encountered a lot of people from a wide variety of professions ranging from emergency workers to scientists to sanitation engineers. SHID was a pretty slapdash affair, but I could already see the method to their madness.

It was clear that, despite everyone's best efforts and reassurances to the contrary, that they were of the mind this Red fever would spread throughout the Moon. They were trying to assemble as comprehensive a group of people as possible to deal with it.

They just didn't want to *look* like they were doing it.

The problem was that this was trying to shut the barn door after the horses had escaped. It was an idiom older than even the kind of media I consumed, but it applied here. Right now, all we could do was maybe slow down the spread and I wasn't even sure if that was possible at this point.

"Because there are no ideas that aren't a waste of time," Lucy muttered. "While keeping this secret, that is. The public needs to know and institute immediate quarantine measures. Masks, immune boosters, and isolation. At least until we can get treatments or vaccines made."

"I'm pretty sure everyone will try to flood the space ports, blame the government, and start hoarding," I replied, remembering how smaller pandemics on Mars had gone. "I'm not saying that you're not right, but I think having an actual plan of what to do and how bad this is going to get is better before releasing information."

"That's what Shinobu believes," Lucy said.

"Your sister is a wise woman," I replied, wondering where Barksley had gotten to.

"My sister is a raging psychopath," Lucy said, dryly. "She burned down our elementary school."

I stopped in mid-step. "She what now?"

"It was in protest of the school's new curriculum," Lucy replied. "Governor Barnum had decreed that it would be illegal to teach people about labor relations. My mother made it all go away by claiming Shinobu was just severely mentally ill and paying for a sexbot for the school administrator. My sister ended up being tutored by private instructors until she was twenty."

Moon people are so goddamn weird. "Well, now your psychotic sister is plugged into the Moon's most powerful computer and has access to nearly unlimited data as well as power…. Huh. That sounded more reassuring in my head."

Lucy couldn't help but smirk before frowning again. "I can't trust her fusion with Armstrong if it leads her to believe your evil ex-partner needs to be part of this task force. What can a borking slaver—and I don't mind saying that aloud here—contribute to our cause?"

"He's a Karma Corp executive and they're presumably the people who can make enough medicine to treat everyone on the Moon?" I suggested. I mean, I hated Karma Corp and thought they were the worst of the megacorps the same way Ares Electronics was "the best", and that was a matter of degrees rather than kind. But there was no one else who could possibly do the job even among Earth's most advanced government labs and research facilities. Money talked and Karma Corp had the best scientists it could buy.

Lucy shot me back a death glare.

"Oh, right, that was rhetorical," I said, already seeing how our partnership was going to suffer from our personal life being disrupted. Everything I was saying seemed to irritate her and I found myself far more willing to make unnecessary jabs.

This was not good as we both needed to be in top form if we were going to do anything about this. Either way, we headed out of a door under a sign marked EXIT that contributed to the apartment building's general retro 21st century aesthetic.

The apartment building was in a part of Crater Town that was still under development, and probably would be for years. The hundred-story craggy building looked ancient but that was a trick of the fact the duracrete was of poor quality and graffiti covered everything. Governor Hopewood had cleared out the locals and there was already a holographic sign in front of the place promising a cleaner, prettier, and more stable building that, to me, honestly looked like a newer version of the same construction. There was also a large blue tarp wall around the place that disguised the full parking lot of STRIKE vehicles as well as the civilian transports of everyone Kate had assembled for this mission.

It was a poor disguise since anyone could just fly overhead and see the STRIKE vehicles, but half-assing everything was the government employee way. I knew because I was one now. I had to admit a vague disquiet with that realization because I was suspicious of all things political. Even now, knowing Governor Hopewood was trying to build decent affordable housing for the locals, all I could think of was that her version of "affordable" probably was very different from that of the average Crater Towner. Also, I had to wonder where the locals evicted for her planned revitalization had been forced to go until then.

"I don't trust your ex-wife or Nigel and, bluntly, Neal, it bothers me you do," Lucy replied.

"I don't trust Nigel in the slightest," I said, annoyed she thought I did. "He's a resource or at least was as long as we were working for the

Slavers Guild case. Right now, though, and I never thought I'd say this, we have more important matters to deal with."

Lucy stopped and turned around. She was trembling with fury. "You act a lot more calmly around a man that shot off your leg and burned you alive than a normal person should. Every time I see that man, all I want to do is pull out my gun and put him down."

"Yes, because I keep forgetting that," I said, sarcastically, annoyed that Lucy and Barksley kept bringing it up.

Nigel never attempted to justify or explain what he did, but I got the impression he expected me to think it had been some sort of backhanded way of saving my life. After all, I'd killed something like fifteen human traffickers in a shootout that I'd gotten ridiculously lucky during. I'd fired my gun like three times before that day and never killed anyone. He'd arranged for me to be taken by Karma Corp medics and transformed into a posthuman without telling me. As if that would make up for betraying my trust and the evil things he'd done.

Lucy and Barksley couldn't understand why I hadn't put a bullet in his head, considering I'd killed a lot more people since then. They couldn't accept how calm and collected I seemed around the man, as if I'd forgiven him. Lucy was furious on my behalf and the fact he'd hurt me meant that she wanted to kill him. She may have dumped me, but I didn't doubt she cared for me. Part of the reason why I'd pushed her so hard—too hard in the end—to admit it.

But what they didn't understand was I wasn't angry at Nigel because I'd passed beyond that into something more resembling confusion. I'd been the best man at his wedding and thought we'd been like brothers, yes, and the man I'd known never would have done the things he did. They did not fit my image of the man so much that I couldn't reconcile the pieces. It's like those stories of interviewing the neighbors of serial killers and them always saying, "He seemed like such a nice man." You never got the response, "Yeah, no surprises there. Dude was a terrifying monster."

I couldn't be furious at Nigel in the way I'd be at other perps because the man who'd wronged me was a total stranger to me and utterly inscrutable. The person I'd known had been a mask and probably had been his entire life. That was my working theory: Nigel was a psychopath and incapable of human feeling or sentiment but with a masterful ability to fake both.

The problem with that was that didn't make any more sense because he'd gone to such lengths for me as well as his ex-wife that he'd made this deal to get her cured of Deimos Syndrome. That he was willing to risk everything he'd achieved—millions in credits and a cushy executive job—to help me take his bosses down.

I'd discounted a second theory that, somehow, he was undercover, or guilt-ridden by his actions. If he was, he showed no sign of it. Which left me with a third possibility: Nigel was not a psychopath but capable of doing things that no normal person should be in the pursuit of his goals. Which might be making a fine distinction, but there was one. It would mean that he could turn off and on that part of his brain which empathized with other people when necessary. Either way, whatever my assessment of his character, being mad at him was pointless. It's why I redirected my fury at the organization behind it and we'd seen how that worked out.

"I'm sorry," Lucy surprised me by apologizing. "I know you're unlikely to forget that, but I'm unable to put the pieces together. Your former partner sends us on a tip to a massive gangster and suit meeting that ends in all of them dead at the hands of your ex-wife. Then she recruits us to deal with a massive viral outbreak the next day."

"You think it's all connected somehow?" I asked.

"How could it not be?" Lucy asked. "Especially since that lunatic and his fellow bioterrorists tried to hit us this morning."

I put my hand over my heart. "A moment of silence for the Purple Rain. It was a truly tacky ride."

Lucy rolled her eyes. "I'd say this was all a hoax, but Shinobu confirmed the threat was real."

I didn't say out loud my next thought, that as much as I loved Shinobu like a mad bomber kid sister, I wasn't sure she was 100% trustworthy since her merging with Armstrong either. The Moon's central AI had its own agenda that it had made abundantly clear. It considered us to be useful tools, but tools, nonetheless. Instead, I said, "Then I guess we better focus on solving this issue. Whatever Kate and

Nigel's agendas are—assuming they're not one in the same—will have to wait."

Lucy lifted her activation key and tapped it, causing one of the flying cars to honk its horn. Both of stared at the vehicle.

It was a crimson Red Dragon X8, which rivaled the Caliburn for being a luxury vehicle, yet also having elements of a sports car. The cars were *ridiculously* expensive and primarily bought by actors, executives or people trying to be as cool as those people while having no sense of what practical spending was. The thing was all smooth and sharp lines that seemed incongruous to our surroundings. It was the kind of car that guaranteed its owner—whichever gender or orientation—would confidently state, "I will never sleep alone again."

"What in the world," I said, staring at the vehicle with my mouth open.

"Should I leave you two alone?" Lucy asked, staring at me.

"You can join in," I replied, going with her joke, and one-upping her. "We need to set some ground rules first."

"My mother has three X8s," Lucy said.

"Yes, and your mother lives in a magical world of privilege and awesome that few of us mere mortals dare dream of," I said. "Why the hell would we be driving that?"

"It seems like your wife is trying to bribe us," Lucy said.

"It's working," I replied before adding, "*ex*-wife."

"Mmm hmm," Lucy muttered, clearly not believing any past feelings were settled between us. Probably because she was an actor and assumed that things worked like television. You couldn't just wave your hand and make the pain of a sudden and sharp separation go away. It was enough to shock me out of my car-induced fugue.

"Speaking of untrustworthy people, what's with Captain America?" I asked, looking at her.

"Who?" Lucy asked, doing a double take.

"You know, the guy made of muscles and hair," I replied, thinking about him. "The one you used to date."

"Really, Neal?" Lucy asked, approaching the car. "You're bringing up my exes when yours show up out of the blue slicing and dicing with a horde of drones?"

"Yes," I replied, following. "Yes, I am."

Lucy shrugged. "It was before Dick and after I'd left the Knights. Cyberlife was just getting started and the Lunar Rangers were sent to train us. He said all the right things, made all the right moves, and wasn't overly impressed with the fact I was an ex-TV star. Nor did he dismiss me as a cop because of it."

"Must have been pretty serious if he was willing to invite you to marry his husband and him," I said, trying not to be weirded out by that. Polyamory was fine but introducing marriage into it was way too much legal hassle on my end.

"I considered it," Lucy said, an unsettled expression on her face. "But there was a side to him that wasn't... great."

"What do you mean?" I asked, rubbing my hand on the surface of the Red Dragon. It was so sleek that I almost drooled over it.

"He got... religious," Lucy said, pausing. "The Church of Money."

"Ah," I said, grimacing.

The Church of United Prosperity AKA The Church of Money was one of those things that popped up and you wondered how anyone got sucked into it but somehow just kept growing and growing. If their nickname wasn't an indication, their grasp of theology was questionable at best, and included a bunch of ideas taken from other religions as well as things made up wholesale to sell it to the space colony generation. Things like God being an alien and your success in life being determined by donations. It was the world's first virtual religion and forty million people jacked in every day to experience the Gospels according to Reverend Cash. Which wasn't a pun, that was just his last name.

Well, it was now Reverend Cash Junior and his daughter, Penny Cash, whose name I assumed was the evangelist dynasty having at least some self-awareness about their brand. If it sounded like I didn't respect them, it was because I didn't and thought of them as less an actual religion than a corporation taking advantage of people looking for meaning in their lives. They were especially blatant about it, too. "God needs you to fund a new starship so missionaries can convert the heathen aliens." The church had been heavily involved in politics and backed the Neo-Militants as a bulwark against the godlessness of whoever was pissing them off this week. I'd dated one of their missionaries briefly before she'd tried to get me to heavily invest in communally owned real estate,

"Do you believe in God?" Lucy asked one of the three questions that could make or break any relationship alongside, "Do you want to have kids?" and "How much money do you make?"

"Someone's out to get me," I muttered, entering the driver's seat. "Which isn't sarcasm. That's an actual statement of belief."

The interior had beige leather seats and that new car smell, with a dashboard that looked like it had the computing power of a space station. The Red Dragon X8 was easily worth more than I would make in three years, let alone a year, and probably more if I bought it new versus from someone who'd stolen it from its rightful owners. How the hell had we ended up with this thing?

"I'm serious," Lucy said, sitting in the passenger seat.

"So am I," I replied. "Let's just say my relationship to religion is complex. Got no use for churches but one of the nicest ladies at the Gordon Foundation, the closest thing I had to a mother, believed. So, I do for her sake. What's the worst that could happen? You?"

"My father believed in Zen Christianity," Lucy said. "My mother believed in herself. I'm still figuring it out."

"And Steve went full online cultist, huh?" I asked, trying to figure out how to work the machine.

"It wasn't like that," Lucy said. "Or maybe it was but he had his reasons. Steve was part of the Gray Heaven Riot."

I stared at her blankly.

"Right, not a lune," Lucy said, pausing. "It was a prison riot on one of Karma Corp's domed labor plantations. Well, Fiddler's Green's domed labor plantation. 17B-7 AKA Gray Heaven."

That was another fucked element of Moon society that, for such a freedom loving people, they had a really messed up legal system. Because so much dangerous nasty work was needed to keep the Moon functioning, particularly food-wise, prison labor was a mainstay of its economy. The Reformers were determined to outlaw prison labor, but Karma Corp was determined to keep it as long as possible. But seriously, if someone ever uses the word "plantation" describing something they own, they're probably the bad guys.

"I'll avoid rooting for the prisoners out of respect to your ex," I replied. "Unless it ended acrimoniously, in which, go rioting criminals."

Lucy side-eyed me. "The conditions on Gray Heaven were bad even by Moon standards and it's a reason I would never be a civi cop. Exiling people to work in those places is something I'd only wish on the worst of the Moon's criminals. However, the Gray Heaven Riot wasn't a spontaneous uprising of disadvantaged and abused prisoners. It was an organized massacre by the Syndicates to try to free Marcus Calivari. He was the Razor's father. It was timed for when a bunch of Reformer observers were visiting along with other civilians."

"I take it things went bad?" I asked.

"To say the least," Lucy said. "Three hundred and fifty-three people died and the prison dome was locked down for thirty days. The Lunar Rangers were sent in, and it ended up being a massacre as the prisoners had armed themselves with illegal weapons the Syndicate had smuggled in. Steve lost almost his entire unit and had to take a medical discharge."

Ouch. "He seems a lot better now. Has his job back too."

Lucy didn't respond. "The Church of Money has a lot of friends in high places. All I know is he went to a very dark place I tried to help him with before he rejected me. His new husband brought him to the church and when we next talked, he had a lot of *opinions* on what was causing our planetoid's woes."

"Ah," I said, not inquiring as to what those opinions were. I could tell by the tone of her voice that they weren't things Lucy agreed with. She was as close to a progressive anarchist shitkicker as you could get while being part of the oppressive government—which was every bit the contradiction it sounded like. Just as I chose to believe the lie that the police were there to protect the innocent even from the rich and powerful, so did Lucy believe she could fix stuff from the inside. It turned out both of us were wrong. "So, he's not the kind of guy I should befriend."

"I dunno," Lucy said, smirking. "You might be his type."

"Okay, I can't figure out how to turn on the biometrics for this thing," I muttered, referring to the X8. "Could you check the ID box?"

Lucy nodded and did so, discovering a manual and plastisheet paperwork. One look at it caused here to bang her head against the back of the passenger seat headrest.

"What?" I asked.

"This is Rodan Yadlav's car," Lucy said, referring to the dead Syndicate Inner Council member we'd witnessed get killed by Kate earlier.

I stared at her. "First she kills the guy, then she steals his ride?"

"So, it seems," Lucy muttered.

"I like her style," I said, poking the vehicle dashboard a bit. "Interface, a little help?"

The car started up immediately.

"Yes!" I said, making a fist.

Lucy cleared her throat and lifted the activation key. "Ahem."

"Oh," I replied. "How retro."

"Should we wait for Barksley?" Lucy asked.

"I'll give him a call," I replied, looking at her. "Little guy can't have gotten far."

That was when Doctor Frankenstein walked in front of the Red Dragon with Barksley in his arms, a concerned expression on the doc's face. "Hey, guys, I need to bum a ride with you. Tommy Calivari is my son-in-law, and I don't want my daughter caught in the crossfire when he inevitably tries to kill you both."

"Sorry for getting lost," Barksley said. "I got caught up talking with the doctor about trying to make a cure for the disease using posthuman blood. By the way, is this our car? Ugh. What an ugly piece of poo. It doesn't even have fins or glowing hubcaps."

CHAPTER ELEVEN

Visiting Scarface

The Red Dragon X8 handled like a dream and even though I had it on autopilot, I pretended I was driving it as it soared through the artificial atmosphere of the Luna City dome. Lucy just looked at me like she was irritated with my handling of the car and, I admit, she had a point since she was an incredibly talented stunt driver while I was just savoring the rich playboy feel the car engendered.

A feeling somewhat undercut by the people in the backseat.

"Can we stop by Big Hawaiian Burger?" Doctor Frankenstein asked. "I admit, one of the benefits of having virtually the entirety of your insides replaced is that you can eat just about anything you want. That includes the artificially flavored cardboard they pass off as food here."

"Oh yes," Barksley said. "I need to keep my biology hydrated and I'd love an Electric Lightning soda with extra syrup."

I stared forward as if willing there to be an ejector seat for them both. "There is to be no eating in this car. It shall be kept pure and innocent like a young lady in a nunnery."

"Shakespeare would have some choice words regarding the other meaning of nunnery," Barksley said.

"I went to Catholic School and that was a complete failure," Lucy replied. "A lot of situational sexuality, though. It's how I met Priss."

I opened my mouth. "I have questions."

Doctor Frankenstein, realizing his attempts to ease into the conversation weren't succeeding, just repeatedly bringing up the subject he really wanted to talk about. It was the second time he'd done so since climbing into the vehicle without permission. "So, neither of you are interested in the whole bit about my daughter being married to a crime lord, my belief you're going to get killed there, or the fact I need samples of both your blood to try to cure the Red fever."

I stared at the luxurious skyscrapers under the light of the Sun that lasted thirty days on the Moon. "Nope! Already got way too much riding on us now, we don't need to add anyone else's problems."

"Well, I want to hear it," Barksley said, "and since you owe me a car, you are all my slaves until I get a new one."

"Blackmail, is it?" I asked.

"No, extortion," Barksley corrected.

"Fine, tell us about your daughter," I said.

"Well, she's not so much my daughter as someone who is like a daughter to me," Doctor Frankenstein said. "Also, not so much like a daughter as nonexistent. Mostly because I needed to get into the car."

I turned around and glared at the cyberneticist. "Really?"

"Well, I am really worried about you getting yourselves killed," Doctor Frankenstein said. "I figured you'd buy me claiming some incredibly contrived connection to an important part of your case because between you both, you know everybody on the Moon within six degrees like Kevin Bacon."

"Who?" Lucy asked.

"Guy from a town who outlawed dancing," I replied. "Not really a fan."

Barksley gasped in horror.

"The part about you going to die if you go is true," Doctor Frankenstein said. "The criminal underworld is in chaos after the mass assassination yesterday in the Depths."

Yeah, technically that had been yesterday. I hadn't had a chance to sleep since it had happened, though.

"Oh yeah," I muttered, clenching my teeth. "I heard about that. A lot of executives and gangsters got killed."

"Well, we were there so, oh, right," Barksley said. "You're making a joke."

"Yeah," I replied. "What, do the Five think we killed them all?"

Doctor Frankenstein stared forward. "Yeah, that's what the rumors are saying. You somehow lured a shit-ton of bigwigs to the middle of the Deep and then polished them off. That's why Chief Deckard suspended you because the Syndicate, Trikuza, and Golden Tigers have all put a black mark on you."

"A black mark?" I asked, doing a double take,

"It's a hit on a cop," Lucy explained. "Except, it's not as bad as a red mark."

"There's something worse than a hit?" I asked, suddenly wondering why this wasn't brought up earlier.

"Yes, a black mark is a hit, but it is more like permission," Lucy replied. "A red mark is a bounty. Whoever kills a black marked cop doesn't get paid for it. Which means that they're only likely to kill us—"

"If we walk directly into the lion's den," I muttered. "Great. I suppose we should cancel this trip then."

"You can't," Barksley said.

"And why is that?" I asked. "I'm not an idiot."

"All evidence to the contrary aside," Lucy said, before grimacing in embarrassment. "Sorry, I forgot I lost my friendly teasing privileges with our breakup."

I gave a dismissive wave. I didn't care. "As I was saying, I'm not an idiot. I take these kinds of threats seriously."

The fact no one was willing to pay for my execution was both comforting as well as weirdly insulting.

"You can't because you still need to recover the tainted Loop and sending another agent will take too long," Barksley said. "Every minute could count. Also, you need to clear this up pronto."

"And you think the best way to do that is talking to a drug lord," I replied.

"Calivari has been moving into the food trade," Lucy said, as if that didn't sound utterly ridiculous to anyone from a planet where drugs were more regulated than casseroles. "The easing of the Food Prohibition Act, much to Karma Corp's irritation, has allowed a lot of independent operators to get into it. So, he's technically a food baron as well."

"Like an incredibly handsome, tiny, intelligent dog," Barksley said. "I mean, allegedly."

"Do I need to state, again, how utterly weird the Moon's entire War on Food is?" asked.

"It's not weird at all," Doctor Frankenstein said. "Karma Corp makes 90% of the food on the Moon and they don't want any competition. Even if people go malnourished in the meantime. I admit, none of the people who grew up in the 21st century had Big Farming as the chief evil megacorp of the 22nd century."

"Technically, Karma Corp would be Big Farm-Pharm. Which is combining farming with pharmacy in a portmanteau," Barksley said, showing once more that he'd been made as an educational toy for children.

I kept the car heading toward Calivari's. "Fine, I'm willing to take the risk if you are, Lucy. We're technically federal agents now."

"No technically about it," Lucy muttered, clearly not happy about it. Being a soulless corporate enforcer was a lot less shameful than being a, *gag*, government agent on the Moon. "But I'll do anything to stop this plague before it spreads."

"Which brings me to my next request, I'd like both of you to donate blood and other tissue samples to my lab," Doctor Frankenstein said. "I know both of you are posthumans and I think it might be our ace in the hole."

"It took three weeks of surgery to make me a posthuman," I replied.

"Yeah, but you were burned alive," Doctor Frankenstein said, showing a remarkable amount of knowledge about my condition. "Ms. Westenra only took forty-eight hours to be transformed."

"You're awfully well-informed," Lucy said, uncomfortable. "I was also drugged by my so-called friends to get upgraded. Take note, I know you're one of like three individuals on the Moon capable of making the kind of upgrade I went through."

"Well, I didn't do your upgrades," Doctor Frankenstein said.

"Would you tell me if you did?" Lucy asked.

"Oh, hell no," Doctor Frankenstein said. "You'd just been shot, though, and I considered it a medical procedure. The fact is that turning the Moon's people into posthumans is impractical anyway."

"So, Interface says," I muttered. "Plus, there's the whole stealing your soul thing."

Posthuman technology had one rather major drawback, the fact was that its users came in "Willed" and "Hollowed." Willed posthumans were holders of original recipe posthuman tech that came straight out of the package. That was the kind I'd gotten. Willed had the ability to make more posthumans but the ones they created were the Hollowed and were basically second-tier versions that could be dominated by their Willed creators.

One of things that made me doubt the Community's inherent decency was the fact that all Hollowed were subject to that sort of mind-control. Your personality and beliefs could be overridden by your interface like you were turned into a vampire by Dracula. The Knights had done that to Lucy even though they'd never intended to ever exercise that power in hopes of making her semi-immortal like themselves. I'd had my nanites checked three or four times since then to make sure that Nigel hadn't made me Hollowed.

YOU ARE WILLED, NEAL, Interface said. I CAN CONFIRM IT.

Yeah, but you would say that, wouldn't you? I pointed out.

FAIR ENOUGH.

"But if I were to put samples of the virus into your blood, I could see whether it generates specific auto-immune responses and enzymes that will allow us to harvest them with a bio-printer," Doctor Frankenstein said. "It's a brute force solution to an advanced scientific problem but theoretically possible. It would still be months of testing before we could use it but might be the difference between life and death for many patients. Especially if the nano-samples are self-replicating in organic matter beyond their initial gene-locked symbiotic host."

"You're just throwing together random science words now," I said, annoyed.

"Magic blood make cure, beep boop," Barksley translated for me.

"I'll do it," Lucy said.

"Really?" Doctor Frankenstein said.

"Anything to save lives," Lucy said. "I can get the Knights to contribute as well."

Doctor Frankenstein's expression told me he'd gone to them first. "And you, Mr. Gordon?"

"You stand to make a lot of money from cracking the secret of this," I replied. "Karma Corp would pay a lot."

"They'd pay me with a horse head in my bed *at best*," Doctor Frankenstein said. "More likely it would be two bullets in the back of my head. This has a slim chance of working but if it does, the good scientists at K-Company have had months to work out something I came up with in an afternoon. The fact we don't have a treatment or vaccine already ready means it either doesn't work or they're holding it back for some reason."

That was a disturbing but very real possibility. At the end of the day, all the megacorporations were ultimately loyal to their stockholders over any nebulous greater good.

"Alright, you have my help." I decided to make a phone call. *Interface, contact Nigel Blackwood.*

Interface seemed surprised, probably because I was at my own idea. ARE YOU SURE?

Yes, I responded. *Just make sure it's encrypted with whatever freaky-deaky alien super-tech you possess.*

I'D EXPLAIN THAT'S NOT HOW IT WORKS BUT IT WOULD BE FUTILE, Interface said. CALLING NOW.

Nigel and I normally arranged our meetings in the Deep where surveillance was far less stringent and, even then, we used a bunch of analog old school spy techniques to make sure we weren't followed or recorded. It would have honestly been better to have a face-to-face meeting at the SHID HQ, but we already had a mole there, so I was willing to risk an infolink call between our posthuman brains.

An image of my former best friend appeared in the right top corner of my vision, visible only to me. He looked unhappy. *This isn't a good time, Neal. You're also taking an awful risk using the Posthuman Network.*

Three questions" I said, internally. *Did you arrange that hit yesterday? Do you know who did? Also, what the hell is going on with this plague business? Oh, and what's Project: Jenner?*

That's four questions, Nigel pointed out.

Oh, I'm so sorry and fuck you, I replied, not in the mood for semantics.

109

Nigel nodded, clearly not offended by my response. *No, I did not arrange the mass assassination of the heart of the Slavers Guild. I have no idea who did, and I was operating under the decision that it was actually you're doing.*

Me? I asked.

I figured you finally got tired of being led around by my breadcrumbs and decided to go Medieval on their asses, Nigel said, sounding almost disappointed. *When I heard from one of the survivors that a quote-unquote sexy murder hero had been responsible, I figured you had Lucy do it.*

I imagined Lucy in the outfit then shook my head. *'Fraid not.*

Well, that's bad, Nigel replied, an unreadable expression on his face. *Especially since I've already claimed credit for the massacre, thinking I was protecting you.*

I blinked. *Why would you do that?*

It's better to be assumed to have done a violent coup to move yourself up the ladder than to have utterly failed to protect a bunch of your fellow suits as chief of security, Nigel replied. *But, to answer your next question—your real next question—no, Karma Corp had nothing to do with this plague. Nor did the Slavers Guild.*

I was skeptical to say the least. *And you expect me to believe that?*

"Are you talking with someone, Neal?" Lucy asked.

I nodded.

If Nigel noticed, he didn't comment. *The Slavers Guild is in complete disarray and has nothing to gain from a pandemic either way. Karma Corp is in a state of panic and is devoting every possible resource to resolve this.*

I thought they'd be ecstatic over a plague, I replied. *It's the one time anyone has anything positive to say about your company.*

It's a threat to Project: Jenner, Nigel said, finally bringing the conversation around to question four. *The buyout.*

I stared at him or at least would if not for the fact his image was already being projected into my brain. The concept of "buyout" and "megacorporation" were not really words that went together. The megacorporations, even before they became transtellars, were rich enough to be their own nations. As such, no one could buy them out except another megacorporation and Karma Corp was the largest one of them all. The Reformers had considered breaking them up as part of their efforts but that was such a ridiculously difficult task that it was underneath a hundred other priorities and probably impossible.

No one on Earth can buy Karma Corp, I said, making a guess.

Exactly, Nigel said, sending a chill down my spine. *The Albion Commerce League, which is a corporation by any other name, wishes to purchase Karma Corp and it has the resources of several planets to back it up. The only thing standing in the way of purchase is Earth isn't necessarily keen on selling its biggest economic body to off-worlders, even if they're mostly humans.*

You said that this threatens Project: Jenner, I asked. *How?*

Karma Corp's next one hundred years of economic growth is tied up in cloning farm animals, bio-engineering foodstuffs, and creating inoculations for the off-world colonies. The destruction of Nergal has everyone spooked and considering shutting down expansion, Nigel replied. *Without the fifty-world deal, the Guild isn't interested in buying Karma Corp, which threatens everyone's billions. They want this resolved without giving up Earth's claim to any of its worlds. Trust me, for once, Karma Corp is entirely on the side of the angels.*

I sincerely doubted that, but it explained how the cover-up of Nergal had occurred. The transtellars had put a gag order out to protect its bottom line. Karma Corp had lost a lot of its influence with the fall of the Neo-Militarists and had moved a lot of its sketchier business to the colonies. That was where its real money lay. It might even be the missing link between Lady Zero AKA Kate, and the Slavers Guild if someone was cleaning out Karma Corp's skeletons before a buy-out. That didn't seem to fit with anything going on with the Red fever and Sons of Mithras, though, which meant this could be unrelated tragedies intersecting only in how they affected the greater markets.

God, I hated thinking like an accountant.

Thanks, I said, absently. *You've given me a lot to think about.*

One final thing, Nigel added. *Don't trust your ex. Kate's not an SHID agent, she belongs to Department One, Oversight, and is much, much deeper and more connected than you realize.*

I almost scoffed. *That is rich coming from you. End Connection.*

The little window showing his face disappeared.

"So, what did Nigel have to say?" Lucy asked, correctly guessing who I'd been talking to.

I gave her a rundown despite Doctor Frankenstein's presence. At this point, I didn't care who knew he was our contact. I did leave out Nigel saying not to trust Kate, though. I didn't want to open that can of worms.

"So, effectively, the producers of Earth's food supply might be owned by foreign powers in a few years," Lucy said, softly. "Because that's worked out so well for the colonized people of the universe throughout human history."

"Above our paygrade," I replied. "But it does paint a more coherent picture."

"Of what, though," Lucy said, staring forward into Luna City Bay that we were now approaching. Calivari lived on the water of the artificial sea that had been created primarily to provide drinking water to the organics of the world but had been converted into a tourist trap. "The Sons of Mithras weren't leftover from the construction of this place. Those people liked being on the Moon and probably have been here for generations. So how the hell did they get here? There's only so much traffic from the off-world colonies and even less official immigration. What little trade we get from the Community is in parts for the gravity manipulators and atmosphere processors."

Yeah, there were pretty much only the colony ships and missionaries going back and forth. They might have hitched a ride with the Postal Service, but that didn't strike me as likely. Either way, we'd run out of time to discuss this because the Red Dragon started descending to the surface of the bay.

Tommy "The Razor" Calivari lived on a massive super yacht that was four stories tall and had room to park flying cars on the deck as well as to the side. It was heavily guarded by a combination of armed guards and security robots. It was lacking in the usual beautiful men, women, or both that typically accompanied the criminal kingpin lifestyle. I'd heard he was married but knew almost nothing about his spouse, which had led me to believe Frankenstein when he'd told me he was her father. Compared to most lunes, Calivari was practically a monk.

112

A monk who lived on a super yacht.

Okay, bad example.

"Did you transfer our credentials?" I asked, our vehicle hovering a few feet above the water and creating waves around us.

"Yep," Lucy said. "It says Calivari is eager to meet us."

"Well, great," I muttered. "That's a good sign. Super."

"I wonder if he likes the movie *Scarface*," Barksley said, climbing up in between the front seats. "I have the entire soundtrack downloaded. The Pacino version, not the Terry Crews one."

Shame.

The Terry Crews one had been awesome, even if he'd been a bit old for the part at seventy-seven.

CHAPTER TWELVE

Dude Just Needs a White Cat to Stroke

"So, what do you think our chances of walking out of here alive are?" I asked, standing there on the deck beside Lucy and Barksley with Doctor Frankenstein behind us. We were presently surrounded by Calivari's goons and a couple of floating drones, but the man himself had yet to make an appearance. They were also distinctly on the silent side.

The yacht exterior was spartan and had more guns than little martinis or deck chairs. I could see into the interior, but it wasn't exactly screaming with the personal touch. It looked like the place had been left exactly like you'd buy it from a dealership, not that I'd seen many yacht dealerships.

What I did know about Tommy "The Razor" Calivari was he was curiously absent most of the habits of his fellow crime bosses. In addition to the lack of the usual hot and cold running women or men—they don't discriminate on the Moon—he wasn't known to sample his own product, nor did he make the kind of extravagant purchases that typified his class of bad guy. Indeed, a note on his profile, made by the late Dick Grayson no less, suggested he only did business from a super yacht because he needed something to impress his wealth upon others to be taken as a big deal.

Whether it was because he didn't derive any pleasure from materialism, was an enormous cheapskate, or, hell, had some sort of fetish or kink much darker than the usual kinds didn't matter, though. What *was* known was the fact that Tommy was linked to more murders than three wildly successful serial killers. He'd worked his way up from the Deep and still had a lot of ties down there that meant he could generally call upon an endless number of replacements should he lose soldiers in fights with other gangs.

The old joke about some people being willing to kill for a pair of sneakers down there was a lot less funny when you realized that was the only pair of shoes some of those guys had. Maybe I'd vote when someone moved to help those people. I didn't know if Calivari's current bodyguards—of which there were apparently fifteen or so onboard—were among these individuals but they wore thick vests underneath tropical shirts and sported intimidating, but somewhat useless in close quarters, PO-17 assault rifles. They were basically knock-offs of the more expensive Atlas Security MR-9000s and relics of the Unification Wars. Like most street criminals, the way they handled their weapons wasn't professional like a soldier's, but quantity had a quality of its own.

"I think that strongly depends on whether or not he believes Department Four qualifies as law enforcement or not," Lucy replied. "The black mark against us was probably helped along by the fact that we were suspended from Cyberlife."

"Fired," I said. "Suspended means they might intend to let us back on."

Lucy grimaced at that. She was still having difficulty reconciling herself to the fact she was no longer a member of the force. I wanted to be more sympathetic, to comfort her, but I couldn't bring myself to do so because I was also fuming mad. She had chosen the same moment to push me away, too. Emotions were complicated.

"Deckard was probably paid a hefty sum to shovel you out of Cyberlife," Doctor Frankenstein said, surprisingly calm despite our surroundings. "If the other gangs took you out while you were still cops, then he'd be obligated to retaliate. It's why if you want to kill a cop on the Moon, you always have a fall guy already set up or you pay to have other cops take him out or both."

I blinked at the casual nature of that revelation. I mean, it made sense, but the very fact that they had a system for how to kill cops on the Moon was a pretty shocking revelation. It also made me look at

Lucy, who was undoubtedly thinking about the execution of Dick Grayson, which hadn't been given a fall guy or done by police— probably. That had been a message from the Syndicates. "You're not helping, Doc."

"I wouldn't worry too much," Doctor Frankenstein said. "The Razor has been known to kill cops but has a rule that he only kills dirty ones."

"So, he's willing to kill cops," I replied, dryly.

Lucy shot me a glare.

"Fine," I corrected. "Lucy will be good, but Barksley and I are screwed. Just last week, we lifted eight gees in Black Lotus to sell to keep our next-door neighbor from getting kicked out of her home. We also lifted a wheel of real cheese worth half as much for her niece's bat mitzvah."

"I didn't hear that," Lucy muttered.

Barksley looked up to Lucy. "Don't hate the player, hate the game."

It was on that surreal note that our erstwhile host made his appearance. He was, in simple terms, a beast of a man. He looked more like a professional wrestler than a crime boss, though that was merely stereotype at work. The only other member of the Five I'd met in person had been a nebbish reed of a guy who looked like he stalked women with drones.

Calivari had a long mullet, a white suit that looked like a much more expensive version of the one I'd had damaged this morning and topped about two meters with muscles on top of muscles. He was a good-looking sort of guy, if you liked beefcake, and had a sour expression on his face until his gaze turned to us. That was when a bright smile appeared and he marched right up to us, passed me and Lucy by, then bear hugged Doctor Frankenstein.

"Papa!" Calivari said, genuine joy in his voice. "Why didn't you tell me you were coming. I was just preparing the mechanical shark."

"Mechanical shark?" I asked.

Calivari pointed over the side of the yacht to a large fin of an enormous underwater construct. "Best money I ever invested. It doesn't actually digest anything you feed it, but the effect is still impressive."

"Uh huh," I said, not even sure he was threatening us so much as casually mentioning he had planned on having us killed. "So, Papa, huh, Doctor F? You were lying about lying?"

"No," Doctor Frankenstein said. "Papa is just what a lot of the children of the old neighborhood called me. Call me."

Calivari shook his head. "Doctor Saint Croix—ignore all this Frankenstein stuff—was a saint to many of us growing up. He arranged for many cybernetics to be harvested from corpses from the rich then sold off or transferred to us down to the Deep. Regularly needed organs as well. Saved thousands of lives. As the medical examiner, he is barely a cop to us."

"I didn't hear that," Lucy muttered.

"I've tried to follow his example," Calivari said, smiling. "Things have improved significantly down below since the fall of Governor Barnum, and we've opened many new smuggling routes to get more supplies down there. Not just food and narcotics but actual medicine-medicine. The new civi-cops are much more bribable these days."

Great, he was a "civic minded" gangster. I hated those. Gangsters loved to cultivate the people's touch and it was rarer than the alternative. It was just good business. People wanted to believe there was a heart in the local mob bosses even if they tended to be every bit the psychos that stalked women with knives in scare movies as the other sorts of gangster. I knew one guy back on Mars called Giovanni "Gifts" Chang who had a funeral attended by forty thousand people weeping over the death of a man who'd built schools and frozen rent throughout a job strike. He'd also had a sixteen-year-old girl's throat slit because she *might* have seen his son snorting Red Dust off a male hooker's backside.—Yes, they *did* discriminate on Mars. It's about the only thing the Moon has over the Red Planet.

Lucy smiled. "I did not hear that."

"Not our job anymore, Lucy," I replied, forcing a smile.

"He's a real philanthropist," Doctor Frankenstein said, trying to let me know I should play to that angle.

"I've heard a lot about you from Doctor F," I said, lying. "Says you're a real salt of the earth—or Moon in this case—kind of guy."

I extended my hand, but Calivari didn't take it, looking at me like he was still debating over whether to murder me. "You know, they have a red mark on you on Mars. The Golden Tigers

"No surprises there," I said, pulling my hand back. "I did kill quite a lot of them."

"You, I also recognize," Calivari said, turning to Lucy. "Loved *Lucy Westenra, Vampire Hunter.*"

"Super," Lucy said, giving a smile so forced that she looked like she had hernia. Unlike her time with the Knights, Lucy had nothing but ill feelings regarding her time as a TV star. Not the least because she was legally obligated to keep the same name as her character for twenty years.

"In any case, you stirred up a shitstorm with what you did," Calivari said, crossing his arms. "I could earn a lot of street cred by killing you. I'm curious about what could possibly bring the two most infamous cops in the Moon to my home. Especially, after I heard you're no longer protected by the LCPD."

"I'd hardly trust them with my protection if I was a citizen, let alone a cop," I said, sarcastically.

Calivari struggled not to smile at that. "But because my dear, dear friend is here, I'll give you thirty seconds."

"Plague," I said.

Calivari paused, his expression changing to something like a mixture of concern and curiosity. "I'll give you a minute."

"A bunch of humans from another planet have been producing a crap-ton of Loop at rock-bottom prices and practically giving it away in bulk," I said, knowing far less than we should. "We have reason to believe they've covered the latest batch in a designer disease. In the interests of whole bunches of people not dying, presumably starting with your customers, we'd like to buy it from you so we can burn it."

Calivari seemed to process what I was saying, then he grabbed me by my shirt, staring into my eyes. "Do you think I'm stupid, *fra?*"

"Back off." Lucy charged a fusion pistol at his chest point blank range. She'd had it hidden on her and they'd stupidly avoided patting us down. Calivari should fire them.

That, of course, led to Calivari's goons pointing their guns at her head as well as at me and Barksley.

"It's true, Tommy," Doctor Frankenstein said, raising his hands. "There're some crazy-ass people out there and they've done something exceptionally stupid. Lucy and Neal are here representing the feds, not the cops."

Calivari dropped his hands from me. His attitude was complete disdain. "Just because you're barely a cop doesn't mean you're still not a cop, Saint Croix. I've heard plenty of bullshit about these new Department agents and everything about them smells. I'm not going to be roped into one of their sting operations and let you set up whatever the fuck you're planning."

The sad fact was that I would believe the exact same thing in Calivari's position because—and I know this because of who I am—cops lie. There's no legal obligation for us to tell the truth and the old myth about cops having to tell you when they're screwing you is one we perpetuate ourselves. Unless you get it in writing, plenty of times they'll blow all sorts of smoke up your ass then stab you in the back because, hey, you're just a criminal. I'd feel guilty about it except for, well, most of the guys screwed by this are real assholes.

Note I said most.

"This isn't a set up," Doctor Frankenstein tried futilely to explain as, of course, that was exactly what a guy setting someone else up would say.

"Throw them overboard, the dog too," Calivari said.

"Now that's just rude," Barksley said.

This was about to end in all of us getting gunned down or eaten by sharks, though I was pretty sure I could get Calivari and maybe five other guys with my enhanced posthuman abilities. Our chances were slim, but Lucy and I might be able to survive. Frankenstein was probably screwed, though, and I gave even odds we'd also be gunned down before we managed to get to the car. Taking Calivari hostage was about the only move I could see that didn't end with us as mechanical shark chow.

Did mechanical sharks eat?

Great, now I was going to die thinking that.

One of the goon squad moved to grab me and I prepared to go for the drug lord with my own hidden pistol. Then the sound of an explosion sent us all to the deck instead. Windows shattered from the detonation as gunfire was unloaded onto the guards and Calivari's drones by unknown attackers.

"Mothersucker!" I shouted.

"What the hell is this!" Calivari screamed as the closest of his bodyguards got up and started firing, only to end up riddled with bullets that penetrated his body armor.

"Someone is trying to kill you!" Lucy shouted, lying on the ground beside me.

I didn't correct her because, well, I wasn't an idiot to be focused on that right now. It was equally likely someone was trying to kill us.

THREE ENEMY DRONES DETECTED, Interface said, providing me a scan that showed more high-end killing machines were attacking. SHALL WE ENGAGE COUNTERMEASURES?

I don't know what that means, but yes! I snapped.

INITIATING ENHANCED COMBAT MODE, Interface replied, and I suddenly felt my body jerk as I drew my Herakles-7 pistol and started shooting as the world around me moved in slow motion, targeting reticles appearing in my eyes around the drones as I fired. It would have been badass if I'd been the one doing it, but I instead felt like a passenger in my own body.

The Herakles-7 bullets were designed for piercing the armor of cyborgs as well as plastisteel soldiers, basically making the gun a hand cannon. I'd had it customized further since acquiring it from Shinobu, mostly by letting the adorable mad tinker improve on it. But even I was surprised at the detonation that followed each shot. It was like something from a movie.

ADDITIONAL TARGET DETECTED, Interface said.

I noticed yet another drone coming up from the other side of the yacht, its targeting system looking firmly focused on Calivari. That one was taken out by Lucy, her firing three blasts in quick succession into the machine. The drone, yet another *Assassin*-class, went down into the water beside us.

Something was not right here.

"Is everyone alright?" Barksley said, removing his paws from where he'd been covering his glasses. "Are you alive, Mr. Drug Lord?"

Calivari looked shaken but quickly recovered, climbing to his feet. "This is your doing!"

The funny thing was that the damage wasn't that bad. I mean, it sucked for the five dead guards scattered around the yacht, but the destruction could have been a lot worse. They could have pelted the super yacht with enough rockets to destroy it outright or just plain old sink us. No, it was a horrifying and very directly targeted attempt to scare us. Which certainly worked but might have the side effect of getting us shot as Calivari's goons looked ready to open fire on the people who had just saved them.

"No, it's not. This was a hit on you, and we just saved your life," I said, doing my best to calm him down while lowering my gun. Which might not be the best move even if I did suddenly have powers from *The Matrix*.

YOU HAVE BARELY EXPLORED YOUR POSTHUMAN CAPABILITIES, Interface said.

Yeah, well, you don't come with an instruction manual, I replied.

YES, I DO. YOU NEVER BOTHERED TO READ THE FILE.

I ignored the pseudo-AI.

Calivari responded by going to one of his goons and reaching past his unbuttoned Hawaiian shirt to pull out the guy's own Herakles-7 hand cannon from his side holster. I couldn't fault the man's taste in weapons. "You think I'm going to buy that crap? You arrive and ten minutes later, the hit happens!"

Yeah, it absolutely was suspicious as hell. "The Moon's underworld is in turmoil and it wasn't because of us. Someone's making a major play and we witnessed the first move but there are probably a dozen other ones being made now."

Calivari aimed his gun at my face. "Drop the pistol, Action Dan and I might spare the dog."

Lucy narrowed her eyes.

"It was an honor working with you, Neal," Barksley said. "I'm sorry we didn't get to make loads of money we could swim in."

121

"Alright. Alright," I said, not immediately dropping the pistol as I fully intended to shoot the guy in the head and then hope ten guys could be taken down easier than fifteen.

That was when one of the ship's crew dressed in all white, not part of his guards, crew, ran up from below deck. "Mr. Calivari, we're getting reports of attacks against our businesses. It's the Golden Tigers. They're using drones!"

I looked at Lucy, whose expression was unusually even. She appeared to be concentrating.

Calivari made some mental calculations. "Fuck. Alright, Neal, Lucy—"

"*Agents*," Lucy corrected.

Calivari narrowed his eyes. "Agents. Fine, I believe you. I'll tell you where the Loop is. However, you don't know just how much money is involved here. Those crazy missionaries sold me a literal ton of Loop. I don't know where they got the chemicals but we're talking crates of it. I've been able to double my business."

"And we'll pay street prices," I said, softly. "With a ten percent discount. Because you owe us."

It wasn't my money; it was the government's, but there's no way in hell Calivari would treat us as on the level if we didn't bargain.

Calivari stared at me then burst out laughing. "Ha! I don't see no cash on you, Agents."

"It's ready for transfer," Lucy asked. "However, we'll first need bank accounts for it and confirmation of the location. Remember, if we did cheat you, you know where we live."

That wasn't a great thing to say, Lucy.

Calivari smiled. "Fine, let's talk biz."

The remainder of the negotiations took place over a thirty-five-minute period where we ended up transferring roughly ten million in EarthGov credits as well as an additional twenty million in Atlas Security credits to the crime boss. I was surprised the money was there but apparently both SHID and Armstrong had come through. Atlas Security lending its significant financial resources to try to protect their investment on the Moon was going to be controversial at the next board meeting even if they spent twenty million credits of their own cash on a month of recruitment ads to teenagers.

It was how they got me.

Eventually Calivari calmed down considerably once he had the money in his accounts and regained some of his friendly demeanor to Doctor Frankenstein. The dead bodies were carried down to his super yacht's freezer and he even slipped the location of one of his competitor's Loop warehouses, probably not realizing that we intended to make the same sort of deal with the other members of the Five. Still, I wasn't going to turn it down. A man like Calivari would talk all the livelong day about honor among thieves and never snitching but he'd turn on his fellow crooks the moment it was convenient.

When we were all done "negotiating" and loaded back up in the Red Dragon X8—with Lucy in the driver's seat—she said what I was thinking, "So, your wife absolutely attacked us with her drones, didn't she?"

"Yeah," I muttered, having reached the same conclusion. The passenger's seat somehow felt wrong when I was in the Red Dragon. Which I knew wasn't exactly a priority at the moment. "That was just to make us look good."

"It worked, didn't it?" Doctor Frankenstein said, sitting in the back with Barksley. "Mind you, I think I'm off Calivari's Christmas list."

"To think I was going to make him a business proposal," Barksley said. "The maple syrup cartels could always use more distributors."

"It was murder," Lucy said, softly. "I hope you realize that."

"I do," I replied. "But whether it was justified or not can be decided on if we manage to contain this."

Lucy didn't respond.

"Lucky thing that the Golden Tigers attacked when they did," Barksley said.

"It wasn't luck," Lucy said. "That was me."

I did a double take.

CHAPTER THIRTEEN

I Can Feel It Coming in the Air Tonight (and It's Plague)

"You'll have to explain that," I said, letting the Red Dragon X8 transport us to the location of the warehouse. We'd already transmitted the coordinates to SHID and hopefully they would be able to wrangle together enough people to gather the infected Loop safely then burn it all. With luck, the other four members of The Five were cooperating and we could nip this thing in the bud.

Yeah, I didn't believe that either.

"You're not the only one with superpowers," Lucy said, reminding me of her posthuman status. "I datasliced Calivari's network and faked a call from his gang about the Golden Tigers attacking. He's going to be pissed when he finds out they didn't."

Doctor Frankenstein whistled at her audacity.

"I'm sure the thirty million will compensate," I said, not entirely sure it would. Calivari was the kind of guy to order an attack on the Golden Tigers before verifying who was attacked, when, and where. Starting a gang war was, unfortunately, just the least of the kind of things that we might have to do to stop this.

"I'll drop him a line once we verify the contents of the warehouse," Lucy replied, showing she was a much better person than I was. "In any case, SHID managed to get the warehouse locations from the other members of the Five."

"Really?" I asked, surprised at her knowing that and curious. "Good news makes me suspicious."

"As well it should," Lucy said. "It's now the Three anyway since Priss and company ended up crashing a meeting with two. They ended up gunning them down but got the locations from some of their lieutenants."

I facepalmed. "This is why soldiers don't make good cops."

"That applies to you too, Neal," Lucy said.

"I stand by my statement," I replied, before pausing. "How do you know what they're up to anyway?"

"I'm linked to the Knights through my nanotech," Lucy said, bitterly. "Just like you have a singular interface, we have a shared network. It means even when I want to be apart from them, I can't be. That's why I can't really forgive them for what they did."

Ouch.

"Wait, if your AI is a shared consciousness among all the other Knights, does that mean whenever you're having sex, it's always with everyone else participating?"

Lucy looked at me with a bewildered expression on her face.

"I'm asking for science's sake," I said.

"You're a sick man, Detective Gordon," Lucy said, sighing. There was a smile on her face afterward, though, that told me she'd found it as funny as I'd intended. "I'm going to miss that."

I wanted to tell her that she didn't have to miss it, but I had my pride. There were plenty of other fish in the sea. You know, just not gorgeous ex-rocker girls and actresses with minds every bit as dirty as my own. Okay, now I'd depressed myself.

Barksley glared at the dashboard. "It's going to take a ridiculous amount of time to program my music playlist into this thing."

"You don't have it backed up?" I asked.

"Of course I have it backed up, but it's the little things," Barksley said. "I mean, the slight lag whenever I played the soundtrack to *Miami Vice 2128*. This just isn't a substitute for the Purple Rain."

"It's not actually our car, Barksley," Lucy said, sighing.

"I know," Barksley said. "It's *my* car. I wonder if we can trade it in for something decent. Maybe a car with fins."

What followed was an argument about music that lasted about twenty minutes until we arrived at a warehouse, which was

125

surprisingly in Luna City itself rather than Crater Town, let alone the Deep. It was already being surrounded with police cars, STRIKE vans, and even an armored personnel carrier that seemed ridiculous for what we were trying to accomplish.

The warehouse was near the bay and was officially a sailing equipment and supply warehouse for something called Sailing Equipment and Supply. Wow. The originality here on the Moon. It had a little life preserver logo and several trucks parked in the front. The place had several garage entrances that were all closed, and no windows. No sign of exterior guards or staff, which put me on edge.

"I've got a bad feeling about this," I muttered aloud.

"I can't imagine why, what with this being a mob boss' warehouse full of plague," Doctor Frankenstein said. "You know, this reminds me of the time I used to hang out with the Gordon Foundation's founders."

"Excuse me?" I asked, looking at him sideways.

"Kei and Case Gordon," Doctor Frankenstein said. "The founders of the Gordon Foundation."

"Yeah, I know the Trikuza queenpin and the head of Atlas Security," I replied.

"They're both more into spy shit these days," Doctor Frankenstein said. "I always wondered why they got into children's charities. Now I think they must have been building an army of quirky but capable weirdos to do their bidding. At least between you and Rogers."

"I'm my own man, thank you," I said, annoyed. "I don't know the Gordons from the Princess of Wales even if we share a surname."

"Is that still a thing?" Lucy asked. "I thought they dissolved the monarchy."

I shrugged. "I think they live in Canada now."

The Red Dragon descended inside the perimeter created around the warehouse and we settled ourselves behind a gunship that was the best way to intimidate anyone inside. Unfortunately, the guy standing outside in full tactical gear and his SHID badge hanging on a chain around his neck was Captain Steve Rogers Hudson.

I really didn't want to deal with this guy.

"Masks on," Lucy said, pulling out a plastic bag from underneath the seat. It contained four breath masks that had little filters and gas mask-like attachments on them. I was surprised it was there and wondered if I should have paid more attention to the briefing's orientation bits.

"Aren't we immune to this shit?" I asked.

"We're setting a good example," Lucy said. "Help Barksley get his on."

"I am a robot dog," Barksley said. "So, this will be ridiculous and stupid looking. But I hope children will follow my example."

"Gimme," Doctor Frankenstein said, wiggling his fingers in the air. "I may be just a brain and spinal cord these days, but I don't take any chances. I want to live long enough to get uploaded to a porn site for the rest of my life."

"Choose wisely," I replied, putting on my mask first. "There's a lot of sites that would be a digital Hell rather than Heaven."

Lucy muttered something under her breath as I helped Barksley get his mask (badly) on and the three of us exited the car.

"Do you even want to be here, Doc?" I asked, my voice sounding like a demon from Hell.

"You have your reverberator on," Lucy said.

"No shit," I said, before pausing. "The plans you refer to will soon be back in our hands."

"Can you take anything seriously?" Lucy asked, flipping a switch on the side of my mask.

"I think we know the answer to that," I replied, my voice back to normal. "Why do they even have a function for this?"

"It costs more to add it per unit," Doctor Frankenstein said. "Anyway, you need some medical personnel here even if I'm usually into forensics these days, and that's primarily dead people. I notice this place should be surrounded by ambulances and doctors but all I see are cops and soldiers."

"Maybe someone should have advised our murderous Red Queen of that," Lucy replied, not hiding her disdain. Then again, all she knew about my ex was she was a repeat mass murderer. Okay, wait, it sounded bad when I said it that way.

"Let's get going," I said, waving to Lucy's ex. "Yo, Captain America! We would have words with thee!"

Steve waved back, a broad smile on his face that made me uncomfortable. I hated cheery people; they were always hiding something. I, by contrast, was always cheery sarcastically.

"Howdy, Gordon!" Steve said. "Glad to see you here."

"Sure," I said.

"What's the situation?" Lucy asked, keeping this professional.

"In addition to being storage, this is also a narcotics assembly line," Steve replied. "Apparently, the civi police knew about it long before we did but didn't decide to share that information until we asked about it."

"Sounds about right," I said. "That means there's actual staff inside?"

"We detect fifteen people inside with scanners," Steve said. "Only a couple of them are moving around and have heat signatures."

I stared at him. "That's not a good sign."

"No," Steve said, dryly. "It is not. We've made a few calls in to demand the survivors come out, but no one has responded."

I think it said just about everything that needed to be said that the best possible reason for this was that Calivari called ahead and had everyone inside murdered.

"Someone has to go in," Doctor Frankenstein said.

"Tell me something I don't know," Lucy said, about to volunteer by her posture and sucking in her breath. "I—"

"I had a walk on part in a movie back on Mars," I said, interrupting. "I didn't know it was a porno, though."

Everyone stared at me.

"I mean when I saw all the naked people, I guessed," I replied. "I volunteer to go in first."

"This really isn't the time for jokes," Lucy said.

"I use humor to cope with the horrifying nature of reality," I replied. "I said I'll go."

"May the Sun be with you," Steve said, giving a weird blessing.

"Yeah, I'm sure Jesus loves cops after what happened to him," I replied, making a joke even I thought was going too far.

Steve gave an enigmatic smile.

If any in our audience of readers were confused why we were hesitant, it wasn't because we were afraid of infection. Well, maybe on that unconscious primal level that you could never quite completely remove from yourself. We'd been assured we were immune to the disease due to our posthuman status and that was probably why we were picked for SHID, though my wife and so many other people I knew being involved offered other possibilities. No, the hesitation — and it was only a few moments mind you — was because even cops, especially cops, are reluctant to walk into place they suspect is going to be a charnel house.

I'd put way more bodies in the morgue in the past couple of years than I ever wanted to, and most soldiers did the same during a war, but that didn't make it any easier. I'd have nightmares about the five bodies we'd made earlier if I didn't have any about the ones with the Slavers Guild massacre — and only then because a sexy ninja massacring them made it all too unreal.

My choice to head in lost a lot of its drama, though, when the door to the side of the sailing equipment warehouse opened and a man stumbled out of it. He was coughing violently and there was blood beneath his chin that looked like he was straight out of a horror movie. Plus, the rash.

"Yeah, I think we can safely assume infection," Doctor Frankenstein said, rushing to the guy's side and catching him before he fell over. He then started demanding medical supplies. In that moment, I officially developed full-on respect for the man.

"Go in and check the building for any other survivors," Lucy said.

Steve started calling for the doctor's supplies.

"Sure," I muttered. "Barksley?"

"I'm good!" Barksley said, standing still.

"Of course, you are," I said, heading into the warehouse through the open door.

The interior of the warehouse wasn't an abattoir. It looked distressingly normal, really, with boxes and boxes. I couldn't smell anything with my mask on, but it wasn't difficult to guess what it stank like, and my eyes watered.

It was two levels with the ground floor having a larger-than-normal office space that had a pair of double doors that were tied with a chain and padlock, and again, no windows. On the ground, there was the corpse of a man who looked like he'd vomited himself to death. He had probably died eight or nine hours ago. He'd just been left on the ground to rot and there were other signs that the people here had been hit hard by the Red fever.

There was another body propped up against a bunch of crates but far fewer bodies than the fifteen Steve had mentioned. This guy looked to be in his forties and was lying in his own waste, but a couple of hacking coughs later, I realized he was still alive. Going to the guy's side, I checked him and saw, yeah, he was alive but not exactly in great shape.

"I'll get you help," I said, looking at the man. "But I need to know where the others are. Plus, the Loop. It's contaminated."

The man managed to look up to me with his deep brown eyes. "No, shit, really."

"Okay, stupid statement," I said. "Still, I gotta know."

"The Loop is in the assembly room," The man said with a rasp. "Twenty million worth."

Okay, we'd been hustled. I was really going to have to figure out a way to put a good spin on paying an extra ten million.

"The people?" I asked.

"They got sick early," the man said, struggling for each breath. "They're Deepers. Worthless trash. Sell their own mothers for a nickel. We keep 'em here on site. They bunk in the next building. Work 'em for food and water. We figured we'd... we figured we'd lock 'em up until they died off and the disease was clean off the Loop. Guess we tried to check it too early. I need a doctor man. I can pay."

What the man described was monstrous but all too believable. Still, I had to see. I got up and immediately went to the padlocked door before looking for a bolt cutter. I couldn't find one and grabbed the chain before seeing if my posthuman status granted me superhuman strength. Much to my surprise, the metal bent and snapped after putting my back into it. Letting the chain fall to the ground and panting for a second, I opened the door and stared at what was inside.

130

I'll spare you the gory details, but the disease had ravaged the workers of this drug smuggling operation. They'd all been infected but the disease only had a fifty percent mortality rate if you got proper medical treatment. No, these people had died because they had been left to die of total lack of care, with thirst and hunger combined with the disease. They appeared to have been left here for almost a week. The Loop was in boxes to one side, looking like it was going to be smuggled in cardboard boxes full of packing peanuts. Enough to make a man extraordinarily rich. But I barely paid attention to it because of the age of some of the "workers" here. Some were barely out of adolescence.

"Son of a bitch," I said, walking back to the man I'd left up against the wall. I pulled out my Herakles-7 and aimed it at his head. I'd never extrajudicially killed someone and didn't want to start now, but I wanted to put the scare in this piece of garbage. I aimed it right at his face and tried to think of something to put the fear of God in him.

It was pointless.

He was already dead.

"Dammit," I said, putting away my gun.

Lucy entered in a few seconds later. Maybe it was minutes, I lost track of time. "Neal?"

"Yeah?" I asked. "Yeah, we need to burn this place to the ground."

"Neal..." Lucy trailed off.

"No survivors," I said, shaking my head. "We need to check this place for records to see where it's shipped and—"

"Neal," Lucy said.

"Yeah?" I asked, turning around to look at her.

Lucy looked defeated, even with the mask covering the lower part of her face, and that was a rare expression for her. "Nigel and his cronies have been over to the Sons of Mithras cell's apartment. They've checked all their drug lab's equipment and determined that they made five large shipments, one for each of the Five. There's evidence that it's one of several cells operating on the Moon, though."

"How many did we get?" I said, suspecting where this was going.

"Neal, it's—" Lucy tried to soften the blow.

It was pointless.

"Please," I said.

"One of the warehouses was completely cleaned out," Lucy explained. "It's owner, one of the ones killed earlier today, shipped the product almost immediately. We're trying to track down who they were shipped too, what dealers, what stash houses, and so on, but it'll be difficult. Every person they sell to, every person that takes it, every person they interact with after that—"

"How many are out there?" I asked. "Pills, I mean. Infected ones."

"Up to twenty-thousand doses," Lucy answered.

Crap.

CHAPTER FOURTEEN

Betray Your Friend or Betray Your Country

The next month was among the worst in my life.

We worked two weeks straight tracking people, breaking down doors, and quarantining them while struggling to test as many people as possible. We always seemed one step behind, and the story broke just as we were about to (seemingly) get a handle on it. Honestly, I was surprised it took as long as it did to do so.

There had been something akin to two hundred thousand reported infections and the actual number was probably much greater due to the fact no one was really checking on how the Deep was coping with it. That was when the state of emergency was officially declared, most of the traffic to the Moon was shut down, and panic set in. The SHID operation went from a bunch of handpicked operatives to coordinating a million medical and relief workers, and police.

It was insane how quickly the Moon seemed to change. The streets of the cities were largely empty, and people were isolating in their homes, trying to keep themselves safe. Fears of shortages led to hoarding. Anger, long suppressed, was bubbling up and several food riots of the kind that hadn't been seen in decades started up again as did government protests.

I punched a prison warden in the face when I found out he'd let the disease run rampant through his convict "guests" because he didn't think they deserved treatment. There was no inquiry because he died of Red Fever a week later himself.

Lucy and I were sitting in the front of the Red Dragon on our way back from a protest where a bunch of Nationalist Moon Front (translation: militant hate group) members had been planning to burn down a neighborhood of former Deep dwellers that had somehow made their way into Crater Town. The civi cops had, of course, been very upset when we'd told them to break up the guys wearing Man on the Moon novelty helmets while tossing Molotov cocktails and firing guns in the air. Both of us looked like we needed sleep, a hot shower, a good meal, and to live anywhere else but the Moon.

I'd managed to get a replacement for my fedora and trench coat, though Barksley had also given me a bow tie and suit that he was forcing me to wear. It turned out my government salary wasn't quite enough to cover my current debts and the dog was covering for me if he got to use me as his personal action figure to dress up. Lucy had adjusted to wearing a black bodysuit, long coat, and military-grade shades that made her look like a comic book secret agent or action movie vampire. She'd also dyed her hair blue, which was an interesting fashion choice.

Barksley was snoring behind the passenger seat, looking adorable even as a little cord stuck to the bottom of his belly as he recharged from the car's infojack.

"Prayer is the only thing that can save us now," the voice of Penny Cash spoke from the car radio. "The godless Reformers have brought ruin to us with their embrace of deviant alien religion. We need to return to the Sun's Light. The lizard men have infiltrated our society since—"

"Do we have to listen to this crazy woman?" I asked, looking over at Lucy. She was driving while I was going over paperwork. We were still no closer to finding out who the mole was, and we'd had several more leaks since then.

Lucy sighed. "The Church of Money is growing rapidly during this crisis. They've been heavily preaching that... whatever. Bad things. Send us money. Don't wear masks. Don't stand five feet apart. Don't wash your hands—"

"That last part gets me," I said. "I mean, gross."

"The Red Queen wants us to find something to threaten Penny with," Lucy said, referring to Kate by her nickname, which was increasingly less hostile as every extreme measure seemed more and more justified. "I don't think Kate understands free speech is absolute on the Moon until you throw a brick. Which, unfortunately, a lot of people have been throwing lately."

"I was there," I muttered, exhausted. "At least Earth has managed to contain any infection. They've kept quarantine down so that it's only the Moon that's really effected."

"Fuck Earth," Lucy muttered, looking up through the dome above our heads at Earth above. It was now the night period of the Moon's rotation. "We should declare our independence and drop rocks on it until they surrender."

I stared at her.

Lucy blinked. "Wow, I don't know where that came from. I'm not usually very revolutionary. Nationalism isn't in my blood."

"Anger from helplessness comes out sideways," I replied. "We're all well and truly sick of this."

"Yeah," Lucy said, sighing. "I know. We're also nowhere near finishing this either. The earliest projections for a vaccine are still a year away and we haven't even begun testing. That's assuming one is even possible and it's not some alien superbug that will kill us all."

"It's a human disease made by humans," I replied. "We'll figure something out."

The fact Karma Corp hadn't yet figured anything out had done a lot to diminish the power of that organization even with their three-month head start. Governor Hopewood had finally broken down and begged for assistance from the Community. It had gotten her impeached but not removed from office. The Moon's Colonial Council was a group that was willing to tolerate just about anything from its leaders, but showing weakness was not one of them.

"Thanks, Neal. I needed the reminder." Lucy looked in the rearview mirror down at Barksley. It was a novelty, really, because the car had rear cameras like most vehicles of its type. "Well, at least someone is getting a good night's rest."

"Do android dogs dream of chasing electric cars?" I asked, looking back at Barksley.

"What?" Lucy asked, confused.

"Never mind," I muttered. "What do we have to do next?"

"We can catch a couple of hours sleep if you want," Lucy said. "Both of us are running on fumes. Then we have to tackle an investigation of stolen medical supplies."

I wasn't eager to do that because they were likely taken by Calivari and being sent down to the Deep. Despite the fact the guy was a monster, or at least employed them, he was apparently sincere in his charity. Earth was still sending plenty of food and other supplies to the Moon, but only for its official population. There were plenty of shortages that were only made worse by profiteers. The only upside was that violent crime was way down and Big Brother, Rashid's website, had exposed the massive stockpiles of food Karma Corp had been sitting on to drive prices up. *That* had been a blow to their stock prices. Also, it meant no outright famine at least.

For now.

"Sounds good," I said, deciding to sleep for a week once I discovered the secret of cloning and dumped all my work on my hapless double.

So, of course, that was when we got a call from headquarters. We were still operating out of that apartment building if you could believe it. Well, at least the "inner circle" of SHID was. We also had a public office building with ten thousand employees fielding phone calls and that one was connected to several other offices who directed calls to other services.

"Answer," I said, already guessing it was more work.

On the dashboard, a holo of Kate appeared in a rumpled suit. She looked about as bad as I felt. Kate was burning the midnight oil every bit as much as we were. She'd technically failed in her mission to contain the disease and could have passed this down to local authorities, but she had spent every waking moment trying to reduce the body count. According to Doctor Frankenstein and Shinobu, we were doing a helluva job, but it certainly didn't feel like it.

"You have reached the message service of Neal Gordon. Neal Gordon is not available right now. He's off having a bottle of tequila on a better planet with a cover girl of LADS magazine. If you'd like to leave a message—" I started to say.

"Neal, I am not in the mood," Kate said.

"Bzzt, bzzzt," I said, raising my hands and waving them. "You're breaking up. Interference. It must be the aliens! They're finally invading."

Kate turned to Lucy. "Lucy, I have a job for you."

"Is it pushing Neal out of the car to his death?" Lucy asked, smiling, "Because I'll do it."

"Hey, the cover girl could be you," I pointed out.

"That was one issue!" Lucy snapped.

"Not today," Kate said, referring to tossing me out of the car at a thousand feet. "We've identified one of the leaks."

"That's awesome!" I said, genuinely impressed. "You've found out who ratted us out to the Sons of Mithras?"

Trying to track down the other Sons of Mithras operating on the Moon was like trying to find a needle in a stack of other needles. The Albionese had been subject to heavy discrimination upon the discovery of the Sons of Mithras hailing from their world and for every tip with solid evidence, there were a few hundred thousand fake ones.

Vitellius had finally broken down and started spilling his guts after an involuntary rehab program and getting a Mithras priest to lecture him. Unfortunately, one of the things we'd discovered for certain was the man was an idiot. Well, idiot savant. He could cook high-quality Loop but had been left out of the details of his cell's activities. Probably because he'd have been shouting the details from the rooftops if they'd let him loose. The biggest thing we'd gotten out of the man was that apparently there were non-Albionese working with the terrorists who'd made the arrangements to import and house them all. Unfortunately, they'd paid in cash and the landowner had only noticed they looked "respectable."

Which didn't narrow it down, even on the Moon.

"Wait, you said one of the leaks?" Lucy clarified. I must have been too out of it to notice.

"Unfortunately, it's not who betrayed you to the Sons of Mithras, if they even exist," Kate admitted. There was still always the question if they could have found out about our arrival via a bug in someone's office or by other means. I didn't believe it, though. "No, Priss and Nina have been feeding classified information to Rashid Al-Fariq AKA Big Brother."

Lucy and I exchanged a glance.

"And?" I asked.

Kate stared. "Can either of you bother to pretend to care about operational security?"

"No," I answered for us both.

I had my questions about the effectiveness of amateur journalism. Dataslicers like Rashid poked around in other people's business with no regard to privacy, let alone the law. However, I also felt they were generally harmless unless they were actively spreading lies and misinformation like some of the assholes out there. His Big Brother site might have a slightly conspiratorial tone and put the worst spin on just about everything the government, cops, or corporations did, but that didn't mean it wasn't telling the truth.

There was also the fact that Rashid was, unlike most of his fellow infonet anarchists, a snitch. Which I meant in the nicest way possible. He'd helped us with my crusade—he really hated that word—against the Slavers Guild, as well as against several other unpleasant criminals. In return, Lucy had helped him escape from the Fleur de Lis gang and their Syndicate masters. She'd even set him up in her mother's guest house, or one of them at least. Which, honestly, probably wasn't a good look for Lucy.

"You need to go there and shut down his website and take him into custody," Kate said, staring at us. "You also need to arrest both Nina and Priss. They were last seen heading in that direction as well."

"Yeah, that's not going to happen," I said, calmly.

"Neal," Lucy muttered, clearly not ready to torpedo her career in the middle of a massive crisis where she was vital to people surviving.

Something I was.

"They're good people and I follow an age-old adage," I said, noting that seemingly no one else seemed to have this attitude. "That if I ever

138

had to choose between betraying my friend and betraying my country, I'd have the courage to betray my country."

"That is a horrible, *horrible* attitude for a government agent," Kate said.

"His best friend also burned him alive," Lucy said.

"*I* am his best friend now," Barksley said, waking up.

"Can't you just let this go?" I asked, knowing the answer. However, pointing out that hiring Priss and Nina in the first place was something bound to blow up in SHID's faces. Frankly, I was surprised they'd limited themselves to whistleblowing.

"This *is* me letting it go," Kate responded. "The fact Black Briar mercenaries aren't breaking down the door to Rashid's home to execute him has cost me every bit of cachet I have with the Colonial Council and favors to Nigel, which is another reason he's onboard. So, I want the information that Rashid has received retrieved and for you to offer him a deal: work for us and help coordinate attacks against misinformation campaigns and track down who is benefiting from all this."

"He won't accept it," Lucy said. "It took me years to build up a relationship with him and he still doesn't trust me."

"Then offer him a plea deal of six months in the whitest white-collar prison there is," Kate said.

"He may prefer a supermax," I replied.

Rashid was stupid that way.

It was a good deal, though, and a lot better than he'd receive from anyone else. The one thing both Neo-Militarists and Reformers hated equally was whistleblowers. Both threw the book at anyone who tried to publicize their secrets with charges like espionage, treason, and other loaded words that Nixon wished he'd thought of a couple of centuries ago.

"What about Priss and Nina?" I asked.

"They both have to be discharged," Kate said. "I'm sorry."

Both Lucy and I stared at one another and resisted the urge to laugh. Neither Priss nor Nina would consider that to be a punishment. Despite my earlier attitude, I figured it would be worth presenting the option to both people. It also wasn't worth playing the card, "Oh, Kate,

I know you're actually a mass murdering vigilante." Blackmail rarely worked out the way that people thought it would as it had to be in the sweet spot between something people would pay or do favors to cover up but not be so dire as to warrant killing you over. Given the enormous discrepancy in our powers, if I did try that move, Kate might just have me shoved out an airlock onto the Moon's lifeless surface. Besides, I didn't want to betray her like that either.

"Yeah, I think we can work with that," I said, pausing. "What about you, Lucy?"

"We have an obligation to present it to him at least," Lucy said.

Kate glared at us. "You're not Rashid's lawyers."

"God no," I said, sharply. "I have some standards as a poor corrupt official. That's a quote from *Casablanca* by the way."

"No, it's not and that guy was working for the *Nazis*," Lucy pointed out.

I grimaced, embarrassed. "Right. I forgot about that part."

"I'm starting to understand why you two were fired from Cyberlife," Kate muttered.

"Starting to?" I asked, confused.

"Goodbye, Neal, Lucy," Kate said, reaching for the control panel in front of her console.

"One last thing," I interrupted her from signing off. "Does Shinobu know about this?"

As the avatar of Armstrong, Shinobu had a lot more power and influence than might readily be apparent. Despite technically only being his interpreter and mouthpiece, Shinobu had the "ear of the king" and the amount of knowledge and soft power she had might have been SHID's best advantage on the Moon. They were intrinsically linked, too, and Armstrong couldn't just fire her and appoint a new one.

Kate blinked. "Why would she care?"

"Rashid and she have been dating off and on for over a year," Lucy said, trying not to relish sharing this bit of news.

Kate closed her eyes as I could feel her oncoming migraine vicariously. "Of course, she is."

"Do you still want us to bring them in?" I asked.

"Yes," Kate said, firmly. "Because plugging these leaks is important to finding out who is leaking dangerous information. One of our undercover agents was killed yesterday while investigating the passports the Sons of Mithras were using to get here in the first place. Putting out fires with the megacorps by going after leakers is comparatively a low priority."

I didn't entirely disagree with her and that bothered me. We all needed to be focused in one direction: defeating the Red fever. Rashid was one of the best dataslicers on the Moon and if anyone could sort through the massive amount of data to find any clues we'd miss, it was him. Well, him or an AI, and most of those were hardcoded to be unable to do that due to people's paranoia about them doing exactly that.

"Gotcha," I muttered. "Will do."

Kate signed off.

"Do you think they're still at your mother's?" I asked, turning to Lucy.

"Unfortunately, yes," Lucy said. "Housing an infamous cybercriminal is exactly the sort of thing my mother loves to do. Ugh, this means I'll have to interact with her again."

"You poor thing," I said, noting that at least she had a mother. Mine had probably been some random teenage girl who'd gotten knocked up but carried me to term anyway before abandoning me on the Gordon Foundation doorstep. Mind you, Ayanna Breeze was a *terrible* mother by all accounts, but more incompetent than malicious.

Besides she had what settled most parental problems: money, and lots of it.

"Do you have any of that Loop leftover?" Lucy asked.

"You're kidding," I said.

"We need to wide awake for this," Lucy muttered.

"Sorry, I burned it out of solidarity," I replied, making a sentence that sounded good but didn't mean anything. "That and the last one I broke a tooth on."

"Then we need to stop by a bio-fuel station and get ourselves some synth coffee," Lucy said. "Lots and lots of synth coffee."

"Amen."

CHAPTER FIFTEEN

Party Like It's the End of the World

L ucy and I were sufficiently caffeinated when we headed to the
Tranquility dome that was up there with Las Vegas and Dubai
for "biggest waste of money making an inhospitable wasteland
into a playground for the rich" in human history. Specifically, it had
converted the Sea of Tranquility into a bunch of massive estates.

The vast majority of the Moon's populace lived below the poverty
line, and you could measure that in physical space as the poorest
citizens lived deeper in the Moon like frigging Morlocks. However, it
had been fashionable for a time for the one percent of the one percent
to buy themselves homes on Luna in hopes of displaying just what an
ostentatious piece of crap they really were.

I wasn't a class warrior and normally kept my opinions limited to
quiet envy, but it was hard to do when we passed through the UV light-
equipped doors of Ayanna Breeze's estate. A light antiseptic mist
coated us while we listened to the loud music of Ayanna's brief but
disastrous pop career. "I'm Rich and Pretty" and "Live Forever" were
at least appropriate music selections.

The place was jam packed with A-list celebrities, movie producers,
politicians, and their hangers-on that included wannabes as well as
never-weres. The alcohol and expensive food were flowing freely to the
point I suspected a vomitorium was probably somewhere on the
premise. Which was wasteful as hell; a bathroom worked just as fine.
There was a fire dancer performing and a couple of aliens pretending

to be royalty unless they really were giant pill bug princesses and princes.

"I think Edgar Allan Poe wrote a short story about this," I muttered, noting that this was probably a super-spreader event in the making. I was wearing a mask like the rest of my team but that made us stand out here even more than our lack of fame or wealth. Well, my lack of fame and wealth. Lucy was still remembered as a cult classic star and Barksley was a genuine maple syrup lord if his collection of Purple Rain replacements back at the apartment building was any indication.

"We should only be so lucky," Lucy replied, showing she was not so hesitant about her opinions regarding the super-rich. Mind you, she was still the regular kind of rich and I'd always found that a wee bit hypocritical.

"Oh, there's the King of Thailand and Councilor of Commerce," Barksley said, looking at them. "Oh my, those aren't their spouses."

Lucy tilted her head to one side and blinked. "I think that's inappropriate behavior for a public location."

"It's not so bad," I replied, following her gaze. "They're both adults and, oh, you were looking past them. Yeah, that's something to keep behind closed doors. I guess the Power Rod 5000 needed a news spokesperson."

"I prefer the real thing," Lucy said, dryly.

"In any case, Priss and company aren't here in the main house," I replied, giving the place a short once-over. "Why? Because—"

"Because they would have burned the place to the ground?" Lucy asked.

"Damn, that's better than the zinger I was going to use," I muttered. "But yeah."

"She'll be at the guest house with Rashid if she's anywhere," Lucy said. "However, we can't go there directly without getting my mother's permission."

"Aren't we representing the Deep State?" I asked. "Come on, what's the point of belonging to a quasi-legal emergency service with shades of secret police if we can't abuse our authority?"

Lucy looked at me sideways. "Somedays, I can't tell if you're kidding but no, I don't want to go without talking to my mother because she got authorization from the government to install lethal countermeasure security. She felt threatened by the plague."

"Lethal countermeasure security," I repeated, glad we were being ignored by the majority of people here. "You mean like drones and security turrets?"

"Yes, everything on the Moon is legal but regulated unless it involves kids," Lucy said. "Then you're effectively the property of your parents until eighteen."

I stared. "I feel like there's a story there."

"My legal challenges for emancipation at thirteen and sixteen failed," Lucy replied. "In any case, let's just find her and get going."

A beefy shirtless man in Speedos and a bow tie carrying a tray of champagne passed by as I picked up a flute before grabbing a shish kabob of real meat.

"Really, Neal?" I asked.

"When in Rome, check out the orgies," I replied, biting into the meat. Mmm, God, that was good, the real stuff.

Lucy rolled her eyes.

"I hope you brought enough for everyone," Barksley said, looking up.

"You can't eat real food," I replied.

"I can eat it, just not digest it. Besides, that's not the point, now, is it?" Barksley replied.

We managed to find Ayanna Breeze at the center of the party, everyone gathered around the couch like she was Marie Antoinette holding court. Which you'd think was an exaggeration if not for the fact she was presently dressed as Marie Antoinette, for some reason. Later, I would find out she was dressed as Madame de Pompadour but that wasn't relevant at the time.

Ayanna Breeze was considered by many people to be the world's most beautiful woman. Most of these people were heterosexual and bisexual men as well as a surprisingly large number of queer women, who usually had different tastes than the XY brigade. I wouldn't necessarily go that far in complimenting her looks, but the buxom blonde Eurasian woman had the best body that money could buy mixed with a powerful personal charisma which would have propelled

144

her to superstardom if not for the fact she was an objectively terrible actress. But she was an *entertaining* terrible actress, I should add, and that was the difference between a career and obscurity.

Plus, Ayanna Breeze was very good at the real secret in Hollywood, Bollywood, and whatever equivalent the Moon had: managing her friendships. As the adage went, it wasn't what you know but who you know and that was certainly on display here. Sitting beside her was Zoe Hopewood, military governor of Luna, and Penny Cash, the woman on the radio I'd rapidly developed a not-so-irrational hatred of. Both women were sensibly dressed, which made them look incredibly out of place in this bacchanalia.

Governor Zoe Hopewood was a short-haired, Afro-Canadian woman who looked like she taught kindergarten and was a bit on the larger side. She'd cultivated that inoffensive persona even though she'd ruthlessly pursued power as one of the Reformers from the time she was a Green Foods marketing exec. Most lunes didn't like her and considered her a foreigner appointed to be their ruler, which was correct even if she'd been approved by the democratically elected Colonial Council after three weeks of hearings and would "eventually" be replaced by a governor voted on by the populace. Don't ask me how the system works, I just live here.

Penny Cash, by contrast, was a bio-sculpted, raven-haired goddess who looked exactly like the kind of people who did news reports on Channel 51. Supposedly, she'd been a beauty queen in her youth, but it was notably the Church of Money that had sponsored most of those pageants. Her eyes were very striking, though, and were a steel gray that resembled the Moon. It was only when I caught her gaze that I got a chill.

Like I've told people before, I've been a cop awhile. I know the difference between the victims of society, the bent but not broken, the poseurs, and the genuinely evil. Looking into Penny Cash's eyes, I saw something that I'd seen before and it never got less unsettling: the kind of person who simply did not care on any appreciable level about other beings. People were not even things because things had value. To someone like Penny Cash, others were just background noise, petty annoyances to be stepped around or on as it benefited her with no other regard any more than a traffic jam or other inconvenience. Hers were the people I considered to be evil. You may find me weird for judging her as a narcissistic psychopath after a single gaze but, well, I also had her public persona to draw from.

"And who are these two?" Penny asked, looking at us as if we were pieces of poo that had somehow moved physically into her presence.

"Oh, this is Neal Gordon, the solar system's greatest detective!" Ayanna Breeze said, introducing me first for some reason. "Incredibly dashing secret agent and rogue policeman who doesn't play by the rules. He's killed dozens of people. I've optioned the rights to his life story."

"You have?" I asked. "With whom?"

Barksley bumped my leg with his butt, looking embarrassed. "We're still working out details."

"This is my clone-daughter, Lucy," Ayanna said, as if it was ridiculous. "I know, she used to look identical to me, but she had to go and ruin her good looks."

"Yes, I'm hideous now," Lucy said, looking like she was entering her happy place to avoid killing her mother with a spoon. "We need to talk to you for a moment."

"You shouldn't wear masks here," Penny said, looking on in disapproval. "They're the government abridging our freedom."

"They're setting a good example," Governor Hopewood said, defending us despite not wearing one herself. This party was notably violating numerous restrictions on government officials that she, herself, had laid out. "In any case, I'm putting out a motion to freeze rent for the duration of the crisis while people can't work. Obviously, they'll have to pay back what they owe to their landlords eventually, but they won't be kicked out on the street during the pandemic."

"I'm telling you, invest in Panacea topical cream," Penny said, ignoring us. "It's better than a cure."

I could have pointed out that what she was shilling had no effect whatsoever on the plague but I'm pretty sure my readers, the audience, and probably Penny herself knew that. We'd gotten to the snake oil period of the epidemic and con men were making a killing. I was just surprised that the Church of Money was getting in on it. Then again, she hadn't said to take Panacea topical cream, she'd said to *invest* in it. Which was a different beast altogether.

"I dunno, I trust the science," Governor Hopewood said. "Wait, by the way, Detective Neal—"

"Gordon," I corrected.

"Detective Neal Gordon," Governor Hopewood said. "Can we get Doctor Saint Croix to show up and do weekly talks to the public?"

"The medical examiner?" I asked, confused as hell. "I mean, you could order him—"

"He's just so virile looking," Governor Hopewood said. "Plus, that voice. Ooo, so sexy and commanding! I think he looks exactly like the kind of expert that we need to reassure the public everything will be fine."

Well, she obviously knew Doctor Frankenstein like I knew jump space physics, which was to say not at all. He'd tell the truth to everyone live and walk out flipping the bird. He was the kind of guy who'd lie to his wife about where he'd been the night before but always tell you when you were being a screwup.

"Please, Mother," Lucy said. "I'm not sure I can take any more of this unwitting social satire."

"Huh?" Ayanna asked, confused.

I almost pointed out to Ayanna that she was making a living argument for the French Revolution for how to deal with the nobility, but it lost some of its punch with her outfit. "She's saying could you turn off the killbots in your backyard so we can go talk to the folks in the guest house."

"Oh," Ayanna said, giving a dismissive wave. "Aurelius deals with all of that now. Go talk with him. He's in the kitchen or something."

"Your *pet therapist*," I said, trying to remember what the guy's job was.

"Oh no, I promoted him," Ayanna said. "He's now the household info media consultant. He maintains my mansion's various accounts and daily promotional content. You can recognize him by his purple attire."

A lesser man would have done something foolish and perhaps asked, "Wait, your house has its own social media account manager?"

However, that would have resulted in her answering and that was a rabbit hole I did not wish to go down.

"Right," I said, doing my best to not sound sarcastic and only half succeeding. "We'll just be going then."

"You shouldn't trust him," Penny said, speaking to Ayanna rather than us. "Albion immigrants are absolutely riddled with extremists. They don't think like us."

"Praise Jesus," I muttered, knowing he'd be whipping the shit out of everyone here. There wasn't an eye of a needle large enough for any of these pricks.

"May the Sun be with you," Penny said, cheerfully.

I got the impression I was missing something about their use of the word Sun (as in the Sol system's star) instead of Son (as in Jesus) but wasn't sure why that detail stuck with me. Cops often got obsessed with the idea that their instincts were better than evidence and ninety percent of the time, which was bullshit. Yet, I knew that detail would stick with me. Maybe there was a connection I was sensing unconsciously but not putting together yet.

Oh well.

Ayanna, to her credit, just rolled her eyes and waved us off. "If you three ever want to quit working for the government, remember I always have room open in my security division."

"I could never take the pay cut," Barksley said, trotting behind us as we departed.

I continued munching on my shish kabob and drank my champagne while following Lucy.

"I feel like taking a flamethrower to this place," Lucy muttered.

"It's not so bad," I said, surprising myself. Then again, free food was the basis of how our ancestors made peace in the caveman days. "Your mother was the least offensive person there. I'm pretty sure I'm voting for the other guy next election, though."

"They'll probably be worse," Lucy replied. "Do you have any idea what we're going to say to Priss and company? I know we're offering Rashid a job."

"Are we sure they're here?" I asked.

"I can sense them," Lucy replied, referring to her connection with the Knights.

I looked at her. "That would have been really helpful last year."

Lucy blanched, having unwittingly given away that she'd been working to protect her friends during the whole Posthuman Legion thing. Personally, I didn't hold it against her. I'd made my opinion clear on whether you should side with the people you cared about versus the government. I was, as the ancient board game they played at the Gordon Foundation described, firmly, "Chaotic Good."

Well, good-ish.

Mind you, I was rapidly developing friends on both sides of this conflict and wasn't sure how to deal with this. Kate and I hadn't exactly had to reconcile despite her standing offer of dinner, but she'd shown herself to be about as decent a leader as I'd met. She wanted to save everyone she could on the Moon, and it was only an issue over how to do that that presently put us up against Priss' group.

"We all need to be focused in one direction," Lucy replied. "Not undermining faith in the government's handling of the crisis."

"As badly as they're doing it," I replied, finishing my food and drinking the last of the champagne down.

Lucy shook her head and the two of us entered the kitchen that was bustling with a bunch of overworked, annoyed servants packed from wall to wall. The place had a long, central table where food was being prepared and a trio of doors at the end. It was the kind of place you'd be lucky to find in a high-end restaurant let alone a mansion. Giant ovens, walk-in-fridge, and an area specifically for chopping vegetables were all in the central kitchen. A separate room for cleaning dishes was visible through an alcove. Nobody seemed to be suffering any symptoms of Red fever, but it was an invisible killer until it suddenly wasn't. The asymptomatic cases were among the worst. Like Typhoid Mary, they potentially carried doom wherever they walked and didn't know it.

Aurelius Saxon wasn't difficult to find in the group as he sort of stood out in a crowd. Indeed, he was wearing purple attire, but Ayanna hadn't exactly been telling the whole story. His suit was purple, a very loud purple, with an interior shirt that looked like a radioactive cheetah had died to make it. His hair was brilliant white spikes, and he was from a Eurasian ancestry that couldn't really be directly traced anywhere. Not that such things mattered on the Moon, but it made me wonder what sort of racial composition other than the descendants of Britons existed on Albion. A pair of tri-holo sunglasses rested on the bridge of his nose, shifting colors every few seconds. The guy looked like the kind of guy who had gotten his start as a pet therapist, though, or maybe a hairdresser. I had no doubt he would fail upward to become a movie producer at some point.

Call it detective's intuition.

Lucy waved at him and shouted over the din of the workers, "Aurelius Saxon, we need to speak with you! We're agents of the federal government!"

In hindsight, this was probably not the most reassuring way to begin a conversation. However, I hope you can appreciate the surprise that we had when Aurelius' demeanor instantly changed from one of control to absolute apeshit panic. Aurelius froze up, spun around, and pulled out a small compact box that looked like a cheap men's electric razor. This object proceeded to shoot out a continuous beam of glowing red light that caused the top of the ceiling above us to explode and shower us with plaster.

"Holy milk bones!" Barksley said, covering his head with his paws.

Both Lucy and I were momentarily shocked into inaction as complete panic spread through the kitchen staff and everyone either hit the deck or started fleeing. Aurelius used this as an opportunity to make a break for it, heading to the other end of the kitchen and out one of the doors.

Lucy, former action star that she was, leapt onto the kitchen table and knocked over plates of food as she ran after him. "Don't let him get away!"

"Yeah, because I was going to do that," I muttered, grabbing one of the kitchen staff by the arm. She had been frozen in place by the sudden burst of plasma fire. "Which way does that door lead?"

"Outside, monsieur," the lady said in an exaggerated French accent. "The courtyard."

Where all the lethal security was.

Shit.

"Come on, Barks!" I said, pushing past her and drawing my pistol. I really hoped that Cash woman hadn't been right because the last thing we needed now was to deal with a terrorist when we were just here to stop our own teammates from informing the public about the danger that they were in.

Huh.

When phrased like that, it made us sound like the bad guys.

"I'll save you, Ms. Westenra!" Barksley said, running ahead. He was, after all, based on a herding dog breed.

I was the last out the door and a part of me was terrified that I'd find the golf-course-like estate covered in the remains of my partners. Thankfully, I'd forgotten the ancient truism that just because something cost a lot didn't mean it wasn't a piece of crap. That, in this case, applied to the lethal defense measures of Ayanna Breeze.

The area was littered with drones and a couple of the turrets had exploded, apparently having been turned upon one another by either Lucy hacking them or being hard coded not to kill the clone/daughter of their owner. Lucy had managed to grab the legs of Aurelius Saxon with her vibrational whip, and it was seemingly set on "stun" since it hadn't cut them off. Aurelius had gone for his laser weapon, but Lucy managed to get it from him before Barksley clamped his mouth down on the guy's arm.

"Stay down, Pet Doctor," I said, pointing my pistol at him. I admit, I felt a little embarrassed that I'd proven completely unnecessary here.

"Gah ahood," Barksley said, with a mouthful of arm. "Maak mah dah."

"Who are you?" Lucy asked. "Really? Are you with the Sons of Mithras?"

It was a ridiculous set of questions, almost as bad as, "why did you run?" But I wasn't about to begrudge her after she'd saved herself and captured the bad guy. If bad guy he was. Maybe he was worried he was being investigated for tax evasion.

"No, I'm not one of them!" Aurelius said, reacting to the group's name with visceral disgust. "By the Sun, no!"

"Then who are you?" I asked, doing my best growly voice.

"I am Aurelius Saxon," Aurelius said, pausing. "I'm a Watcher, well, intelligence agent, for the Community."

Oh, for fuck's sake.

CHAPTER SIXTEEN

The Ridiculousness Continues

I gave my opinion on Aurelius' claim. "Bullshit."

"He's telling the truth, Neal," Lucy said.

"Yes, he clearly must be of a new breed of spy that dresses like they raided Prince's closet," I replied.

"Which prince?" Lucy asked, confused.

Barksley stopped biting our prisoner's arm. "I am deeply disappointed in you, Lucy. Prince Rogers Nelson, the only Prince who matters. I'm going to take back the raspberry beret I gave you for Christmas."

"I hate that thing anyway," Lucy muttered.

"My cover identity is loud on purpose. It's called misdirection. No one suspected someone so flamboyant was a spy," Aurelius said, looking offended. "Yet my insertion here provided me access to the corridors of power as so many important officials prostrate themselves at the foot of your demigods."

You could tell Aurelius was from outer space at least because while he could speak English just fine, he was just ever so slightly off in his word choice. His accent was also something similar but slightly different to Vitellius' own, like they were from different regions of the same country.

"Uh huh," I replied. "Well, you're under arrest."

I wasn't sure if SHID agents could arrest people. Technically, just about everything we did as investigators was deferred to the Advanced Crime Unit, Cyberlife, or civi cops. We had very broad authority but that mostly meant other people had to listen to us when we made recommendations like, "throw the book at this guy."

"For what?" Aurelius asked.

"For pissing me off!" I snapped.

HE'S ATTEMPTING TO CONTACT THE *HEART OF SORKA*, Interface said, surprising me. HE'S GOT POSTHUMAN IMPLANTS AS WELL. MORE ADVANCED THAN OURS.

Block him! I snapped.

YOU REALLY DON'T KNOW HOW MY ABILITIES WORK, DO YOU? Interface replied. BUT IT'S ALREADY BEEN DONE BY MS. WESTENRA.

Huh, I said, mentally. *Well, that's good news. I guess he is telling the truth about being a spy for them.*

SO, IT WOULD APPEAR, Interface replied.

Aurelius looked dejected at the realization he couldn't contact his people or maybe just being arrested by what I imagined he thought were a pair of country yokels. Or whatever the galactic equivalent was. "I am not a member of the Sons of Mithras. Indeed, that is why I have been deployed here, to prevent the extremist group from spreading its toxic message."

"And a bang-up job you've done," I replied.

I noted there was a crowd gathering outside of the mansion and realized that it wouldn't be too long until we were deluged with questions by the uber-rich. Pulling out my own personal pair of magnetic cuffs—and no, not for fun times… usually—I slapped them on him and helped him up as Lucy released her vibrowhip's grasp. We started marching him around the mansion to the parking valley, since lot really didn't describe the place.

"Listen, you must understand, the Sons of Mithras do not represent the majority of Albion," Aurelius said. "They are a reactionary Far North imperialist branch of religious zealots that do not embody the true teachings of the Sun. Disaffected and lost youth who—"

"Save it for the interrogators," I replied. "If you guys really cared, you'd be sending boxes of medicine rather than spies."

My opinion on accepting help from the Community, incredibly controversial as it may be, had been cemented with the first dead child.

In the words of the great Marcellus Wallace, "Pride never helps. It only hurts. In the fifth, your ass goes down." Okay, that last part wasn't necessary, but you got the gist. We should have groveled like the Community was an ex-girlfriend.

"I have all of his files," Lucy said, staring forward as if looking at something I couldn't see.

"That's ridiculous!" Aurelius said, staring at her. "Our encryption is beyond anything your planet could make in a century."

"I used my interface's military override to access the records from your civilian implants that included memory collection," Lucy said, sounding like gibberish to me. "That included all of your passwords. It collaborates your story and should help us coordinate efforts against the Sons of Mithras on the Moon. Which is something you should have been doing from the very beginning."

"We all have our masters," Aurelius said, sounding defeated. I gathered he wasn't someone who necessarily agreed with his superiors' decisions any more than I tended to with mine.

"Anything good?" I asked.

"I'll have to have Shinobu sort through it," Lucy said. "But it confirms there are at least eleven cells operating on the Moon, and we eliminated only one. They're also working with collaborators. People who may not necessarily know they're doing the Sons' bidding but are undermining the Red fever response. Agitators and criminals."

"Great," I muttered. "Well, this is a red-letter day."

"My people will pay a tremendous ransom for me," Aurelius said. "Embarrassing as that may be for my family."

"I don't care if you're royalty where you come from, friend," I said, unimpressed.

"I am," Aurelius said. "Or at least aristocracy. You also should care since that ransom might be paid in medicine. My house's patriarch could well force our parliament to send you the relief medicine your planet so desperately requires."

I paused, looking at Lucy who looked back at me. "Which means you could have been helping from the beginning."

"My sympathetic words about your system's appalling conditions have fallen on deaf ears," Aurelius replied, insulting us in three ways without probably intending to. "The Sons of Mithras may be loathed in my world's government but that doesn't mean Earth has many sympathizers. What could not be achieved through mercy, however, could be achieved by avoiding embarrassment."

Ever have a conversation where the person you're talking to is trying to be subtle, but you have no idea what they mean? Maybe there were some cultural clues I was missing on. "So, you want us to take you prisoner so we can get life-saving medicine from your own side, because the Albionese high muckety-mucks will pay for it to get their spy back but not give it to us to save millions of people?"

"Yes," Aurelius said, sounding like he was speaking to a particularly stupid child. Which was such a common enough treatment of my intellect that I recognized it immediately.

"I think you're more likely trying to save your ass," Lucy said. "However, I think this is worth bringing to Special Agent Roebuck. If there really are eleven other cells, it's no wonder we've had no luck containing this thing."

Honestly, the terrorists could have done a lot worse in spreading the disease indiscriminately among the populace, but they were possibly allowing it to fester so a maximum panic could be achieved. Earth, which may have been their original target, had intercepted all attempts by the infected to spread the plague. Only a few hundred people had been infected by various parties on Earth and all of them successfully quarantined. Mars was a little worse off, but not by much.

Still, one thing you learn is that life is gambling and playing the odds. It was probable it wasn't some sort of magic bullet to slay the disease and even if we could trade Aurelius for a cure, that wouldn't be something we could do. That would require the Reformers to approve, and God knew how many other people before we could even make the offer. There was no knowing how many people would die in that time, but it was AOP (Above our Paygrade).

"Well, let's get him to Kate," I muttered. "Rashid can wait."

Lucy paused. "No, no he can't. I'll take Aurelius back to HQ by myself. You and Barksley need to handle this."

"I don't like leaving you alone with this guy," I said. "Backup is important for any agent to have."

Lucy nodded and then pressed the handle of her vibrowhip against the back of his neck and delivered a paralytic shock that sent him down to the ground.

"How many modes does that thing have?" I asked.

"A lot," Lucy said. "It's of alien design."

"I got that from its hyper-advanced but wholly impractical nature," I replied, looking down at Aurelius. He was still twitching.

Lucy picked him up like a rag doll, reminding me she was as enhanced as me and tossed him over one shoulder. "He'll be out for an hour. If he was serious about ransoming himself back to his side, he'll forgive us. If not, well, he was a fucking spy who took advantage of my mother."

"That's not going to cause trouble for her, is it?" I asked.

"Please," Lucy said. "My mom will be all over borking a spy. Just... be gentle with Priss and Rashid."

I paused, wondering in what universe Lucy thought her six-foot-tall Amazon ex-bandmate (and possibly more) needed to be treated gently. Rashid might be a different case, but I never forgot everyone's favorite dataslicer used to be a gangbanger. He was a lot more dangerous than he let on, idealist activist persona be damned.

"Sure, I'll be gentle as a kitten," I replied.

"I'll watch his back, Lucy," Barksley said.

Lucy nodded. She then got an expression on her face that showed a huge chunk of emotion: regret, care, and even love. It brought a wellspring of other emotion back to me before I saw she regretted showing such feelings. Then she started to say something that would probably be, "Neal, we may not be dating anymore but I still care for you." Which I absolutely could not hear right now.

Lucy started to speak. "Neal, we might not..."

"Yeah, sure." I turned and walked away before anything else was said, scooping up Barksley along the way. The issue between us wasn't getting any better and we just sort of zig-zagged between flirting and awkward silence. Our dynamic was basically what it used to be—except when it wasn't—minus the physical intimacy. It was maddening and I wasn't sure it could continue. Which was troubling because aside from Barksley, she was my best friend.

157

Damnit.

I made a mental note to get drunk tonight and find someone to sleep with. It was a pissy and immature way of dealing with what I was feeling, but it was a tried and tested method by both sexes for the past ten thousand or so years. I wasn't sure if they had alcohol past that point in history or it'd probably be longer. I think the Chinese invented it when they discovered rice went bad in a fun way in clay pots. Thankfully, whoever had designed the posthuman upgrade had left the ability to get drunk in or the Community's special operations soldiers would have all gone insane.

"You should really sit down and talk with her," Barksley said, sounding unusually somber.

"Ain't no point in talking when no one is listening," I said, pausing. "Besides, what do you care?"

"You're both people I love," Barksley said. "In a strictly pet-owner situation. Speaking of which, we need to get your shots updated."

"Ha, ha," I replied, heading to the guest house that was just one of several on the property. It was a two-story building with its own basement and easily could have housed its own family. It had a large porch, several transmitters on the roof , and a micro-fusion generator that could provide its power needs for the next millennia.

Ayanna Breeze typically kept her boy and girl toys in the buildings but, as far as I knew, Rashid just stayed there because Lucy had asked Ayanna to put him up for a few days only for him never to leave. I think it said everything you needed to know about Ayanna's level of wealth that she hadn't apparently noticed or cared. If Rashid was smart, he would have the place locked up tight and made himself scarce.

He had done neither.

Putting Barksley down on the porch, I checked the door and found it unlocked. The first floor looked a great deal different from when I'd last been there. It was now full of empty beer cans, discarded take out, and many musical instruments. Oh, and grenades. There was a box of them on the table next to an antique assault rifle was in the process of being cleaned. The large number of Ayanna Breeze posters that usually dotted the place had been replaced—when they weren't outright defaced—with band posters. Given Rashid rarely left the basement and was significantly tidier, I used my deductive powers of reasoning to determine the other two Knights, Lina Gibson and Sylia Trinity, had been holed up here the entire time.

"If the Moon had ants, this would be how you got ants," Barksley muttered. "Well, this part of the Moon at least. They're an important part of a biosphere."

"Poor Rashid," I said, shaking my head. "Forced to share his house with two gorgeous rocker chicks."

"I don't think Rashid is their type," Barksley said, following me into the house. "Versus each other."

"Oh," I paused, realizing what he was saying. "Okay, I have to ask, was that the band's *thing*?"

"Their *thing*?" Barksley asked, knowing exactly what I meant.

"You know," I said, looking for signs of the house's occupants. "Being *together*. I understand that's a thing on the Moon."

To clarify for future generations, my reason for wanting to know this wasn't because I had a prurient interest—well, no more than basic biology as a 99% heterosexual male entailed—but to get a sense of just what sort of shitstorm I was stepping into if I ended up having to try to bring in Priss or Nina. Not that I probably could, but there was a difference between arresting someone's friends versus their ex or exes. I also was still no closer to understanding Moon polyamory. I had enough trouble managing one relationship at a time.

Barksley looked up at me skeptically. "Are you actually asking me about Lucy and her friends' sex lives when they were a hyperpunk band? The talking dog designed to teach kindergartners?"

I realized the sheer ridiculousness of the question. "Forget I asked."

"Probably wise," Barksley said, sniffing the ground like a bloodhound. "It's also no use being jealous now."

"I'm not jealous—" I said before being interrupted by a crashing noise from the basement. I went to the door in the kitchen.

"And as far as I know, Ms. Aim and Ms. Westenra are both straight," Barksley said, immediately undercutting his dignified response to my earlier question. "Ish. Ms. Asimov is uninterested in romantic entanglements and only has sex for the pleasure of friends. Indeed, I'm certain the wild nature of their parties and behavior are highly exaggerated. If for the only reason that several blocks in Crater Town are still standing that should otherwise be ruins."

I opened the door and cursed myself at being more curious about this than I was about confronting Rashid. Deciding surprise wasn't going to help matters, I called down, "Rashid, this is Detective Neal Gordon, now of Department Four and underpaid civil servant! I'm coming down. Please don't shoot me. Otherwise, Barksley and his descendants will be required to avenge me."

"What now?" Barksley asked.

"What?" I asked, looking down at him. "I'd avenge you."

"Yes, but that's because I'm adorable and fluffy," Barksley said. "I don't know if revenge is really within my programming. I mean, I'd certainly feel bad but—"

"Stop it, Barks, you're killing me," I said, shaking my head.

"I'd send a card to your funeral!" Barksley said, smiling to let me know he was taking the piss. "I mean, I'd even show up unless it was raining. Also, what was that about my descendants? Are you planning on shackling them with a blood feud? I don't have any progeny, but I hope I'd raise them better than that."

I didn't move from my position as I let our insane conversation continue. "Listen, Barks, you're going to have a bunch of descendants, train them in the martial arts, and send them to kill Rashid. Each will be mutated, humanoid, and wield a different weapon: sais, bo staff, katana—"

"Now you're just describing the Teenage Mutant Ninja Turtles," Barksley said, annoyed. "Either that or you came up with that on your own and I don't know which is worse. Yes, Neal, even I have limits on ancient pop culture I love."

"I'm not going to shoot you, Neal!" Rashid said, calling from the bottom of the stairs. "However, if you keep having these meaningless conversations that I'm forced to listen to, I may just shoot myself."

"That's fair. I'm coming down!" I replied, putting my hands in my pockets and descending the stairs.

Barksley reluctantly followed. He really hated going downstairs. "Curse my stubby little legs."

At the bottom of the stairs in front of a massive computer rig that included several shelves of servers, three monitors linked together, and a RealDream chair that probably cost upwards of a hundred thousand creds—something he absolutely could not afford—was Rashid Al-Fariq. He was Afro-Arabic in descent with dreads, brown skin bordering on black, and the fashion sense of a guy who ran a smoke shop or music store. He had baggy jeans, a ratty bootleg t-shirt, and shoes that had seen better days.

Rash was presently packing up his "slicer den" with a lot of plastiboard boxes full of old-fashioned books, documents, and the nick-knacks one tended to accumulate in life. He was a lot tidier than the Knights upstairs, but that was a bit like saying that I had less hair than Barksley. I couldn't read the code displaying on his computer, but I suspected he was in the process of decrypting something and that was probably why he hadn't gotten the duck out of Fodge.

There was a distortion in the middle of the room, a slight bending of light that wouldn't have been noticed by most individuals. It was optical camouflage and while you could theoretically hide anything under there, I was pretty sure that it was the Knights.

"Hey Rashid," I said, waving. "Hi, gals."

Seconds later, the optical camo dropped, and the world's only all-female special operations unit turned hyperpunk band appeared beside me. There was Priss Aim, now dressed in civilian leathers with her trademark long coat; Nina Asimov, who was an adorable pink-haired ball of fun; Sylvia Sterling, who was a Japanese woman with graffiti pattern kimono; and Lina Gibson, who looked a lot more punk than the rest of them combined. Lina had half of her head shaved and piercings across that side of her head. You could tell just by looking her that Lina had grown up in a house of rich assholes.

Barksley did a double take and pointed with his nose. "Ah ha! I knew there was an off smell here."

"Sure, you did," I said, dryly.

"You're not taking Rashid," Priss said, positively growling.

"Okay," I said, dryly. Then I turned back to Rashid. "Assume I made a big dramatic speech about following the law and how there's a right way and a wrong way to inform the public they're all going to die. Otherwise, the terrorists win."

Rashid blinked. "You really are a terrible cop."

"I mean, Lucy would probably be able to fake actual concern, but we all have bigger fish to fry in this case and I'd rather you be working with us than against us. For that I'm willing to give you more access. We need to find the mole in Division Four, and I know everyone in this room can be trusted as well as Lucy and Barks. Otherwise, this could well be some kind of sick plan to reduce the size of the surplus population or sell more cat dewormer as a treatment."

"Please don't mention worms," Barksley said.

Priss looked suspicious and her team looked mostly confused. Priss spoke first. "You trust us that much?"

"Lucy does," I replied. "Despite what you did to her."

"I'm currently working on a project," Rashid said, gesturing to the computer screen beside me. "Karma Corp is going to be releasing its own alternative to Loop that's way more addictive and dangerous but supposedly clean of disease."

"This is more important," I said. "Probably. But you can do both. Besides, there have been some developments. Did you know Aurelius Saxon was a Community secret agent?"

"The radioactive cheetah shirt guy?" Nina asked, showing she and I apparently shared a brain.

"I know, right!" I said. "I'll feed you information if you need it in exchange."

"I'm not hearing any of this," Barksley said. "I'm listening to the 2115 *Miami Vice* remake theme now. It's drowning out all this conspiracy"."

"Indeed," I replied. "Barksley and I are the Crockett and Tubbs of the Moon."

"He's Crockett, I'm Tubbs," Barksley said.

"I mean, obviously," I replied, once more feeling like I had to remind Barksley he wasn't black. More a golden-white color.

Priss narrowed her eyes. "I'm not sure I trust you."

"Fair," I said, shrugging.

"We'll need some guarantees," Priss said, her voice trailing off.

Moon City Vice

CHAPTER SEVENTEEN

The Morning After

I woke up with a monstrous hangover not even Interface could entirely cure me of, in a bed covered with silk sheets, next to a table with a mostly empty bottle of Martian tequila. It wasn't the only thing I'd drank and taken that evening. Oh, and Priscilla's naked body was next to mine in the bed, which is probably burying the lead.

Yeah.

Apparently, guarantees were spy-speak for, "bribe you with sex, drugs, and a wild party." Which, honestly, was far from the worst strategy anyone had ever employed against me. The Knights had ushered me out of Rashid's basement while he finished transporting stuff and we'd ended up at a high-rise Luna City penthouse that I was 100% sure they'd broken into after slicing the security system.

I think it said everything about my hypocritical nature that I thought very ill of Ayanna's party, but I thought everyone that Priss and company had invited was just having some much-needed unwinding time. Then again, I seemed to recall everyone wearing masks even when they were screwing against the wall.

Sliding out of the bed and thumping against the ground, I proceeded to crawl to my clothes, put on my boxers and head to the kitchen. I passed a couple of interesting visuals along the way in the two-story penthouse that I leave to your depraved imagination to guess at. Suffice to say, everyone was alive and seemed content as they slept off the Knight Palooza Fest Thursday of this Month (as I nicknamed it).

Which was more than I could say about some parties that involved this much hardcore recreation.

Well, almost everyone was content.

When I entered the kitchen, Barksley was notably staring at me from the kitchen counter, an annoyed expression on his face. The dog had the "I am very disappointed in you, Neal" look on his face. But maybe I was just suffering too much of a headache to properly judge his actions.

"I am very disappointed in you, Neal," Barksley said.

Nope! Got it in one.

I reached over to Barksley with both hands. "Fluffy dog pillow. I must use you to rest my head until death releases me."

"Not funny," Barksley said.

I took the dog in my arms, rested my head upon him, and started snoring on him. I was mostly joking. Well, I may have accidentally fallen asleep on him but only for a few seconds and because whoever had created him had made him extremely comfortable.

Barksley responded by licking my face.

"Gah! Dog lick!" I said, bolting backward. "No fair, that's cheating!"

"I am *not* a fluffy dog pillow," Barksley responded, pausing. "Despite that being one of my advertised features."

"Well, it's just until my hangover passes," I said, looking for more alcohol. It was the best cure for a hangover in my opinion. And no, it's not supposed to make sense.

I ended up settling for black coffee—the real thing—which cost roughly a thousand credits a bag when imported from Earth. It took thirty seconds to make, and I put it in a mug saying Moon's Richest Man. If anyone complained, I'd put it down to being vital for my case of investigating police corruption. There was, after all, a federal agent breaking into rich people's apartments to sleep with anarchist chicks before stealing their food on the loose.

"Yes, well, I repeat I am very disappointed in you," Barksley said.

"So, you said," I said, staring. "Why?"

"Lucy!" Barksley said, offended as only a close friend can be.

"Lucy was telling me she wanted to see other people before she broke up with me," I said. "Mind you, I'm not sure how much one-night stands with ex-bandmates qualifies."

"I don't mean that," Barksley said. "This is the Moon. A healthy sexual appetite is considered a proper part of one's mental health if you're on the attraction spectrum."

I had no idea what that meant. "What do you mean, Barksley? Pretending I care."

"I mean you said you'd handle this," Barksley said. "You made a promise, and you broke it! Which is just... rude!"

I stared at Barksley then blinked. "Uh huh."

"What if this is all some scheme to blackmail you?" Barksley said. "Or to compromise your effectiveness as an agent."

"I mean, that is what bribes are for," I said, pausing. "But I'm pretty sure if they recorded this, all it would get from most people would be a windmill high five. Especially on the Moon."

Barksley sighed. "What if you and Lucy get fired for barking this up?"

I contemplated that. "In the words of the late great Brad Pitt: Nah, I don't think so. More like chewed out. I've been chewed out before."

"I still don't think he's dead," Barksley said, pausing. "There's a very real chance he was taken by aliens."

"Uh huh," I muttered, not interested. "Either way, Rashid is hopefully setting up shop someplace safe so he can start working on finding our mole."

"Do you really think he can find out who did it?" Barksley asked, thankfully dropping the Lucy issue. I knew he wanted me and Lucy to get back together but that was really something out of his paws.

"I think it's probably one of three people," I replied. "Nigel, Kate, or Steve."

Barksley blinked. "Really? Your wife?"

"Ex-wife," I replied. "Nigel is a suspect because, well, he's evil and has tried to kill me before. The fact he's tried to be nice about it and make up for the burning me alive thing ever since just makes me think he's even more screwed up in the head than I initially thought. Kate is because she was clearly on some sort of extrajudicial mission before the plague broke out. She also knew when and where we were going so could have warned the Sons of Mithras. Steve? Well, that's a lot more circumstantial."

"You really think Lucy's ex could be involved with terrorists?" Priss said from the kitchen door. She was wearing my shirt and nothing else. She was also wearing it a lot better than I ever did. "Give me the coffee and I'll let you live."

I slid it over to her and went to make myself some. "The early circle of SHID agents was pretty small. It could have been a listening device of some kind, or they could have been tracking the Purple Rain rather than knowing where we were going."

"Impossible," Barksley said. "I always swept my beautiful car for bugs and listening devices."

I stared at him. "Really?"

"Until *someone* got it destroyed," Barksley said, narrowing his eyes.

Priss drank my coffee in three gulps then gestured for my new cup that I'd just made. I sighed and slid it over. "My team was organized for the rescue at a suspiciously quick time. Almost like we were intended to arrive but just a little too late. Steve could have sent a message to take you out but I'm not sure of his motive. He doesn't hate Lucy that much."

It was also possible Priss could have been involved in it, but I discounted that for a very stupid and unscientific reason: Lucy trusted Priss. She was still mad at her for making her a posthuman against her will, but I had faith in Lucy's instincts far more than I had in my own.

"That's the confusing part," I said, making my third coffee. "*Cui Bono.*"

"Who?" Priss asked.

"Latin for 'who profits?'," Barksley said.

"Common police tactic," I replied. "The question of who stands to gain the most from any given crime is probably the guilty suspect. Another way of saying it is, 'follow the money.' That's the thing that bothers me here and what I want to figure out first: someone has to be a making a killing off this plague, no pun intended, and once we figure out who then we've got our bad guy."

"Unless it's not motivated by money," Priss pointed out. "Quite a few people are motivated by beliefs, not cash."

"Plenty of people are motivated by both," I pointed out. "The Sons of Mithras are true believers but someone rubber stamped their visas, set them up with housing, and arranged for them to be sleeper agents until this plague. That's not one person, that's an entire organization."

"And what does the big bad government think?" Priss asked, daring me to answer.

I finished my coffee, finally, and it started to relieve my headache. "SHID's following up the Albion angle. They think some rich immigrants who stayed behind to help make the Moon livable for their fellow humans laid the groundwork for the Sons of Mithras."

"But you don't believe that," Priss said.

"No," I replied. "Rather, it's not my first guess. The kind of people who would want to unleash a Biblical disaster on the Moon, angry pagans being the culprits aside, aren't the kind of people who would be rich enough to do what we're describing. You draw terrorists from people who are desperate, angry, and stupid. At least the soldiers. Rich backers might fund the terrorists, but they wouldn't spread a massive disease at their feet."

"Thin," Priss said. "Very thin but I follow your logic. Why Steve?"

"I dunno," I admitted. "Why are *you* zeroing in on him? You were at SHID too and know Nigel's dirty secrets. Also, you hate Kate enough to undermine her at every turn."

Priss blinked, clearly not having expected me to turn this around on her. "I was the one who introduced Steve and Lucy."

"Oh?" I asked, blinking. "I heard a different story. That she met him while she was training in counterterrorism. I also thought you two were on the outs after she left your band and she only met Steve later."

Priss frowned. "Lucy and I have tried to make amends several times before last year when we made our furthest stride to mending our friendship. It just never sticks. Special operations units are a small community, and Steve and I knew each other from the post-war period. He fought for the Neo-Militarists up here. I fought for the Reformers down below."

I nodded. "Go on. Lucy said he was really messed up after the Gray Heaven riot."

"That's putting it mildly," Priss said. "Steve married the Knights' manager, Glorious Godric Gwydion, and tried to get with Lucy but the three never really gelled. As much as I hate those hypocrites for their corruption of Jesus' message, the Church of Money did a lot of good for him. At least it looked like they did. Mind you, they're all sorts of heretical."

I blinked. "You're a believer?"

Priss looked up. "My second single was 'Jesus Christ, Anarchist'."

Oh. Right. I admit, I'd always skipped that one. I also kind of thought she'd been ironic. Like Celestial Madonna or regular Madonna. "Something happened, didn't it?"

"He disappeared for two years," Priss said. "Triple G, that's Glorious Godric's stage name—and yes, his actual name sounds like a stage name—and Steve are still technically married but that's just because Glorious never bothered to divorce him. It turned out Steve spent all that time as a missionary off-planet."

That gave me pause. "Albion."

"Got it in one," Priss said. "But would a fraudulent church that insults the whole 'blessed are the poor in spirit' ministry with its very existence really work with a bunch of pagans?"

"If they'd get paid for it, maybe," I said. "But that's not accusing just Steve; that's accusing the entire Church of Money."

"It should be noted that the Church of Money recently bought the settlement rights for Nergal," Rashid said, at the door, fully dressed and having been conspicuously absent from the party. "The rights were only up for five minutes before they made their bid and received approval from Governor Hopewood, who is supervising the Colonial Settlement Plan with a bunch of corporate-owned councilors. They plan to open it up to believers wanting to live in their own New Eden, ticket prices at fifty thousand Earth credits. But owning one's own planet and managing a successful colony is a payoff in the *trillions*, not billions."

That was also circumstantial as hell but suddenly painted a very different sort of picture for the Church of Money, Red fever, and the

Sons of Mithras. A colony world is depopulated by a horrible virus and the contract firm that had already been set up for it goes belly up with the Moon suffering a similar condition. They raise a ton of capital in a short time because people pray harder when times are tough, and their leaders shmoozed with the governor at Ayanna Breeze's party before securing a deal to buy their own recently plague-ridden planet at a vastly deflated price.

It didn't tie anything together and just showed them taking advantage of the current crisis for their own benefit versus being behind it. However, land and religion had a pretty lengthy history and that was something people were willing to kill over. Particularly when you were a televangelist-adjacent group like the Church of Money.

"Where the hell have you been, Rashid?" I asked, diverting the conversation as I mulled that over in my mind.

"Downstairs in Nigel's office," Rashid said, pausing. "I've been working all night. Thankfully, the place is soundproof."

"I'm glad you're not into the orgy scene," Barksley said, showing he couldn't say "fuck", but he could say "orgy". Man, his programmers were not very thorough.

"Yeah, certainly not without Shinobu," Rashid said, giving me far, far too much information in one sentence.

"Wait, this is Nigel's apartment?" I asked, pausing.

"Yeah," Priss said. "Dude barely visits it. You have a problem with that?"

"Absolutely," I said, grabbing a trash bag and starting to fill it with the most expensive shit I could.

Priss practically choked from laughter. "I'm starting to see why Lucy likes you so much."

I paused, halfway full of filling my bag with goodies. "Not enough, really."

Priss didn't respond. "She's the flame to many moths."

It was a confession of love and loss, though perhaps not sexual. It was certainly one that I knew and understood, however. It also left the next few moments of our existence very awkward as no one was speaking.

"I'm going to keep prying," Rashid said. "Honestly, I could use Lucy's help in investigating this. She's a better dataslicer than I am. That's how we met in the first place. She was the one who caught me stealing from the Fleur de Lis till."

I raised an eyebrow. "I thought that was because you'd decided to turn against them because they'd become involved in the Syndicate's organ trafficking."

"Also, you wanted to go straight and be a journalist," Barksley added.

Rashid shrugged. "Becoming a journalist isn't cheap."

I shrugged, not giving a shit. Rashid was among those criminals driven by circumstance as opposed to actual malice. In terms of categories, I put him as a genuinely good person who just happened to do a lot of illegal things. Certainly, he'd done a lot of it to get himself and his sister out of the Deep. "I'll try and get Lucy onboard with this. Ex or not, it seems she has her own suspicions of the guy."

Priss sighed. "Before Gray Heaven, I would have thought he would never be involved in this. Now?"

"Now?" I asked.

"Now I think he'd do anything for money," Priss said. "The Church of Money won him over by saying that was okay. Righteous even."

I nodded, understanding that mindset. Some people didn't want to be told to be good even if it was merely hard. They wanted to be told what they were doing was good even when it was awful, if it was profitable. "I think I'll have a conversation with them both when I get back to SHID headquarters. A shame I couldn't find you guys."

"Don't risk yourself on our account, Neal," Priss said, surprising me. After all, I thought the sex and party had been to make sure I had a reason to not betray them—the possibility of more in the future being the lure. "We're going to be our own thing and that will take us far away from SHID's influence. We just needed to work with them for a while to get what we needed."

"Which was?" I asked.

Priss smiled, letting me know she wasn't going to say. "Let's just say we're a little closer to decapitating Karma Corp."

I should probably have followed up on that, but I didn't. "Good luck with the revolution against the corporate scum."

"From the corporate mercenary," Barksley said, dryly.

I shrugged and threw the garbage bag full of stolen goodies over my shoulder. "Ho-ho-ho. I'll go steal a fresh shirt from Nigel. Plus, I need to get my pants and shoes."

"I think one of your shoes is in the fish tank," Rashid said, looking back out into the lounge.

"Right," I said, pausing to think of something to say. "Stay safe, Rashid. The people you're pissing off have finally noticed you and I don't want to end up pulling you out of Luna City Bay."

"I have some friends who have kept me alive until now," Rashid said, implicitly referring to me as one. "But I've gotta try to keep the public informed."

I really didn't think nearly as many people cared as Rashid hoped and that the truth—whatever that was—was frequently drowned out by the noise of day-to-day life. I wasn't going to try to crush the kids' spirit, though. "Sure."

"One more thing," Rashid said, pulling out a data crystal. "My sister had this."

"Farah?" I asked.

"She goes by Cherry Pie now," Rashid said.

I raised an eyebrow. "Is she a hook—"

"Yes," Rashid said. "Either way, she says she thinks there's something going on related to that other thing you and I were doing."

"You mean the Slavers Guild?" I asked.

Rashid stared.

"Oh, that was you being secret," I said, mocking him ever so lightly. "I'll check it out."

"Please do," Rashid said. "My sister hates everything I do and thinks it's put her and her friends in danger. Which it probably has. So for her to reach out, it has to be important. Just promise me one thing."

"Which is?" I asked.

"Don't sleep with her," Rashid said.

I rolled my eyes. "I don't sleep with—"

Barksley glared at me and Priss rolled her eyes.

"Okay, not the best place or circumstances to make that argument," I replied. "I should probably put on pants first."

Rashid nodded.

CHAPTER EIGHTEEN

Unexpected Developments

So, Steve Rogers Hudson was dead.

That was certainly unexpected.

My arrival at SHID headquarters hadn't been greeted with the kind of, "Where the hell have you been?" I expected. In fact, everyone seemed much-much busier with other matters and given the circumstances, I don't blame them. The arrival of Aurelius had been accompanied by a second primary outbreak of Red fever that was already being attributed to another cell of Sons of Mithras terrorists. I only heard about Steve's death third hand while trying to find out where Lucy and Kate were.

I found both of them in a garage that had been turned into an impromptu forensics lab. There, a burnt-out flying car was being disassembled by a team of Cyberlife professionals working with civi cops and the Advanced Crime Unit. This was an all-hands-on-deck situation, it seemed.

Both Lucy and Kate were supervising the investigation, neither of them looking particularly in the mood for my nonsense. It was also overkill since Kate should probably have been coordinating with other agents given the nature of things. The death of a member of your team, whether you were a cop, or a spy hit harder than almost any of the other deaths that were bound to happen over the course of your job. It wasn't fair and there were exceptions, especially when dealing with the mass death we were dealing with during the outbreak, but now was probably not the time to bring up my suspicions Steve was probably the mole.

There also was a guy wearing—and I didn't think this was possible—an even louder outfit than the one on Aurelius. It was difficult to put into words, but basically it was a suit that glowed neon shifting colors that I worried would probably cause seizures in certain individuals. He also wore a pair of RealDream augmented reality glasses that I couldn't imagine were more than a fashion statement since the only places they were useful were theme parks, and Tokyo.

"Well, crap," I muttered, looking at the remains.

"You've got to find the son of a bitch who did this," the loudly dressed man in sunglasses said, speaking in a high-pitched voice with an Italian accent vaguely reminiscent of a Joe Pesci chatbot. No, I didn't know why those were popular. "Let me at those terrorists and I'll get them to spill their guts, literally if I have to."

"We're doing everything we can, Mr. Gwydion," Kate said, trying vainly to reassure the man.

"Yeah, I can tell you're just doing a bang-up job," said the man I had presumed to be Steve's husband, Glorious Godric Gwydion. I didn't know what I'd expected from Priss' description of the man, but it turned out to be close to what his name conjured. "Just like this damn epidemic. I tell you, it's the damned lizards trying to sterilize us."

"Uh huh," Lucy said, clearly not up for listening to a xenophobic rant. "I can reassure you, Glorious—"

"Don't Glorious me," Glorious Godric said. "I've got two more husbands and their wives to console. Don't think I've forgotten how you broke poor Steve's heart. We had to spend years putting him back together. But that's what you do, don't you? You love 'em and when things get tough, you leave 'em. Like my sister."

Lucy stared as if she wasn't sure how to respond to that sudden but personal accusation.

"*Mr. Gwydion*," Kate enunciated, stepping in. "We'll keep you apprised of developments in the case. I can assure you that we will find out who was responsible for Captain Hudson's death."

"You better," Glorious Godric said, pointing a finger at her. "I know people far more dangerous than the government. I know people in the music industry."

A couple of STRIKE guards proceeded to extirpate Glorious Godric, escorting him out of the room to his considerable and quite graphic complaints. A couple of his profanities were ones I hadn't heard before and I'd been both a cop and Marine. Seeing both Kate and Lucy looking at me, I reluctantly slid into place in front of them. Barksley had made himself scarce and I felt outnumbered. Not that I could count on the little dog when confronting Lucy.

"Hey guys," I said, waving. "Sorry to hear about Steve's death."

"I sincerely doubt that," Kate replied, looking at me. "How was your sexual liaison with the Knights? Was it the entire band or just Ms. Aim?"

I opened my mouth, but no words came out. "Just the one," I finally mumbled.

Lucy's expression was unreadable, though if I had to guess she seemed less upset than I'd hoped and more vaguely annoyed. Was it wrong that I wanted her to be a little bit jealous? Probably. But it was what I felt. Kate, in fact, looked more irritated.

"Mmm hmm," Kate said. "Well, if you send a dog to retrieve a package of sausages, you shouldn't be surprised when they get eaten."

"I resent that remark," Barksley said, popping up behind me and making me jolt.

"We've had some developments in the past twenty-four hours," Lucy said, calmly.

"You don't say," I said, not sure how to react or how Lucy was feeling. After all, Steve was her ex even if I suspected she was suspicious of him as well. "You think Steve was assassinated?"

I felt stupid as soon as the words left my mouth.

"Yes, well given the fact he was decapitated, and his body burned to a crisp in his car, I'd say that's a strong possibility," Kate said. "We still haven't found his head."

"Ah," I said, pausing. "Yeah, that does sound like assassination."

"Our working theory is that he realized he was being closed in on and attempted extraction," Kate said. "Rather than take the risk, his employers proceeded to dispose of him as a loose end."

"His employers," I said, dryly, surprised they'd already started on my working theory.

"Either the Sons of Mithras or the Church of Money," Lucy replied. "Assuming there's a difference."

"You were suspicious, too, huh?" I asked, wishing we'd communicated better as we might have come to this conclusion together and sooner.

Kate nodded. "It's taken awhile, but our forensic accountants have finally determined that the Albion terrorists were not recruited from local Moon residents but brought here from their home planet via missionary visas. The records had been erased but we managed to recover them. Steve had also been receiving large monthly payments in his 'holiness fund' at their private bank. That information was obtained illegally by Agent Westenra hacking their accounts, though, and is inadmissible in court."

"I don't know what you're talking about," Lucy said, all but admitting it with her smile.

"All of this is circumstantial, though," Kate said, deflating any expectations. "We don't even know if Steve was involved in this. He could have been feeding his church information to profit from the pandemic instead of outright working with the Sons of Mithras. There could also just be a cell or two of Mithras terrorists among the converts of the Church of Money handling all the paperwork to get here—"

"Or the church's leadership may have arranged everything to make themselves trillions by stock market manipulation via terrorism," I replied. "Like a bunch of goddamn supervillains."

"Yes," Kate said, softly. "Which is thankfully above my paygrade."

I blinked. "Thankfully?"

"I'm passing it up to my superiors," Kate said, simply. "People who have far greater resources than mine. We have our own issues to deal with right now, specifically getting this plague under control. Thankfully, we may have passed a turning point on that."

"How do you figure that?" I asked, thinking about the news of a secondary outbreak.

"Aurelius," Lucy explained. "He was on the jumpcom all night. The Community is willing to make a tentative offer of humanitarian—or alientarian—relief, including bio-generators programmed to mass-produce medicines for existing patients as well as vaccines."

I stared. "Holy shit, that ridiculous ransom plan worked?"

"No," Lucy said. "They laughed at Aurelius for even suggesting it and said they'd prefer to bomb Earth for taking hostages over negotiating for him. I don't think he's a very good spy. He's more someone who was assigned here because he was an otherwise complete screw up."

"I was clued in by his dress sense," I replied. "Then how?"

"Doctor Saint Croix suggested that the plague was mutating and potentially threatened the Albionese minority on the Moon, who are citizens of the Community," Kate replied. "The Community won't do a thing for us but aid for their own people living here is another matter."

I stared at her. "That is the dumbest thing I've heard... well, this week."

"I don't really care either way," Kate replied. "If it works, it works. Our existing treatments for Red fever are inferior to the point of uselessness and Doctor Frankenstein's posthuman blood solution is only lowering the fatality rate by half and is already being illegally used in many hospitals."

I acknowledged her point. "How long until the aid gets here?"

"Months," Kate replied, deflating any elation I would normally have felt. "Six months at the earliest for mass distribution. That's assuming that accepting the aid is fast-tracked through the Colonial Council and EarthGov Senate, then approved by SHID as well as the Food, Medicine, and Recreationals Bureau. Which is why it's imperative to continue to focus on testing, quarantining, and treating everyone we can. Finding and eliminating the remaining cells is also a top priority."

Six months was enough time for Red fever to run through the entirety of the Moon if our existing efforts failed, and they already had multiple times. The populace was already getting restless with the economic and social burden the epidemic was placing on them. Things were going to get worse before they got better. An optimist might believe we could identify and quarantine everyone in that time to bring an end to Red fever but that wasn't me.

"Right," I said.

Kate pointed at my chest and poked me hard. "I need you doing your best work on finding these remaining terrorists. Also, any other work that I send your way because if you think we're understaffed and overworked now, you have no idea what those words mean. I want no more taking the entire evenings off for recreation, got that?"

"Sure," I said, softly.

"Right," Kate muttered, shaking her head. "Otherwise, good work."

With that, she was out of the garage.

"Wow, she is incredibly jealous," Barksley said.

I did a double take, as did Lucy.

"I'm just guessing," Barksley said, pausing. "Weirdly, she doesn't have much of a smell to her, unlike most humans. She has to have the driest shampoo of all time."

"She's not jealous," I replied. "She had a decade to get back in touch with me if she wanted to."

"Maybe she's reevaluating her priorities now that she's a masked vigilante," Lucy said, annoyed.

"Yeah, I don't think we need to speak about that here," I muttered, not sure how Kate would react if she knew we were onto her.

Sort of.

It'd been a month, and we still hadn't done anything with the damning information. That was on me, too.

"She's not wrong, though," Lucy said, quickly switching back to more important matters. "Even if we do have an end to this plague in sight, that doesn't mean we can rest on our laurels."

"I never understood that saying," Barksley said. "Why would you want to rest on a wreath of flowers?"

"How about you?" I asked, ignoring Barksley and changing the subject.

"Pardon?" Lucy asked.

"You... good?" I asked, unsure how to broach the next topic.

"I don't care if you slept with my ex-bandmates, Neal," Lucy said, a little too quickly.

"Only Priscilla," Barksley said.

"Really?" Lucy asked. "That's disappointing. I would have thought you'd have more ambition than that."

I frowned. You see, I knew when she was screwing with me. Usually. "That's not what I meant. Mostly."

"You and Priss are adults," Lucy said. "Indeed, I'm happy for you both. You're both incredibly horny jerks that should make this a regular thing. I suspect your attitudes can only improve. You both get cranky after a week without sex."

"Believe me, I've noticed," Barksley said.

I sucked in my breath and forced down any snarky comments that came to mind. Like, "How would you know? It's only happened once or twice since we've known each other", "I somehow doubt that's ever happened with Priss outside of a desert island", and "I think that's everybody. It's just most people make do in other ways."

"I meant about Steve," I replied. "I just wanted to know where your headspace was with him."

Lucy looked up to me. "If he's guilty, he was a complete monster who deserved far worse than having his head cut off. If he was innocent, then he's just another victim of the people we're dealing with. If you're asking how I feel about both, the fact I can't tell you one way or the other whether I believe he was innocent or not says that anything I might have felt for him before died a long time ago. If you were accused of this, or Barksley, I'd have your back to the end."

"Which is a shame because Barksley is a crime lord," I said, nodding.

"You can call me Heisenberg," Barksley said, making a reference I didn't get. "I have the hat and everything."

"You should get out of the game before the game gets you," I said to Barksley. "The maple syrup trade is a young dog's game."

"Say hello to my little friend," Barksley said, opening his mouth and showing the gun inside.

I shook my head. "I appreciate the endorsement, but I know what it's like to have a friend betray you and show just what they're capable of."

Lucy blinked, clearly annoyed at my attempt to bond with her. "With all due respect—"

"That's usually an introduction to a statement that can be summarized as 'bark you'," Barksley added.

Lucy breathed out, annoyed at that interruption. She then turned around and walked away. "I'm not you, Neal... I don't cling to things that only bring me misery."

"Ouch," Barksley said.

"No kidding," I said, depressed. "I guess I need to accept that whatever we had—"

"She's desperately suppressing her feelings for you," Barksley said, interrupting. "She wouldn't be trying so hard to drive you away if she wasn't passionately obsessed with you."

I looked down at Barksley. "Uh-huh."

"You don't believe me," Barksley said, sighing. Clearly, he was more invested in me and Lucy getting back together than she was.

I pulled out the data crystal that Rashid had slipped me. "Maybe idle paws are the Devil's playground. Why don't you focus on this instead?"

"Is now really the time to focus on the Slavers Guild?" Barksley asked. "Assuming it still exists."

"I have no doubt that as long as there's money to be made, it will continue to exist, either during this quarantine or after it," I said. "Besides, my goal isn't to just punish these assholes. It's also to find the people they've taken."

"If they're still alive," Barksley said. "I don't need to point out the odds of finding them are astronomical. Literally, they could be anywhere in the galaxy."

"Which is another reason to try to take some of these jerkasses alive," I said, pausing.

"You do realize the best probable course of action in that respect is to confront Agent Roebuck and ask what she knows," Barksley said.

"Maybe," I said, pausing. "But first I want to have an edge when I do that. Maybe this will give it to me."

Barksley sighed and stared at the crystal, running an invisible pair of lasers from his eyes and scanning the contents.

"Anything good?" I asked.

"Depends on how you define good," Barksley said. "I don't think this is a Slavers Guild location."

"Ah," I said, pausing. "Well—"

"I think it's the old-fashioned slavers kind," Barksley said. "The kind that have been trafficking in men and women since time immemorial."

I blinked. "Alright then."

"The Hearts of Fire is a particularly high-end hostess club that offers customized experiences," Barksley said.

"What kind of customized experience?" I asked.

Barksley explained. "You chip the young men or women, and an algorithm generates chatter based on your preferences and infomedia profile. Theoretically, you pay for an hour and the prostitutes zone out for an hour then go back to normal after they're done. Everyone wins."

"I know how Puppets work," I said, using the street slang for them. It was the creepiest fucking thing I've encountered in my life, and I'd encountered some creepy shit. It blurred the line between people who'd just want sex dolls versus those who wanted the real thing. The attraction was having a human enslaved to your every whim, so it only attracted sociopaths—at least if you knew they were Puppets.

"Yes, well the owner of this bar isn't letting them back up," Barksley said. "They're kept in their obedient servile form 24-7. You can also buy them permanently. Ms. Cherry Pie is part of the public part of the club."

I blinked a second time. "Well, I guess I know where I'm going tonight."

"This feels exceptionally dangerous," Barksley stated the obvious. "Also, possibly a trap. I don't need to remind you that certain individuals blame you for the massacre earlier this month. As far as I can tell, no one has removed the price on your head. They've just been watching our home more carefully."

182

Yeah, I'd been living here at SHID headquarters too. Mostly, the criminal underworld had been too busy to bother with me anyway. "I may not trust many people, but I trust Rashid. If his sister is cut from the same cloth, I can do the same for her. She had to have taken a big risk passing this information along. Blood will tell."

"I wonder if Abel said the same thing about Cain," Barksley said. "You realize this isn't what you were ordered to do, correct?"

"Uh huh," I replied. "It's something I *can* do, though."

I had no idea where to begin tracking down the remaining Sons of Mithras cells, let alone handling the massive amount of paperwork that had managed to build itself up despite my genius plan to just ignore it until someone else did it for me. Seriously, I wasn't sure why that wasn't working.

"Also, going without backup is what almost got you killed last year with the Cyberpunks," Barksley said, referring to my brush with mortality thanks to the late Ms. White. That had been some genuine Action Dan femme fatale bullshit.

"Who said I'm going without backup?" I asked. "I'm going to have you."

I had some other ideas there too.

Barksley put his paw on his face. "This is such a terrible idea."

"Yeah, probably," I said, putting the data crystal back in my pocket. "You coming or not?"

Barksley sighed. "Someone has to keep you alive. I'm pretty sure I'm going to stick out there."

"Thankfully, I have a plan for that, too," I replied, walking out the door, heading to a nearby elevator, and stepping in.

Barksley followed.

That was when Nigel Blackwood stopped the elevator doors closing and slid inside, leaving Barksley and I alone with him.

This was going to be the mother of all awkward rides.

CHAPTER NINETEEN

On an Elevator Ride with Satan

Yeah, this was not great.

I'd gotten in the elevator to go up to my "office" in the abandoned apartment building where I'd been spending most of my nights to fetch a change of clothes. Now, I was standing right next to Nigel Blackwood, who was the one person with whom I don't need to list all my issues. The fact it was coming after Lucy pointed out that I'd given him a "pass" for his horrific crimes also annoyed me since I felt I hadn't done anything of the sort.

The thing was I wasn't sure that the reason I had let him go—if you could even call it that since he was effectively untouchable by the law— still stood. I'd made a deal with him to go after his conspirators in the Slavers Guild instead of him. It wasn't forgiveness, it wasn't amnesty, it was just good police work. You let some of the little fish go to get the big fish, and sometimes let a big fish go to get a lot of little ones.

But the deal had been of questionable utility from the get-go. Yes, we'd managed to nail some people who would have otherwise gotten away with kidnapping and murder, but not nearly as many as I'd hoped. Our biggest opportunity had also ended up in a massacre by Kate and I wasn't sure how much of the Slavers Guild was still extant. Maybe they were effectively dissolved and now focused on their buyout from Albion. Maybe they were like the mob and new people would replace everyone killed with nary a bump in the road. Either way, I also hadn't been able to follow up on it because of the massive plague.

Which meant I had no reason to be friendly or even appear to be so since I wasn't getting anything out of him as an informant. Yet, there wasn't any benefit to antagonizing him either. Antagonizing him could potentially cut off a resource that I might need later. Which perhaps was the reason why Lucy and Barksley seemed to think I was too nice to Nigel despite his actions.

And maybe I was.

Because all of that seemed like excuses. I was a helluva lot ruder to people who'd done things a thousandth of what he'd done. I didn't want to forgive him—I could never forgive him—but I did want to know why he'd betrayed everyone to become a slaver. It was impossible for me to feel raw anger because I was too confused. If it was just the money, fine, I understood that. People did insane things for money. If it was getting the cure for his wife, I could understand that, too. But I didn't buy that either and he'd continued working for Karma Corp long after he'd gotten Mary Blackwood's Deimos Syndrome treated. No, it was just a puzzle that remained there.

Unsolved.

"So, you've once more heroically saved the day," Nigel said, staring forward.

"Excuse me?" I asked, surprised by him speaking.

"The Community coming with relief," Nigel said. "That'll be six months before even a conservative estimate of Karma Corp's cure. That may cost the company trillions."

"Don't look at me," I said, uncaring. "Lucy and I just found a guy with connections to the big old space empire. It was by accident."

It wasn't something I'd worked or could take credit for. Hell, I didn't even particularly care about whether it poked Karma Corp in the eye either. I hated Karma Corp—most of the megacorps really—and I actively resented the few I didn't hate. A few trillion lost here or there wouldn't bankrupt them, just make them more likely to charge more for headache medicine.

"And yet it may be the most important action of your life," Nigel said, pushing a button on the side of the elevator's old-style paneling and bringing our movement to a stop. "Millions of lives potentially saved by a random arrest in your girlfriend's mother's backyard when you have struggled so very hard to save just a few here and there. It makes you think, doesn't it?"

Barksley was conspicuously silent, just moving behind my legs and looking away from the doors.

"Not really," I said, honestly. "You can't really know which actions are going to have what consequences in the long run. Butterfly effect and all that shit. So you just have to make your decisions in the here and now to do the best you can."

Nigel snorted as if what I'd said was ridiculous. It was an unusually strong reaction from a man who was typically ice cold. "That is the kind of attitude that most people don't have the fortitude for, Neal. To live each day by day without forethought. They have to try to juggle the numbers and predict the outcomes in order to make life make sense. This becomes especially noteworthy when you wield power because gaining and utilizing it require harsh choices."

If this was an attempt to finally explain himself — or perhaps it was his fifth or sixth attempt and I'd just ignored the others — he was doing a shit job. "Is this where you try and say selling a bunch of innocent people to aliens was for the greater good? Because I'm not buying it."

"*Chinatown*," Nigel said, surprising me.

"Excuse me?" I asked.

"Roman Polanski film, 20th century, starred Jack Nicholson," Nigel said.

"I know what *Chinatown* is," I replied. "You showed me the film.'

Both Nigel and I were Retros, which was basically considered to be a subculture of fanboys who didn't like anything made in the past two centuries. I had my exceptions, but it had grown consistently clear that a huge chunk of humanity thought pop culture was "different" pre-First Contact and preferred it. I didn't know if I'd go that far but I knew much of the Eighties by heart, just like Barksley, and Nigel was an obsessive fan of detective stories from the entirety of the 20th century. Marlowe, Spade, and Hammer were his gods.

"During one of their earlier conversations, Detective Jack Gittes confronts the villain of the movie, Noah Cross, and asks why he was involved with a scheme to steal water from the San Fernando Valley farms," Nigel said, explaining the movie like he hadn't made me watch it five times. It was a good film but depressing as hell.

"Uh huh," I said, wondering where he's going with this.

"Jack can't wrap it around his head why the man is bothering to do all this blatantly criminal behavior as he's already one of the richest men in California. So, Jack asks Cross, up front, what he could possibly get by doing it. 'How much better he could eat,' were the exact words he used, I think. Do you remember what the villain replied?"

"The future," I replied, remembering the line. "He could get the future."

"Yes," Nigel said, as if it explained everything. "You can't understand why I've done what I've done without understanding that each of the steps I've taken has been done, one after the other, as part of a larger chance to enact real change. We both grew up in immense poverty and did what we could to escape it. What is happening now and what happens next are chances to redirect the course of human history. For that, sacrifices must be made. Terrible things must be done. Innocent people will die but change always has casualties."

That mostly slid into place what I hadn't figured out about Nigel. Unfortunately, the resulting puzzle picture wasn't a pretty one. It was just another ambitious man who had realized he could not only go from being a crooked lieutenant on Mars' corporate police to being an executive if only he was willing to look the other way when tens of thousands of people vanished. Then he could tell himself that it was all the price of making the world a better place. Maybe lowering the price of Goop by a nickel or donating to some museums to open a wing dedicated to preserving dogs playing poker. I'd seen plenty of internal reformists go this way, guys who thought they could make the police better from the inside, and almost always they ended up having to preserve their positions over accomplishing any change. It just usually was a side hustle of ignoring drugs and prostitution versus human trafficking.

"You know Noah Cross was an incestuous pedophile, right?" I said, having nothing else better to say to his speech.

Nigel slumped his shoulders and restarted the elevator's movement. "One goes to bed thinking one is the hero and wakes up as the villain. But there is no redemption in Hell and some crimes cannot be forgiven."

"Yeah, I love platitudes too," I said.

There wasn't anything I could say to make him feel better and I didn't see the point of telling him that he deserved to feel bad for what he'd done. That there was nothing he could do to make up for the people whose lives he ruined. Maybe I could have asked him, again, where his victims had been sent but he'd said he had no idea and I unfortunately believed him. The only thing he could do was help me try to bring down more of the Karma Corp officials involved in the conspiracy and I wasn't sure he had much information left on that either.

So, instead, we just stood there awkwardly for a few more seconds as the elevator reached the floor he was going to. The doors opened and he turned around to speak. "There's something you should know, Neal."

"Sorry about trashing your place, Nigel," I said, pausing. "Except not really."

Nigel blinked. "Special Agent Kate Roebuck is not your ex-wife. She's someone impersonating her."

He timed the response just perfectly enough to have the doors close on him before the elevator started moving again.

I stared. "What. The. Bark."

Barksley peered out from around my legs. "Okay, I think he won that round."

"I wasn't aware I was competing," I muttered.

"Then you shouldn't be throwing such serious punches," Barksley said, referring to my remarks on Nigel's justifications. Which hadn't even been intended to strike at his emotional well-being, which was probably why they'd been so effective. "I was afraid he was going to execute us both."

"I think he'd do that outside of the headquarters of SHID," I replied. "Probably."

"Do you think he remembers me telling him to bark off?" Barksley asked.

"Yes," I replied. "Yes, he does. You probably are number two on his enemies list."

"Well, one knows a dog's worth by the quality of their enemies," Barksley said.

"Do you think he was telling the truth?" I asked.

"I think he wouldn't tell you a lie like that," Barksley said. "No, he'd only tell you the truth about something so hurtful. That way it stings more."

I had no idea what Nigel had meant by what he said and wondered if Barksley was just taking it literally. Then again, what other way was there to take that bombshell other than literally. He didn't say, "she's not who you think she is" or "don't trust her." He said she was an imposter. Which was entirely possible with today's technology.

Holy crap.

But who the hell would want to impersonate Kate and why the hell would they want to rope me into all of this? She'd been a special operations officer and involved in some shady black ops stuff even before she'd joined SHID, but you didn't adopt the identity of a spy to do your spywork. Or did you?

A part of me just wanted to immediately go after Nigel and demand answers. But I had a funny feeling if he wanted to share them, he'd just tell me. Instead, I sent him a nasty series of text messages and stepped out of the elevator when it opened up on the fifteenth floor where I kept both my office as well as the futon I used in place of a bed.

No response.

Dammit.

"What are you going to do?" Barksley asked.

"Probably discuss it with Lucy, Rashid, and other people I can trust," I said, not yet adding the Knights despite my recent hookup. As much as I wanted to list "rock and roll Special Forces anarchist chicks" to my list of special friends, I wasn't sure I was close enough to them to call them friends versus friends of a friend.

"And in the meantime?" Barksley said.

"Set up the sting tonight," I said, pausing.

"Really? We're still doing that?" Barksley asked.

I looked down. "I dunno, man, it's a bunch of hookers needing rescuing. What do you think?"

Barksley looked up to me. "That does rather cut to the core of your character, doesn't it?"

"Yes," I muttered, heading past a few other masked agents into my office that smelled of disinfectant. "I don't suppose Cherry Pie left a number to call her at, did she? It'd go smoother if she knew I was coming."

My office was one of the abandoned hotel's many, many rooms but sadly didn't come with any furnishings. Instead, a cheap desk had been assembled inside with some other furniture bought in. The place had a bunch of plastisheets waiting to be signed as well as an infopad that I was certain had a few thousand unread pages on it. As mentioned, I had been sleeping here with a couple of laundry baskets of clothes off to one side. I'd set up a fold-up table nearby for mine and Barksley's impromptu dining on takeout for, well, the entire time we'd been here.

If it sounded like I was roughing it, you'd be correct, but given my general style was "disheveled guy in a suit" anyway, almost no one had noticed it for the past few weeks. I was hardly the only person turning in eighteen-hour days here either. Paperwork may not have been my highest priority, but I'd been doing my damnedest to do everything else I could to stop this disaster.

So had everyone else.

"In fact, she did," Barksley said. "It's an infocom line directly to her cybernetics. Also, I hate to ask but could you set this place on fire and move to a new one? I feel like it's inhabited by some sort of cave troll."

"Bah, it's barely orcish," I replied.

I wasn't a big fantasy fan, but Lucy was, so I'd learned that bit of lingo. "Well, pop the number to me and I'll see if I can set something up."

I didn't discount that this could be a trap. While I was pretty sure Cherry Pie—or Farrah as Rashid still called her—was good people, it wasn't necessarily the case that she was doing this sort of thing willingly. People who found themselves in debt to the mob often didn't have a choice if they wanted to keep their kneecaps.

Still, I wasn't going to make any assumptions until I had more facts. That meant going over what Barksley had scanned as well as making contact. Sitting down at my infopad, I proceeded to scan the data crystal's contents after disconnecting the computer from the larger network. Just in case. Indeed, Cherry Pie's number was there as well as times to make contact. We were about twenty minutes away from one of them, so I spent that time examining what she'd managed to supply me with, information-wise.

The results weren't pretty.

Just as Barksley suggested, the Hearts on Fire was a cover for the Syndicate. Specifically, it was functioning as an illegal nightclub for the people who couldn't stand to give up their social lives during the quarantine. Puppets were listed among its varied services which included RealDream customized fantasies, gambling, VIP conference rooms for any form of business, narcotics, and private parties with all manner of entertainments provided,

Cherry speculated that it went much deeper. Many people had lost their incomes during the lockdown and were seeking alternative forms of employment. It seemed that while the nightclub hired plenty, they also arranged people to be "disappeared" as well. After all, if they were applying for a job at an illegal nightclub then they probably weren't forwarding their last known location. The evidence was light, but Cherry had noticed enough that it was a very easy conclusion to draw.

Notably, there was a lot of curious notations in the nightclub's description. Specifically, the club claimed that it was 100% Red fever free and that any customers who were willing to pay for their platinum package would be immunized to it. Normally, I would dismiss this as hyperbole but the platinum package cost over 100,000 EarthGov credits, and even the super-rich rarely blew that much money on nonsense.

"Yeah, this place needs to be burned to the ground," I muttered.

"You'll need to acquire their client list intact," Barksley said. "Just shutting down their kidnapping ring alone won't be enough."

"Not my first rodeo," I muttered, debating if I should get the entirety of SHID involved. I'd managed to throw my weight around a lot as a federal agent but that had its limits, and this was outside our remit. There was also no telling if the late Steve Rogers Hudson had been the mole or even the only mole in the organization.

So, I decided to handle it in my own way. *Interface, I need you to place this call for me and make sure it's not traceable by anyone else in the universe.*

I CAN'T PROMISE YOU THAT BUT I CAN COME VERY CLOSE, Interface replied. JUST SO WE'RE CLEAR, ARE WE GOING ON A KILLING SPREE TONIGHT?

No! I replied. *I just want to confirm what's going on, collect some evidence, and then arrest everyone.*

WHY ARE YOU LYING TO YOURSELF? Interface asked.

Because I'd seen how the Moon dealt with criminals who had money and power. Because it turned out that only a handful of cops believed like I did that there were some crimes so heinous that they deserved to be dealt with using maximum force regardless of legality. Because I had the sneaking suspicion that sometimes you needed to burn a house down rather than try to fix it. But I wasn't going to admit that to Interface because I was still lying to myself: that the system did better than evil.

The low ringing noise of an infocom call was heard in my brain before an image of Cherry Pie appeared in the left corner of my vision. Presumably that was Hearts on Fire's uniform for its hostesses. Cherry was beautiful, and mostly natural, still bearing a strong resemblance to her brother but softer rather than his harsh and streetwise ones. The Great Programmer of the Universe had been generous with her figure and there was a warmth about her that undoubtedly made her very popular with customers. Cherry opted for pigtails and dyed them pink, which I didn't get as a fashion choice, but it worked for her. Tonight, she was dressed in a corset with a bow tie around her neck.

"I got your message," I said, simply.

"Good," Cherry said, simply. "Send the Marines and burn the place to the ground."

"I'm coming tonight. You need to make yourself scarce," I replied. "I'll have the signal ready when needed."

I had no idea what the signal would be or who I would signal but I'd worked around harder issues.

"Uh huh," Cherry said. "No can do, chief, at least about the making myself scarce. The new owner has a thing for me and has already requested me for his own personal Puppet show. I show up, what little freedom I have as the manager here gets turned off and they find someone else who has a modicum of free will."

That explained a few things, not the least being that Cherry had enough free will to turn against her employers in the first place. Contrary to the appeal of Puppets, they weren't everyone's—man, woman, or otherwise—fantasy. Quite a few of us enjoyed partners with actual brains. It also wasn't possible to make Dummy AI smart enough to manage a hospitality business for obvious reasons.

"Take care, then," I said, pausing. "With any luck, we'll find out where the victims have gone."

"Sometimes you can only just cauterize the wound. When you can't save someone, you avenge them," Cherry said, ending the call prematurely.

I didn't want to think like that.

That was when Barksley cleared his throat.

I looked up and saw Kate had entered the room and was standing over me. "Oh, hey, Kate."

"I need to make sure you're doing your job," Kate said. "Also, talk to you about some things. Personal matters."

I looked at her for a moment, scanning her for any sign she wasn't the woman she claimed to be. Nothing immediately jumped out to me that couldn't be explained by the passage of time. There was also the fact that Nigel Blackwood was, kind of, well, evil, and capable of lying despite Barksley's assumption otherwise. That was when I got an idea that might shed light on her situation as well as potentially give me the backup I needed.

"Sounds good," I said, smiling. "How would you like to stop some slavers? Do some fieldwork for a change."

Kate blinked then gave a look very similar to the woman from my memories. "I'm listening."

CHAPTER TWENTY

Unexpected Twists

"The Red Dragon isn't what I'd choose for this mission," I replied, sitting in the passenger seat with Barksley in my lap. I was wearing a dinner jacket that made me look more like a spy than the typical private dick look I sported. I was also sporting a fake beard and a few prosthetics designed to fool someone who didn't know me well. Kate had really gone all in on this operation, and I was surprised at how much she was willing to splurge here.

"Why?" Kate asked, sitting across from me in the driver's seat. She was wearing a stunning black slit dress that probably cost more than I made in a year. She too had changed her features slightly around the nose and jawline so that she looked more like a sister or cousin than a former SAW. The work she'd had done helped disguise her soldier's build and was perhaps the first advantage I saw for it other than vanity.

"I guess because the word inconspicuous isn't the first word that comes to mind when I see this vehicle," I replied. "Remember when Ayanna Breeze did a remake of that Quentin Tarantino revenge pic? This reminds me of her car in that one in terms of flash."

"Ah, yes, the Puppy Wagon," Barksley said. "Yes, I admit it is a tad bit attention getting."

"We're undercover as the sort of people that can afford to attend the Hearts on Fire," Kate replied. "We're meant to be rich, sexually decadent, and corrupt."

194

"I can pull off two out of three of those pretty easily," I replied. "The rich part might be a little harder."

"You're the least corrupt cop I know," Kate said, pausing. "Which is depressing. However, Shinobu has uploaded false identities for us into Armstrong's citizen registry and I've gotten Nigel to provide an introduction for us. He's not a member of the platinum club but apparently some of his associates are."

Thinking about Nigel telling me she wasn't Kate, I couldn't help but ponder whether that was an outstandingly bad idea or not. "I'm not sure Nigel can be trusted."

"Given he is a traitor to his friend, a slaver, and a corporate shill, I would agree," Kate replied. "I know what he did to you, Neal, and if it were up to me, I'd put two rounds in the back of his head."

If she was impersonating Kate, she was a helluva actor as she really did come off as someone pissed off on my behalf. "Thanks, but I can handle my own revenge if it comes to that."

Kate paused. "I'm surprised it hasn't."

I did a double take to her. "Excuse me?"

"I'm surprised you haven't killed him yourself," Kate said.

Outside, we were driving through one of Crater Town's nicer neighborhoods. The artificial day and night cycle in both the Luna City dome and here was presently set to night. The place was illuminated in a broad twinkling spectrum of lights, and you could hear the humming of the massive machinery that provided atmosphere, heat, and gravity even within the confines of the car. Especially since, for once, someone had managed to wrestle the car sound system away from Barksley.

I wasn't sure if she was making a joke or not. "Do I strike you as the kind of guy who is capable of premeditated murder?"

"Yes," Kate said, before realizing I wasn't going to take that as a compliment. "I mean under the right circumstances."

That was the difference between Kate and me. She'd been with SAW for years before I'd met her, and her missions had included plenty of assassinations among other black bag work. Despite being a Marine—there was no such thing as an ex-Marine after all—I was still a cop at heart. I'd kill people if it came to that, but I wasn't into the murder business.

That included Nigel, though I was honest enough with myself to know there was more going on there. Even though I had my answers that he'd just been overwhelmed with a lust for money and power, that didn't mean I'd suddenly developed a burning hatred for him. Weirdly—and I didn't understand my reasoning any better than Lucy or Kate—I pitied him more than hated him. He was the rare criminal who'd understood what he'd lost by selling his soul. Sadly, that meant he had nothing left to lose.

"Right," I replied, shaking my head. "Well, I have my reasons for not going after Nigel directly. Keep your friends close, and your enemies closer."

"Is that the real reason?" Kate asked, looking skeptical.

I paused. No, it wasn't. Still, I wasn't sure I wanted to open to her about this. So, I lied. "I'm hoping Nigel can lead me to where some of the victims he's sold into slavery are. If we can recover any of them, I'd consider that to be a win."

Kate didn't respond for a moment while she stared forward into the night as antiseptic artificial rain poured down on our vehicle's windshield. Finally, she spoke, "You're not going to find any of the people sold by the Slavers Guild, Neal."

I didn't comment on the fact she used my codename for our enemy. Something she could have only learned from me, Barksley, Lucy, Rashid, or Nigel. Instead, I focused on what she was implying. "What do you know that I don't?"

Barksley was silent, looking at her as if scanning her, which he possibly was.

"Your efforts against them, the group we called Trinidad, weren't unnoticed," Kate said, not looking me in the eye. "However, you're a corpo cop, a police merc, and this is something way outside your jurisdiction. Division One, the organization that coordinates all the other intelligence divisions of Earth, has been investigating the network of kidnappers for the better part of twelve years."

Twelve years? Jesus Christ. How long was this going on? How big was it?

I blinked. "You're not exactly covering yourself in glory then."

"The Neo-Militarists turned a blind eye," Kate said. "It was a trade in people for technology. The technology is then reverse engineered, adapted to humanity, and sold for billions. All of it to buy spaceships and advanced tech that require more people to be sold to maintain."

"*Why*?" I asked, confused. "I don't get it. What do aliens want with human slaves? Especially if there's a whole bunch of off-world humans living out there already. I know Karma Corp uses them for experiments but there has to be more than this."

Nigel had given me an explanation that had relied on a lot of assumptions that humans could be disappeared from Earth without a trace but not so much in the Community. You'd think the opposite would be true, through sheer size alone if no other reason, but the Community's technology meant that their police were much-much better at their jobs. That had never sat right with me, though. It seemed like he was covering up something else, but I couldn't figure out what since nothing he could describe could be worse than what he was already a part of.

Right?

Kate sighed. "There's one area that humanity, specifically Earth, has that the rest of the galaxy doesn't have a benefit from—at least in terms of something we can sell that they will be. Everything else the Community has in abundance, and we couldn't afford if we emptied our entire planetary treasury."

"What?" I asked, finally getting answers.

"AI," Kate said.

"What?" I asked.

"It's incredibly regulated, if not outright illegal in the Community," Kate said. "Due to everything being networked, sentient AI is considered something akin to WMDs and they have bombs that can destroy suns. The fact that Earth has a massive number of AI coordinating its society was initially a major source of concern for our erstwhile allies. That's why they've parked a cruiser inside our solar system. It's not there to protect us, it's there to blast us out of existence if any of our Cognition AI go rogue and try to infect the Community's systems."

"Well, that's just bigoted," Barksley said.

I blinked. "What does that have to do with slave trading? Wait, you're talking about Uploads."

There were two ways of creating sentient AI (i.e., Smart AI) in the world versus things that could just mimic human intelligence (i.e., Dummy AI). The first way was to go through an elaborate training process that took about ten years and had an incredibly high failure rate. This was usually only used for the creation of Cognition AI and the typical cost involved was usually around ten to a hundred billion credits.

The second, much more common, method was Uploads. Basically, you take an existing human being's brain and deep scan it until it creates a copy with all its personality as well as memories. It was considered the Diet Coke of immortality and was basically mental cloning. It was also incredibly destructive to the human brain and left people a vegetable even if one or two copies could be made without severe damage. For whatever reason, only direct scans of the human brain stayed "alive", and copies of copies had a high failure rate unless they were active. Don't ask me to explain the science, I'm not a quantum computer consciousness expert.

If you were utterly unscrupulous—and plenty of people in big business were—you could get someone scanned and then institute a huge number of directives to make them a sentient computer program that was brainwashed into doing what regular computer programs couldn't. They could intuit, decide, and react on their own. It had been the fate of numerous people suckered into it by Upload-hungry corporations and had been the fate of poor Lucy's dad, Alex.

"Yes," Kate said, pausing. "That's the fate of the people being trafficked to the Community's underworld, Neal. If they're lucky to survive a few months, it'll be only so they can be scanned hundreds of times and left as vegetables. Both the Community and EarthGov were working on shutting this down when we got distracted by the plague."

I balled my fists. "That's not what I was told."

"Does it matter?" Kate asked.

I didn't know how to respond so I just said the first thing that came to mind. "No. But it does mean that Nigel must die for this. No number of people he turns over for their part in this can make up for this."

"Could he before?" Kate asked.

"I dunno," I said, shrugging before something occurred to me. "Wait, you said twelve years."

"Yes," Kate said, starting to lower the Red Dragon down. She knew what I was getting at.

"Was our divorce related to the case?" I asked, feeling silly even asking. Real life wasn't so neatly wrapped up.

"Yes," Kate said, immediately contradicting my assumption.

"Wow," I muttered, having just assumed she didn't want to be married to me anymore. It happened after all, and we'd barely been married to begin with.

"I was on a mission against one of the early slave ships," Kate said. "We underestimated what kind of security they had and were overwhelmed. I got captured and was held prisoner for four months."

I stared. "Christ."

"I was recovered—unlike a lot of people—and exported back to Earth," Kate said. "The Community intelligence services has done its best to do that for as many people as well as Uploads as they can. But my mind wasn't what it was, and the government had classified everything anyway. It took a long time to get my brain back in order."

"I'm sorry, I wish I'd known," I replied.

Kate snorted. "And do what? Sit by my bedside? You had your own life to live, Neal. One you've lived well from everything I've learned. People who care about you. I have my own thing now as well."

"And what's that?" I asked. "Revenge?"

Now was probably the time to let her reveal things on her own. Basically, I was expecting her to say, "Yeah, I was Lady Zero and because of my time as a prisoner at the hands of slavers, I'm on a personal crusade to murder the shit out of these guys." Which, admittedly, sounded like the kind of movie Ayanna Breeze would star in.

"Yes," Kate said.

And nothing more was said.

We were outside of the Hearts on Fire now, right in front of the front doors in fact, and I had to admit the place had done a good job of staying under the radar. There were no flashing lights, neon signs, or holographic displays. Instead, it was a closed-up hotel with all the windows covered in heavy curtains and set to opaque mode. It was also right next to a shuttered department store that was exactly the sort of business you could use for smuggling and storage during the epidemic.

The streets of Luna City were all but abandoned at night and a curfew had been imposed the previous week. We were still in the early days of it all, but the inherently contrary nature of lunes meant that every new rule got considerable pushback. I wouldn't have been surprised if this was one of a hundred bars and clubs operating in this district that wouldn't have normally been able to sustain ten. The lure of the forbidden was a powerful incentive even if you were trying to stop the spread of deadly disease.

One benefit of the streets being largely empty at night was that it was relatively easy to spot all the guards and lookouts in the immediate area. The panhandler on the corner, two guys on the roof across the street, and a guy pretending to be one of the homeless who I saw was concealing a shotgun. I suspected there were probably at least three times as many in the actual buildings themselves.

"Are you sure you've got backup you can trust here?" I asked, switching subjects.

"I have people ready to move," Kate replied. "But I want to see if we can get access to their client files before they can be deleted."

"I'm pretty sure that's illegal," I replied.

"That's for law enforcement, not espionage," Kate said. "Visiting Puppets is enough of a public controversy that it could be used to lean on enough individuals to get their cooperation against the resistance we're currently facing in the corporate-dominated government."

"Plus, we want to see if we can rescue anyone before they're made into computer chips," I replied. "Assuming there's any link to the Slavers Guild."

I hadn't seen any with Cherry Pie's information but that didn't mean there wasn't. Still, I was inclined to agree with Barksley that this was another group at work. This was minor leagues versus the Guild's intergalactic syndicate.

"That too," Kate said. "Though old-fashioned slavery exists in human settlements just fine."

"Tell me about it," I muttered, watching the doors of the Red Dragon slide up. I stepped out into the rainy night and waited for Kate.

"Take the car to the security zone and monitor our vitals," Kate said to Barksley. "We're counting on you, little guy."

"I'm not small, you apes are just freakishly tall," Barksley said.

Kate rubbed Barksley's head and departed before joining me at the hip. "I admit, I didn't think this would be our first date out."

I uncomfortably smiled as, contrary to my reputation as a shameless puppy hound—as Barksley would say—I wasn't really interested in renewing my previous relationship with Kate. I know, surprising. However, when I closed the book on something, it tended to stay closed. Booty calls? Sure. Late night drunken hookups? Absolutely. Friendly regular sex when neither of you have something else going on? I used to have weekly appointments with multiple exes. Trying to revive a relationship that was left abandoned over a decade ago? Not so much. Even if I didn't resent Kate for just cutting off all contact without even a Dear John letter explaining what had happened, which I didn't (honest), I would have long since moved on.

Plus, she was my boss.

That *never* ended well.

"Sure," I said, holding her arm and accompanying her into the building's front entrance.

We were scanned as we entered and since no one gunned us down, I assumed we passed the initial check. The Hearts on Fire club that greeted us was a lot classier joint than I expected. I'd been thinking gaudy neon and hookers on display, but this had the feel of an old timey nightclub from the Prohibition Era.

It was a two-story main hallway with a staircase leading up the side and the front was a restaurant where you could dine with your entertainment in snug little booths before heading upstairs to the private rooms. The ratio of male-to-female customers was about 75% men to women, which was common in these establishments but not so much that we stood out. We weren't the only couples here as some men were with their wives, mistresses, or boy toys.

Everyone was dressed up and drinking the finest of champagne and eating presumably organic food served by gold-plated bots. The place had red-painted walls, patterned carpet, and wood paneling that gave the sense of it being somewhere the riff raff wasn't welcome. Light jazz music was playing in the background.

Looks like your kind of place, Kate said to me via our infocom link. I shouldn't have been surprised she'd managed to hack my posthuman connection but was.

I like my women to be conscious when I'm having sex, I said, disgusted. *Get a sexbot if you want someone reading lines about how you're the best lay ever.*

I sensed Kate stiffen at the mention of the word sexbot, but she quickly recovered. *People pay for the fantasy. I can understand the appeal of Puppetry as a profession for sex workers as well. You just close your eyes and wake up without having to deal with any of the memories of ugly, smelly, or rude customers. Plus, get paid more.*

Clearly you never read Neuromancer, I said, remembering one of the books in the Gordon Foundation's physical library, something of an oddity in an age where everything was digitized.

What happened in Neuromancer? Kate asked.

Let's just say never trust that when you give over control over your body to a shady pimp that you're only doing what they promise you'll be doing, I replied.

I didn't a chance to speak more because Cherry Pie walked up in a flattering red Chinese dress with a slit, and her hair bound with chopsticks. She was also wearing particularly high stiletto heels that she moved in gracefully, accenting her already impressive height to being above even me. It was a clash of cultures given her ethnicity, but she managed to make it look fantastic, nevertheless. By her expression, I had no doubt she recognized us despite our disguises. It was annoyance and bemusement rather than relief. I also had a weird buzzing in my head around her that I was trying to identify. Well, other than general attraction and anxiousness about this mission.

"Greetings and welcome to the Hearts on Fire," Cherry Pie said, smiling. "Mr. Smiles wants to speak with you."

Kate and I exchanged a look.

"Mr. Smiles?" I asked, confused.

"He's the acting director for establishment," Cherry Pie said. "He likes to greet all new customers that want to make themselves available to our platinum membership."

"Ah," Kate said, nodding. "Yes, I did make reservations for that. Please lead the way."

I had a bad feeling about this.

CHAPTER TWENTY-ONE

The Frame-Up Job

C herry Pie led us upstairs and along a set of hallways past numerous guests and workers. It was usually very easy to tell the Puppets from the regular employees as there was a kind of unsettling bland pleasantness to the former. Men and women of astounding beauty that had nothing behind their eyes. It was the kind of thing that I found to be a major turn off, no matter how lovely they were, but I wouldn't have been surprised if that was part of the allure for some of the customers here.

However, I was astonished to see that these Puppets were a lot more relaxed and chatting merrily away with their customers. There was none of the usual blandness to their actions and if Cherry Pie hadn't clued us in, I would have just assumed it was a normal sex work establishment—of which I had some familiarity with type not run via slavery.

Still, there was a buzzing in my head when I walked by them that caused me to stick my hands in my pockets. There was a familiarity to the feeling, but I couldn't quite place it. Thankfully, I didn't have to rely on my sometimes-spotty memory. I had Interface to sort through my unconscious for me.

Can you check out these women's chips? I asked Interface. *There's something weird going on here and I need to figure it out.*

SOMETHING WEIRD? Interface asked.

Call it a gut feeling, I replied, hating myself for following this versus the evidence. But, sometimes, you had to do it. *Just do it. See if they have an infonet connection you can access and whether it ties into the brothel's central mainframe.*

IT DOES AND YOU WERE CORRECT TO ANALYZE THEM. Interface explained, surprising me. THEY ARE HOLLOWED,

What? I asked. I knew what the Hollowed and Willed were but wasn't sure what soulless super-soldiers and sleeper agents had to do with a brothel in Crater Town. Unless the prostitutes were about to break out in a bunch of ninja moves on us and while that would be awesome, I hoped reality would reserve something like that for the next Action Dan film.

THE TECHNOLOGY THAT HAS ALLOWED THESE MEN AND WOMEN TO BE MADE INTO PUPPETS IS DERIVED FROM COMMUNITY-BASED MILITARY IMPLANTS, Interface explained. INFERIOR KNOCK-OFFS, DEFINITELY, BUT SOMETHING BEYOND THE TECHNOLOGY OF EARTH. I AM INTERFACING WITH THEM NOW WITH THE HELP OF MS. SHINOBU.

Hi! Shinobu's avatar—a bunny with a machine gun—appeared in my vision. She was shouting. *Can you hear me?*

Yes, I can hear you, I replied, feeling extra ridiculous. *How the hell did you get involved in this?*

Agent Roebuck has me monitoring your feed! Shinobu said. *I can hack anything instantly while hooked up to Armstrong, at least on the Moon!*

It suddenly felt very crowded in my brain.

Can you tell where they came from? I asked, more than a little annoyed that Interface claimed to just be my unconscious at work yet was constantly going off and doing his own thing. If he was just a reflection of me, he was the Jekyll to my Hyde.

YOU MEAN THE HYDE TO YOUR JEKYLL, Interface corrected.

Which one of us is a horny brute? I asked.

FAIR POINT, Interface said. AND YES, THIS IS ALL ALBION-BASED TECHNOLOGY. WHICH INDICATES THAT IT MAY WELL BE TIED TO THE SONS OF MITHRAS OR PERHAPS ITS PARENT ORGANIZATION.

I can use it to ping all the women and men tied to the original technology as well as the greater Sons of Mithras network, Shinobu said. *Wow, look at that network light up. It's giving me the location of their entire system.*

It took me a few seconds to process what they were saying. I didn't have a brain the size of a planet like Interface, after all.

SINCE WE'RE BOTH CONNECTED TO ARMSTRONG VIA SHINOBU, YOU DO, Interface said.

Smartass, I said. *Wait, are you saying that not only is this a base for the terrorists and we lucked out again, but we've got them all?*

Yeah, actually, Shinobu said. *I'm also finding a bunch of financial records here and payoffs. It's funny that the backdoor I needed to access everything was actually in the prostitutes all along. Ooo, I bet there's a dirty joke there. I bet you never guessed you'd be inside so many prostitutes, Neal! Actually, no, you really strike me as the kind of guy who has been in a lot of them.*

I ignored Shinobu making fun of my sex life—I never had to pay for sex since the Marines, thank you very much—because my mind was too busy racing. This was a fantastic stroke of luck, and I didn't believe in those. There was no possible way we'd stumbled onto the Sons of Mithras by accident. No, those were coincidences I didn't believe in.

Someone had laid out a trail of breadcrumbs for us that were falling like dominos now.

You're mixing up your metaphors now, Neal, Shinobu said. *Also, I shouldn't be reading your thoughts. I'm transferring all the data now. Got it, Kate?*

Yes, Kate replied.

We were at the end of the hallway in front of the doorway to Mr. Smiles's office. That was when I realized what I'd been unable to put together until just a few seconds too. The buzz that indicated the surrounding Puppets were Hollowed and mind controlled.

And I'd gotten that buzz from Cherry Pie.

This *was* a trap.

I reached out to grab Kate by the arm, looking at her. "I just remembered we left something in the car. Dear, would you come with me?"

Kate turned her head to me, obviously having her own private conversation going by the faraway look in her eye. The alarm on her expression told me that she'd managed to put the pieces together as well. That was when I felt my head ring louder than it had when I'd been surrounded by all those Hollowed and instead became like it had on that rooftop when the Sons of Mithras attacked. I tried to contact Interface and Shinobu but got nothing but static. Hopefully, that would mean that this place was about to be swarming with SHID agents but that wouldn't help us right now.

Especially when I felt the tip of a gun pointed in my back as I looked to see one was pointed at Kate's, too. It was one of the Puppets and a guard, both staring forward at us with murderous intent. We were hostages and I had to wonder just who had it out for me enough to potentially burn—actually completely burn—all of the Sons of Mithras as well as one of their operations here to get me.

There was one blindingly obvious answer, and I didn't want to acknowledge it because it made me look like an idiot. Who was the guy who was probably the mastermind behind all of this? I dunno. How about the guy who was involved in interstellar slavery, murder, terrorism, and had been playing both sides since the beginning?

Nigel.

Nigel Blackwood.

He could have informed the Sons of Mithras. As a Karma Corp executive, he knew about the whole Charon affair (you know, the colony world first infected with Red Fever), and he had enough personal stake with me to go to such elaborate lengths to take me out after several failed attempts. Plus, he was also rich enough to arrange for the Jesus Loves the RichTM freaks to serve as his middlemen to get terrorists here to spread Red fever.

The asshole had all but confessed in the elevator and I'd been too stupid to figure it out because I was still trying to think the best of him. He wanted to change the world and the best way to do that was to get access to Community technology. The Slavers Guild, Project: Jenner, and this outbreak were all ways to acquire for humanity more access to Community resources with him at the center of it all. Plus, every time one of his schemes threatened him, he just betrayed everyone involved to one of his enemies. It reminded me of the late Giovanni "Gifts" Chang, who'd been the biggest snitch in police history, but his information was always about his enemies. Hell, I think Nigel had worked that case.

All the pieces fit together, and I wanted to beat my head against a wall because of how obvious it had been from the beginning. He'd sent me and Barksley down to the meeting in hopes of probably getting me killed, arranged for me to get fired so I couldn't follow up, had me and Lucy ambushed, plus probably was behind this hostage situation.

The problem wasn't my detective work, it was the fact I'd kept surviving or bouncing back. In large part due to Kate's protecting me. Indeed, the only reason I was probably still alive was because killing me and the head of SHID was probably going to be a lot bigger hassle than killing just me. Hell, Nigel telling me Kate was a fake was probably just to rattle my trust in her since she had pulled me out of several of his traps.

"Please enter," Cherry Pie said, staring forward at last with the glassy eyes that marked her as one of the Puppets.

"And if we don't?" I said, hoping to hear the calvary charging in.

So far, nothing.

"Then things will get difficult," Cherry Pie said.

"This plan is already borked," I said, using the preferred profanity of spacers. "We've already—"

Any conversation I was about to have about the subject—which was probably pointless since I wasn't talking to Cherry Pie but whomever was working her strings—was interrupted by Kate punching the guy behind her in the throat before forcing him into the woman behind me.

That gave me a second to move as I went for the gun that I'd concealed in my jacket pocket. I managed to get it free right as Cherry Pie pulled a tiny Athena-90, a woman's gun that was designed to only carry non-lethal icer rounds.

Which was comforting since she shot me in the head before shooting Kate, causing her to fall beside me. I managed to stay conscious despite the fact my entire body felt limp like a wet noodle, and I struggled to try to activate whatever super-soldier countermeasures that Interface was designed to make use of.

Nothing happened.

Ironically, as Cherry Pie raised her pistol up to my face, I could hear the doors being broken open downstairs. Unfortunately, what happened next was beyond my ability to perceive because Cherry Pie shot me again in the head. At close range, it was 50-50 whether it would lethal.

BLAM.

No pearly gates, demonic servitors, or dolphins thanking me for all the fish greeted me. Neither did cessation of existence because, well, I was aware of none of these things greeting me. Instead, I was only vaguely conscious of going down some sort of ladder, tunnel, and voices around me. If that was the afterlife, it was distinctly disappointing.

My religious beliefs are pretty basic and far removed from groups like the Church of Money, but I was pretty sure that if there was going to be existence post-mortem, it would have more than just empty darkness as far as the eye could see. Well, would see, as my eyes were closed. That was another sign I was alive but paralyzed. Sadly, my eyelids were strongly resisting opening.

Time kind of became difficult to process as I drifted in and out of consciousness. A good rule of thumb is that if you're out for more than fifteen minutes, you're not actually unconscious, you're in a coma and your chances of waking up are increasingly unlikely. I also had very little faith that my captors were going to pay for expensive medical treatment to get me back to 100%. Unfortunately, I was also pretty sure that whatever they were taking me to do probably wasn't going to be helpful either.

The fact I could sort of think, though, was a decent sign. It meant I was coming out of it or at least trying to. Alas, my thoughts felt inordinately slow. However long I had been out—and I was damn sure it was longer than fifteen minutes—it was not so much that I was able to push through it. I'd never thought I would miss Interface, the cybernetic voice in my head that made me think I was crazy, but I did.

Anything to get me and Kate out of this.

JAMMING BYPASSED.

What? I asked, blinking as I felt the words appear in my head.

I AM DEEPLY TOUCHED BY YOUR DESIRE FOR MY RETURN DESPITE THE FACT YOU'VE EQUATED ME WITH SCHZIOPHRENIA.

Wake me the hell up! I said, not interested in chitchatting with my second personality.

MORE LIKE I'M PART OF YOUR BRAIN THAT WORKS MUCH FASTER, Interface said. BUT I AM ATTEMPTING TO DO SO.

Attempt harder! I snapped.

YES, CLEARLY THAT WILL HELP MATTERS, Interface replied. I SHOULD POINT OUT THAT I AM ABLE TO HEAR THE DISCUSSION YOUR CAPTORS ARE HAVING.

I really don't care! I snapped again, feeling wide awake and just not able to move.

IT'S NOT LIKE YOU HAVE ANYTHING BETTER TO DO, Interface said.

Smart ass, I replied.

YES, Interface said. THEY ARE PLANNING ON KILLING KATE AND FRAMING YOU FOR MURDERING HER.

There's no way anyone will believe that, I thought back. *Honestly, I'd buy her murdering me much easier.*

WELL, YOU WILL HAVE COMMITTED SUICIDE AFTERWARD, Interface said. THERE IS MUCH CONFUSION SINCE THEY HAD NOT EXPECTED SO MANY OF THEIR SAFE HOUSES AND BUSINESSES TO BE RAIDED.

It was easy to think how Nigel, if Nigel was at fault, had planned this to go. He'd subverted Cherry and left a trail for me to follow. However, he probably hadn't expected I'd get Kate involved and she'd brought a lot more muscle than he assumed. Throw in the fact that Interface had hacked the system with Shinobu's help and the baddies were all implicated. Nigel might have been planning to burn all his associates, but it was always a bad idea to think your enemies were super geniuses in full control of their plans. It was as bad as assuming your enemies were idiots.

How much time do I have? I asked, suspecting I was not going to like the answer.

SECONDS, Interface replied. ASSUMING I CAN EVEN RESTART YOU BEFORE THEY FINISH STAGING THE SCENE.

I didn't like the implications of that. *I'll give it everything I've got.*

GOOD, Interface said. COMBAT MODE INITIATED. GO.

Adrenaline and probably a bunch of other chemicals I didn't recognize flooded my body as my eyes shot open. I was being handled by three large men in what looked to be a hotel room. It wasn't the Hearts on Fire—the decor was far more subdued—but I didn't pause to take in my surroundings. No, I was too busy focusing on killing people.

I struck out with a throat punch that crushed one of my captors' larynx before kicking him back, smashing my face into the nose of the man behind me, then jabbing both of my elbows back. Everything slowed down even as I attacked the individuals holding onto me with a vicious primal fury.

The three people holding me weren't the only ones in the room, though, and while I got a few surprise hits in, I found them going for their weapons. I couldn't count how many were present, so I went for the gun the man behind me was reaching for, an Apollo-14 pistol and ripped it free before shooting him in the face.

What precisely happened in the next few seconds isn't something that I can put into words because even with my enhanced reflexes and analysis during combat mode, everything happened too fast. The people in the room were themselves enhanced and I had to rely on simple gut instinct to stay alive.

Pistol aiming my way... shoot.

Guy coming at me with his fist... shoot.

Knee coming at me... shoot.

Two pistols aiming at me from separate directions... duck, roll, shoot, shoot.

My last action on gut instinct was raising my knee into the groin of one of my attackers, knocking him to the ground, and shooting him in the head. I ended up double-tapping two more guys bleeding on the ground, one of who grazed my leg with his pistol as a dying gesture. It wasn't my artificial leg either.

Dammit!

Grabbing my injured leg, I fell to one knee and looked around the hotel room. I was surrounded by six dead bodies and there were shouts coming from the rooms around me. Gunfire was a particularly distinctive noise and some of the bullets had gone through the walls, hopefully not hitting any bystanders. Back on Mars, Cheeto—my partner before Nigel—had been a real fuck up and ended up shooting some old lady's parrot while firing a warning shot. Importing the thing from Earth had apparently cost more than a high-end luxury car.

NO FURTHER ATTACKERS DETECTED, Interface said as I felt the world seemingly return to its normal speed and my body calm down to an extent. Unfortunately, that didn't help with the searing pain I was presently feeling.

I don't suppose you've got a massive pleasure boost you can send me, I thought back. *Because I could really use some endorphins now.*

I AM ATTEMPTING REPAIRS, Interface said. YOUR MOBILITY WILL BE LIMITED UNTIL I CAN FINISH, HOWEVER.

No shit, I said, trying to stand but unable to do so. Thankfully, I had a good view of the room and could take in the rest of my surroundings.

I immediately regretted it. I recognized the room was an Imperial Grand Dragon hotel that was basically the same across the entirety of Earth's solar system and for people rich enough to visit all sorts of exotic locations while experiencing nothing new during their stay. There was an open door to the room next door that our late killers had apparently rented as well. I'd stayed in a room like this when I'd been put up by parties unknown after being burned alive but before my assignment to Antarctica. I'd always assumed the government had done it before deciding I was better buried in the middle of nowhere than used as a state's witness or interred in a field to cover up matters.

The room was large with almost two stories of height for no good reason, eggshell blue walls, and a king-sized bed with an enormous infovision entertainment unit in front of it. The floor was covered in blue shag carpet as well as an excessive number of dead bodies from where I'd been temporarily possessed by the spirit of Action Dan. Even with the pain from where nanotech was forcing the bullet out of my leg and reconstituting dead tissue, I was lucky to have somehow pulled it off. No, lucky would have been maybe handling one or two guys. That had been a goddamn miracle.

Unfortunately, miracles were in short supply and the one handed out to me hadn't been shared with Kate. The reason I was describing the room and bodies on the ground before her was my brain was once more trying to figure out something that was so confusing that it wasn't logically registering. It was tragic, horrifying, and bizarre at once. Kate was lying on the bed, her arms spread out, with her throat slashed. She was still wearing her dress from the previous evening and there was no confusing her for anyone else. There was also blood spread all across the sheets.

White blood.

The blood of a bioroid.

The Kate I'd been with last night had been a machine.

Possibly the entire time I'd known this version. Had this Kate ever been the real one? Was the special agent of SHID a machine that had been sent my way to control the handling of the pandemic? Was the real Kate out there or had she died years ago? Was this what Nigel had meant and if so, was he responsible? I was about ready to blame him for everything wrong in my life like he was my own personal Lex Luthor but why would he tell me his own plot? He was possibly a goddamn supervillain, but not a stupid one.

They mention this during their conversation, Interface? I asked the machine in my brain.

WE WERE A BIT DISTRACTED, Interface replied. BUT IT MIGHT EXPLAIN WHY THEY HESITATED FOR A FEW SECONDS WHILE PREPARING TO FRAME YOU FOR HER MURDER AND YOUR SUICIDE. THEY HAD TO WONDER IF THEY'D GOTTEN THE RIGHT PERSON AND THAT GAVE YOU ENOUGH ADVANTAGE TO ELIMINATE THEM.

Great detective work, I replied. *Which I'm claiming credit for since you're always saying we're the same person.*

That was when I heard a voice from the front door of the hotel room. "Open up, it's the police."

Oh goddammit.

CHAPTER TWENTY-TWO

Escape

If someone ever suggests that the only people who ever run from the cops are the guilty then you have my permission to call them an idiot. There are very few things that can say a person is privileged more than a statement like that. Having grown up on the streets of the Los Angeles Refugee Zone, I can assure you I regularly ran from the cops whether I was guilty or not. I'd tell you about my friends who didn't, but I never saw quite a few of them again.

If this strikes you as a strange attitude from a police officer, corporate or not, then you've had your second valuable life lesson today. Everyone had someone to hide and while there were police who tried to put the work in—I'd like to think I was one of them—they would always be outnumbered by the ones for whom this was a job, and the easiest result was the best one.

The easiest result was one that even I had to admit was damning to presume: six dead bodies around a dead bioroid in the bed. AI didn't automatically have the full rights of citizens, first you had to pass the DICK test, but it certainly didn't look good. I also didn't know if these police were in on it given there's no way they'd been called about the gun play and were probably here to find the staged murder-suicide I'd been expected to have starred in. Which was a long way of saying there were better than even odds they were in on it.

I wasn't thinking about that, though, because my instincts were a lot faster than my conscious thought—Interface or not. I rushed to the door to the room, locked it and ran to the opening to the bedroom next

214

door, locking it behind me. None of which prevented the sound of the first door being broken down.

All my decisions in that moment felt justified by the next words I heard through the door sealed behind me. "Halt! Hands up! This is the Advanced Crime Unit!"

The AC police were Karma Corp's version of Cyberlife and pretty much the worst example of badges with guns you could find. They existed primarily to persecute the enemies of the company and abuse their authority in whatever way they could. They were not, however, *lazy* cops. No, they were methodical, efficient, and ruthless in their habits. They were the goddamn special forces of dirty cops and if I had any doubts about a certain person's involvement in all of this, it was gone, since Nigel Blackwood was the head of the AC police.

My leg was still sore as all get-out and dragging with each movement even as fear was keeping me going. Fear and excitement. The normal kind of adrenaline versus the kind pumped into to me by Interface. I tossed the gun in my hands that I hadn't even remembered I'd been carrying and removed my blood splattered dinner jacket before heading out the front door.

If it seemed audacious to try to just walk out of the next room over and hope no one noticed, you'd be correct, but I wasn't exactly swimming in options. I'd been shot in the leg and my biggest advantage right now was the fact that my black slacks would cover up the blood briefly. The hallway was full of terrified looking onlookers, only a few of whom were wearing masks. I don't know why that perturbed me since I wasn't either, but it was the little things that bothered you. The AC police were at the door to the neighboring apartment and making noise that indicated they'd found the bodies and were reacting. I limped toward the end of the hallway, doing my best to look innocent and fade into the crowd.

I don't suppose you have any way of giving me a boost right now, Interface, I said, hoping for some more *deux ex machina* to hit me.

I AM SADLY NOT A GOD EVEN IF I AM A MACHINE, Interface replied. AND NO, I AM USING ALL OF MY ABILITIES TO KEEP YOU FROM BEING IN AGONIZING PAIN AS I REPAIR YOUR LEG.

YOUR INJURY WAS A GOOD DEAL MORE SEVERE THAN YOU REALIZE.

I debated pointing out that, according to Interface, if he realized how bad the injury was and we were the same person that I did realize it but suspected he wouldn't appreciate the word games.

YOU ARE CORRECT, Interface said.

I'd mostly gotten used to the idea of Interface as a secondary personality existing in my brain and possessed of opinions and insights that were close to mine but distinct enough to qualify as a separate person's. Which, in simple terms, meant that the Community had created enhancements for its soldiers that were functionally equivalent to dissociative identity disorder.

DISSOCIATIVE IDENTITY DISORDER IS ABOUT ASSUMING A DIFFERENT IDENTITY. SCHIZOPHRENIA IS WHEN THE VOICES TALK BACK TO YOU.

See? This was what I was talking about. Who in the world had to deal with being corrected by themselves? I didn't care if he had access to all the infonet and could look up everything I thought. It wasn't right.

WHO ARE YOU TALKING TO? Interface asked, making the whole conversation even stranger as you'd think he'd know. What with us being the same person and all, simply part of my brain multitasking due to working so much faster than the rest of me.

I'M MAKING CONVERSATION, Interface said. IN HOPES OF DISTRACTING, YOU FROM THE FACT WE'RE PROBABLY GOING TO BE CAUGHT AND KILLED.

Ah, that. Well, it was going to happen sooner rather than later since I was at the very end of the hall now and about to reach the fire exit. We were probably fifty floors up, so I didn't really see much of a point in providing a fire escape up here since it would probably better to evacuate people from the roof than trying to get them down the flights of stairs on foot, but I wasn't an architect. I did know, however, the moment I opened the door someone would notice my attempt to get away when the AC police had started ordering everyone to stand still. Unfortunately, I was out of ideas to distract them while I made my escape.

To answer your question, I'm narrating, I replied, scanning the area for some way of providing myself a way out.

WHAT NOW? Interface asked, probably just faking ignorance to provide me a distraction while I let my unconscious work something out. Sadly, that didn't seem to benefit from Interface's faster-than-light computational power.

Narrating, like I'm a detective, I replied. *Which I am. It allows me to get my thoughts organized if I'm talking to an audience.*

UH HUH, Interface said, sarcastically. AND I'M THE SIGN YOU'RE CRAZY.

The distractions provided me with an idea. It was a stupid idea but the only thing worse than doing something stupid was doing nothing at all. Spotting a particularly bored and hyperactive looking five-year-old boy rocking back and forth on his heels—his presumed parents a few feet away gossiping—I decided to rely on the universally evil nature of small children.

"Hey, kid, I'll pay you five creds if you pull that fire alarm," I said.

The kid held out his hand and I annoyingly made the transfer. What sort of kid had a digital bank implant at that age? Nevertheless, he went over to the fire alarm on the wall as I managed to hobble to the fire exit. Already, I could hear the AC police demanding that everyone get into lines to have their identities checked.

The alarm went off as I slipped away during the confusion but suspected I hadn't gotten away as clean as possible. Rather than trying to go down the stairwell for, well, fifty flights of stairs, I made may upward. Reaching the rooftop door with my bad leg was something that I managed even as I heard the door opening below and that my distraction hadn't done much in the grand scheme of things.

"I should have killed Nigel months ago," I muttered to myself. "Why the hell couldn't I have been shot in my artificial leg?"

JUST YOUR LUCK, Interface replied. YOU FELT A DESIRE TO REPAY HIM FOR SAVING YOUR LIFE BY GIVING YOU THE POSTHUMAN ENHANCEMENTS THAT CREATED ME. EVEN THOUGH HE WAS THE ONE WHO MADE THEM NECESSARY IN THE FIRST PLACE.

I still remembered the hours of surgery, the medically induced comas, and injections I'd received that had managed to not only save my life but make me someone capable of things I couldn't have previously imagined. But there was something nagging me that was only now coming to the forefront of my mind, though.

Nigel said he was the one who gave me my enhancements and saved my life, I thought, *But do we have any proof that he was the one who did it?*

Interface didn't respond. But that was another angle to explore, that I'd been not only played but played so hard that I didn't even know who the actual players were.

"Get down here or we will open fire!" a police officer shouted from a few floors below. That was right before he fired a warning shot that I have no doubt would have been in my back if he'd had a bead on me.

With nowhere else to go, I pushed my way onto the roof and collapsed on the ground. The artificial sunlight of Luna City's dome illuminated the surrounding skyscrapers and I saw an endless vista of urban development around me. The skies were mostly devoid of cars due to the quarantine, creating an eerie quiet save for the mechanical blowing of the atmosphere generators around me. There was a single flying car on top of the roof, armored like a tank and covered in optical camouflage equipment. It was almost as distracting as the person who was standing in front of it, carrying a pair of thermal katana.

Lady Zero.

"What in the—" I started to speak, staring at the very much alive vigilante dressed in her form-hugging body suit.

"Stay out of my way, Neal," she said, her voice identical to Kate's.

That was when the AC police squad burst through the door behind me, four or five cops in suits carrying Herakles-7 pistols like I favored, and clearly intending to gun me down where I stood. Instead, they were immediately set upon by Lady Zero. There was the sound of shouts, cries, and pain as they didn't have a chance to react before limbs started flying. After a few seconds, it was over and there was a bunch of dead cops on the ground. It was like seeing an actual lightsaber at work and it wasn't pretty.

Thinking that the body count for tonight was now eleven or twelve, I felt strangely giddy as I shook my head and muttered, "I am so screwed. Once you write up three or four police reports with bodies in the dozens, it starts to look like a pattern."

Lady Zero looked over at me. "Are you able to move?"

I looked at her. "I got shot in the leg. I can't—"

THE INJURY IS HEALED, Interface said.

Really? I asked Interface. *Just as I don't need it?*

I'M AWARE OF THE IRONY, Interface replied. YOU'RE WELCOME.

I climbed to my feet, wobbling. My artificial leg wasn't something I normally noticed but I felt good about having it right now. I'd run up the stairs using it heavily as I had favored my wounded leg, and didn't even feel remotely tired from the exertion. My other leg might be "repaired" but it still felt somewhat sore and weak. If I wasn't in the presence of a mass murderer who was clearly not the dead woman in the hotel bed—both looking eerily like my ex-wife—I would have spared more thought to my condition.

"Yeah, I can move," I replied. "Are you the real Kate?"

It was a pretty ridiculous question, what with her wearing a mask and all, but I figured I might as well try my luck. She wasn't killing me right now and she'd had two opportunities to do so, so I counted that as good fortune.

"It depends on how you define real," Lady Zero replied.

"So that's a no," I replied.

Lady Zero stared at me with an expression that told me she was reconsidering the not killing me part. "The Kate downstairs is dead, correct?"

"Yeah," I said. "I'm sorry."

"I don't blame you, Neal," Lady Zero said, pulling one of the corpses from inside the doorway to the hotel below and closing it. "Both of us knew this mission had the potential of ending our lives. Almost all of them do. Come on. These weren't the only members of the AC police special investigations unit, and the remainder will be coming here soon."

"Am I on the lamb?" I asked.

"Please stop talking like a Chandler novel," Lady Zero said. "But to answer your question, if we don't resolve this in the next hour or so then you will probably be an interstellar fugitive and there won't be anything Armstrong or my employers can do about it."

"I prefer Hammett over Chandler," I replied. "Phillip Marlowe was always too much of a goodie-goodie. Sam Spade was more my speed."

The irony was that I'd only read all those classic detective novels because Nigel had forced me.

"Take these," Lady Zero said, picking up two of the Herakles-7 pistols on the ground and staring at them for a second. Their biometric locks, the things that kept anyone else from using them, reset with a click and she tossed them both at me. I caught them by their grips and put the safeties on before sliding them into my pants pockets. Not exactly perfect for holsters but at least my tux had suspenders to keep my pants up tonight.

"By resolving this, you mean—" I started to ask.

"Catching the ringleaders of this plot," Lady Zero said. "Either they will hang for this, or you will."

"Great," I muttered. "Who are you working for? Division Four or something bigger?"

"You ask a lot of questions," Lady Zero said, heading to her car.

I went to the door to the rooftop and wedged one of the late police officers' guns in the handle before jogging back behind her to climb inside the vehicle. The interior was like a spaceship with controls and computer screens that I barely recognized the function of. The seats were extra high and with automatic straps that wrapped around me like a vice. There was a human shaped bundle in the back and I wondered if it was a body before I noticed it was moving around.

"I'm noticeably not asking the most important ones," I replied. "Starting with who you are."

"And why is that?" Lady Zero asked, starting the vehicle up. Seconds later, we were airborne and heading away from the rooftop and any possibility of being apprehended by the AC Police. Especially when the vehicle vanished around us. The optical camouflage wasn't visible (or invisible) from inside, but I could see the controls before us listing that it was active.

"Because I already know," I replied. "Kate, the other Kate, gave me a rundown that more or less explained who she was. I was just too bad of a detective to put it all together."

"You're a very good detective," Lady Zero said, surprising me. "You're just dealing with some very unusual circumstances."

"Yeah, well, you're an Upload," I replied. "Her too. The real Kate, or let's just say, original Kate was caught and turned into a bunch of AI copies."

Lady Zero paused. "Close enough. I remember just about everything about our time together, Neal, right up until I was captured. The same for all of my other sisters."

"How many of those exist?" I asked, not sure I wanted to know.

"A few dozen," Lady Zero replied. "There're a few less these days as we've devoted ourselves to trying to take down the Slavers Guild and their Karma Corp masters. Not exactly a mission profile with a high life expectancy. It's a petty form of revenge, but Division Zero has found us highly motivated, especially since we owe them for finding us before we were sold to be operating systems at some crime lord's slave factory."

I took a deep breath. "What happened to the original?"

I suspected the answer before she gave it. "She never woke up. I can tell you where her ashes were scattered but we've been using her identity collectively among others for some time. It certainly gives us plausible deniability."

"I see," I said, pausing. I mourned both Kates in that moment. The human brain was not built for AI, bioroids, cloning, and other shenanigans so I knew my ex-wife was dead. So was the woman I'd gotten to know as Special Agent Roebuck. "I don't suppose you have any idea how we're going to take down the remainder of the Sons of Mithras."

"I do, in fact, have a few ideas," Lady Zero said. "But think bigger than the Sons of Mithras. They were all rounded up along with their co-conspirators last night thanks to Shinobu's hack of the Hearts on Fire. Its owner really screwed up by connecting the network of his brothel to the other posthumans. Think bigger than the Church of Money, which is just a front for the Watchers."

This just kept getting bigger and bigger all the time. "The fucking space humans are involved in this now?"

"All humans live in space," Lady Zero pointed out, annoyed. "We live in space."

"The Moon isn't in space!" I snapped, having just enough left for one last zinger. "But let me guess, this has all been spy bullshit from the beginning."

"I'm afraid so. The Church of Money is a front for Albion's intelligence agency called the Watchers. These Watchers set up Reverend Cash's family to give them a way to influence Sol system politics but also move people back and forth using missionary visas. Probably to also launder money. I'm guessing they were involved from the very beginning. Perhaps with the original Reverend Cash and his wife being Albionese lying about their origins. Sleeper agents who recruited their own children."

I decided to throw in my thoughts. "Except the Community putting fifty of the planets set aside for Albion to Earth's development pissed them off, so they decided to smuggle a bunch of Sons of Mithras terrorists here. The plan was probably to come swooping in with relief but only after crippling the Moon and the extra-solar colonization efforts that are based from here. But this gets fucked up because the Hearts on Fire people dropped too many clues that Albion and the Church of Money were involved. This disrupted a bunch of other plans like Karma Corp being sold. Which is why you're moving in."

"Oh?" Lady Zero asked, looking in.

I was taking a wild swing here, but I figured it was probably close to the mark. "EarthGov *wanted* the Community involved in all of this. They may have not expected a fucking plague to break out, but they wanted to catch Albion with their hand in the cookie jar as leverage. It's the same with the Slavers Guild. It's all about catching them violating interstellar law to pressure the more technologically advanced government in the Community to make concessions for us at the Big Kids' table. That's where you and the Other Kate came in. You were to eliminate all the Slavers Guild people and shut this down before the plague with Project: Jenner being an exchange of Karma

Corp for Albion updating our technology by, say, two hundred or more years. How close am I?"

"Close," Lady Zero said.

"Which means you and Nigel have been working together on this the entire time," I said, putting the final piece of the puzzle together. "He's the mastermind behind all this."

"No," Lady Zero said. "Pray you ever don't meet the actual mastermind behind all of this."

"And where does that leave me?" I asked.

"Consider Nigel burnt," Lady Zero said. "You can take him down once you help me wrap up Albion's operation. We need one of the Church of Money higher ups or Mr. Smiles alive, though. They're the only people who can tie all this to the Albionese government."

"So, you're offering Nigel to me if I help you blackmail a bunch of Albionese politicians over a million dead lunes," I said. "All so Earth can some new toys and humanitarian aid."

It was monstrous. Every bit as vile as the Slavers Guild.

"Yes," Lady Zero said.

"Deal," I said, making a choice in that moment.

You had to choose your battles if you wanted to win even a single round in this greatest big boxing match called life.

"Good," Lady Zero said.

"Hi!" Cherry Pie said, popping her head from behind the seats of the vehicle.

"Jesus!" I said, practically jumping out of my seat. Well, I would have if I wasn't strapped in like I was on a roller coaster.

"I'm not mind controlled! Well, not anymore at least," Cherry Pie said, answering the question I hadn't been asking. "Also, I was lying in the back because I wasn't sure if you were going to shoot me or not."

"I picked up Cherry during the round-up at the Hearts on Fire. I inserted a jammer chip into the back of her neck," Lady Zero said, explaining something I hadn't been wondering about as well. "It prevents the signal for Hollowed reaching her and forcing her to obey the commands of her Willful controller. Unfortunately, it also prevents her from accessing any posthuman abilities. She can still be used to try to track down Mr. Smiles, though."

"Yeah, no more super hooker," Cherry Pie said. "Which is fine as I was only one for about a week. Seriously, when someone offers you immunity to disease and lack of aging, you should probably be suspicious, but you expect a little body modification in my profession. Plus, the money offered—"

"Cherry," Lady Zero said, interrupting. "Stay focused."

"I'm just trying to apologize," Cherry Pie responded. "Listen, if you want a freebie, I'm fine with it. Blowjob, hands, or even a discount on the full deal. Is your friend alright?"

"She's dead," I said, dryly.

"Oh damn," Cherry Pie said. "That's an all-nighter there."

I'd laugh if the whole thing wasn't so horrifying. "So why is Mr. Smiles so important? Why is a pimp dealing in Puppets so damn important?"

"Because he's got all of the proof we need."

CHAPTER TWENTY-THREE

No One Lives Forever

"So, it all rests on one pimp," I said, pausing. "Operating under a fake name."

I'd met Peter Pans, Freddy Mercurys, Mars Land Rovers, and other strange Moon names, but somehow Mr. Smiles struck me as a kind of obvious alias. Maybe I was just drawing an arbitrary line in the sand to pretend that the world made sense.

"Yes," Lady Zero said. "That is why I have brought Ms. Al-Fariq."

"I don't go by that name anymore," Cherry Pie said, pausing. There was a kind of deep discomfort in her tone that gave me more insight into her character than all the flirting and playful banter. Case in point, she'd chosen Cherry Pie as not just a name for her job as a hooker but apparently a way to fully divorce herself from who she was.

"Whatever the case," Lady Zero said. "He's the guy whose idiocy busted up the Sons of Mithras last night. One of the benefits of posthuman intelligence is you can spread the nanites via a blood transfusion and exert control over the resultant person. It was something he did to his prostitutes in hopes of making a better type of Puppet."

"Yeah, yeah," I said, knowing the basics. The Knights had done the same to Lucy but had been trying to make her immortal. I'd thought Nigel had done the same to me but instead I'd gotten the full posthuman package. "That linked his Puppets together with the rest of the Sons of Mithras and allowed Shinobu to find them all. At least, that's what I heard before Kate, and I went offline."

Lady Zero paused, clearly contemplating the fact someone who was closer than a sister was now dead. "Yes, you've been out a for a number of hours and events have shifted dramatically. Most of the Sons of Mithras have already been captured. The survivors are fleeing to their bolt holes and patrons. Which means that this will be our last chance to get anyone of importance before they disappear forever."

I wasn't sure I believed that, but I was willing to go with it for the time being. "One thing still puzzles me, though."

"One thing?" Cherry Pie asked.

She had me there. I was puzzled by a lot of things, like why Lady Zero dressed like a fourteen-year-old's favorite comic book heroine and why the government had decided to recruit me, of all people, but I figured there were some things that were never going to be answered. No, this question was a little more pragmatic and might give me insight into where our quarry would head next.

"Which is?" Lady Zero asked.

"I get this whole spy versus spy BS for the most part," I replied. "EarthGov doing this and the Watchers doing that. However, why the hell did they bust open the Sons of Mithras last night by letting us, Kate and I, find them all out at the Hearts on Fire? Are they just cleaning up house now?"

"Oh, that was an accident," Lady Zero explained. "In addition to your ability to survive that rivals the noble cockroach, I don't think anyone expected you to think to tap their Posthuman Network. So, congratulations, you really did break the case."

I paused. "So, the guy just linked all of his Puppets together to, what, make a better harlot?"

"Kinda yeah," Lady Zero said, shrugging. "Mr. Smiles is a local asset who has been investing his payoffs into brothels and smuggled vaccines to take advantage of the epidemic. People will pay far more for a Puppet than they will a regular prostitute. Just because he's part of a cult of religious fanatics doesn't mean he can't make a little scratch on the side."

"So, in the end, it was all about the money," I muttered.

"It usually is," Cherry Pie said in the back, speaking for all of us.

"We just need to locate him by facial recognition," Lady Zero said. "Cherry's enhanced brain will contain a complete record of Mr. Smiles biometrics and we can get Armstrong to scan the entirety of the Moon's cameras once I get her to Shinobu. It'll have to be a person-to-person transfer. I don't trust the networks right now. Two of the Puppets tried to commit suicide before we got them all subdued. Apparently, someone figured out they were the leak and tried to eliminate the evidence."

Cherry Pie looked uncomfortable at that.

I didn't blame her.

"I feel like I've missed a lot by getting knocked out," I replied. "So, we're going to meet with Shinobu?"

"Yes," Lady Zero said. "Plus, some other people I feel we can trust."

The stealth car started descending from the sky and I was surprised to find we were landing on the rooftop of the Cyberlife building. It had been so long since I'd seen the tall, black-windowed building that I'd almost forgotten what the place looked like. Still, the enormous, stylized C on the side was unforgettable. I wasn't the sentimental sort, regardless of what you might think, but I was surprised how seeing the place affected me.

I missed it.

The landing pad and communications equipment on the rooftop weren't the only things there, though. Looking out the side window—or more precisely into the integrated camera system that gave us a look at what surrounded us while projecting an artificial field of what was behind us creating the illusion of "invisibility"—I saw the Red Dragon parked alongside a small crowd of familiar faces: Shinobu, Barksley, Lucy, and that goddamn Aurelius idiot.

"This is what qualifies as trustworthy?" I asked, referring specifically to the latter.

"When cultivating assets as a spy, you always look for trustworthy, competent, and controllable," Lady Zero said, pausing. "Then you pick two because no one embodies all three."

I'd have argued with the latter, but I was pretty sure she was right. "You know that even if we get everyone today, the plague is still out there."

"Yes," Lady Zero said.

Nothing more was said and, honestly, nothing more needed to be said. There was a passage in the Bible about God giving you know what you could affect versus the things you couldn't. Unfortunately, it routinely felt like that was always the latter these days versus the former. Either way, I didn't know if it would matter in the long run to nail these remaining bastards, but if I could get Nigel in the process then if it still wasn't worth it, it would at least be close.

God, I'd been such a fool.

The stealth car settled down on the rooftop and made a whirling noise as it powered down. The group waiting for us must have been informed ahead of time that we'd be there because they didn't particularly react to the transparent car settling down beside them. The doors unlocked and my restraints pulled back, giving me the chance to get out of here.

As the door raised into the air, I looked at Lady Zero. "Before we go, do you really remember—"

"You want to know why I left you?" Lady Zero asked. "Why the original one did at least?"

I stared at her then shook my head. "No, not really."

Lady Zero nodded. "The answer doesn't matter anyway. We're all different people these days."

"Or peoples," I muttered.

That was when I noticed Cherry Pie looking at us both.

"What?" I asked.

Cherry Pie blinked. "Sorry, it's just your story is *really* interesting. Like an infonovella. You were married to the person they were cloned from but have recently lost one of them! Yet, you were also in love with the lady cop who was best friends with the woman you slept with who loves her! Like the waves against the beach, so are the days of our nights!"

I blinked and got out of the car. I could have asked how she knew all that but decided I didn't care. Turning to the crowd waiting for me outside, I said, "It's alright, everyone. I'm here to save the day!"

It was meant to be ironic. I didn't know if I had a non-sarcastic side—what other people would call sincere—but the reaction from everyone was strangely very different from what I expected. Instead of reacting to my stupid statement with annoyance or their own sardonic replies, Lucy and Shinobu both ran up and hugged me. Barksley also trotted up and pressed his head against my leg. They were genuinely glad to see me. What a strange feeling.

"Can I have a hug?" Aurelius asked.

"No!" I snapped, staring at him. "What are you even doing here?"

"I'm kind of under penalty of death," Aurelius said, grimacing and tapping his fingers together. "It seems I was not supposed to tell as much as I did. I was supposed to be caught, it seemed, but not fully cooperate. Which seems like something they should have told me in training."

"Uh huh," I said, staring at him. "How did you get this job again?"

"Well—"

"Yeah, nepotism, I remember," I muttered shaking my head.

That was when Lady Zero stepped out of the stealth car on the other side.

"Huh," Shinobu said, pulling away. "You're right, she does look like a stripper ninja."

Lucy glared at her sister.

"What?" Shinobu said. "You also said there was a ninety percent chance we'd find Neal alive and in bed with a woman or two."

"Hi!" Cherry Pie waved from the car.

"So, you were half right," Barksley said.

I pulled away from the circle of love, annoyed. "I can feel the love on display here. Listen guys, we've got one last chance to actually bring an end to this disaster."

"A horde of medical supplies dropped from heaven?" Barksley asked.

"Jesus came back?" Shinobu asked. "Ooo, is he going to smite the megacorporations? Please tell me he's going to smite the megacorprations! Is Buddha helping?"

I turned to Aurelius. "Is this what I sound like? Am I this much of a snarky asshole?"

Aurelius blinked. "Well, I don't know you very well, but yes."

I sighed. "I mean the terrorism. Probably."

At this point, I wasn't sure if it was possible to wrap up all the dirty business on the Moon. I'd settle for as much as possible, though.

Lady Zero cleared her throat. "I assembled you all here because I have need of your particular brand of abilities. Also, because I didn't want to leave Aurelius alone with the rest of my doppelganger's team because they'll probably kill him."

"Your doppelganger?" Shinobu asked.

"It's a long story," I replied. "Sadly, it's one that just leaves me pissed off. Shinobu, can you ask Armstrong to track down someone for us?"

"I'm afraid that's illegal," Shinobu said, turning to me. "Virtually every part of the Moon is covered in cameras and recording devices except for the Deep. However, all of those are inaccessible by hardwired encoding into Armstrong and Deep Thought's primarily programming cores. To access all that data would require a court order from—"

"I'm transferring it now," Lady Zero said, staring forward. "It's part of the state of emergency bill that was voted for and approved by Parliament."

I did a double take. "When was this signed?"

"This morning," Lady Zero replied. "It was submitted months ago but the wheels of bureaucracy turn slowly."

"If at all," I muttered, wondering how much trouble might have been saved if it had happened months before. Then again, we hadn't known who to look for before.

"Would you transfer your memory of the man in question, Cherry?" Lady Zero asked, turning to her.

Cherry Pie walked up to Shinobu and pulled out a wire transfer cord which was practically archaic as a means of moving information from one person to another. Still, they both slotted into the ports in the back of their neck and presumably gave Shinobu everything she needed to find her quarry. There were no sudden last-minute twists like Shinobu being infected with a computer virus or snipers killing our only witness. My life tended to run on dramatic movie logic, but I supposed my ex-wife being cloned into bioroids as my former best friend plotted against me had filled my quota for the month.

"Oh good," Shinobu said, pausing. "Hey, Armstrong, would you be a dear and go look for this Mr. Smiles person!"

I turned to her. "Is it that easy?"

"Kind of?" Shinobu asked. "I am his avatar after all."

"YOU HAVE SUBMITTED A REQUEST TO THE GREAT AND POWERFUL ARMSTRONG!" Armstrong shouted through speakers on the roof. He had an old timey radio announcer's voice that just added to the surreal feeling he was our very own personal Wizard of Oz. "I AM OPENING MY VAST COSMIC SENSES TO SEARCH EACH AND EVERY INDIVIDUAL FACE ON THE MOON! BEHOLD MY GLORIOUS AND AMAZING OMNISCIENCE!"

"Laying it on a bit thick, isn't he?" I asked.

"He's been very bored since the civilian government decided to try to take over all of the jobs he was doing far more efficiently and with less corruption," Shinobu said. "Really, he's an argument for Plato's philosopher kings."

"Plato believed you should censor *The Iliad* because the gods were horny jerks," I said, dryly. "He also believed in a caste system where the workers, soldiers, and philosophers would all be kept separate."

Everyone looked at me strangely.

"What?" I asked. "I read."

"I HAVE DEDUCED THE LOCATION OF MR. SMILES AND HIS REMAINING COHORTS," Armstrong spoke through the speaker system. "YOU MAY BOW BEFORE MY GLORIOUS GENIUS! BOW AND ACKNOWLEDGE THE DIVINE BENEVOLENCE—"

"Thanks, Armstrong," I interrupted. "Where the hell is he?"

"THE LUNA CITY SPACE PORT," Armstrong replied. "THE CHURCH OF MONEY IS ATTEMPTING TO LEAVE FOR THE OUTER COLONIES USING SPECIALLY GRANTED VISAS AND

FORGED CREDENTIALS THAT INSIST THEY HAVE PASSED ALL
TESTING AND QUARANTINE MEASURES."

Dammit, they were making a run for it. If they somehow managed
to reach Albionese space—which was easy enough once, you reached
the end of EarthGov territory—then there would be no finding them.
There were no extradition treaties with the Community and EarthGov
was still trying to establish a permanent relationship with the much-
larger galactic power.

"We have to get there and stop them," I said, trying to hide my
panic.

"OR I COULD JUST STOP THEM FROM LEAVING," Armstrong
said. "I WILL SHUT DOWN THE AIRPORT AND STRIKE WILL
SWARM THE PLACE."

I paused. "Really?"

"YOU DON'T HAVE TO PLAY COWBOY ALL THE TIME,
NEAL," Armstrong replied.

"I'm not playing cowboy, I'm playing detective," I replied,
wondering if it would really be that easy.

"You *are* a detective," Lucy said.

"Sometimes," I replied.

"THE ORDERS ARE GIVEN," Armstrong said. "I SUGGEST YOU
GET DOWN THERE. IT WOULD BE BEST IF SHID HAD SOME
REPRESENTATION."

His confidence was infectious.

"I guess I better change," Lady Zero said.

Yeah, it turned out to be an enormous anti-climax. By the time we
arrived at the Luna City Space Port's private dome, the entire place had
been shut down and every STRIKE soldier on the Moon seemingly
marching around like they'd invaded Normandy. There were other
police and Lunar Military forces as well, mostly hanging out and
pretending they'd done something important. Some of them had masks
and a few were dressed like they were handling radiation in vacuum.

As I understood it, everyone trying to get away had been
apprehended but we didn't exactly know who had really been trying
to leave or how many. I could even hear Penny Cash's lawyers all
complaining about police harassment as I was escorted to a holding cell

to speak with the only person I wanted to. I'd had some time in the Red Dragon to figure out who was who and what was what.

Lady Zero, impersonating Kate, let me have five minutes with Mr. Smiles.

He was sitting behind a desk with his wrists cuffed to the table and I had a strange sense of *deja vu*. Mr. Smiles was handsome, Olympian-like really, and while the face was different, he still carried himself with an identical smug self-assurance. I wondered if Lucy had also figured out his identity and suspected she had but had nothing to say to the man. He was also in her past and anything between them meant nothing today.

I wish I was so good with my exes. "Hey, Steve."

Steve Rogers Hudson was Mr. Smiles. The guy who had been our mole, or one of them, but had just been a middleman. The guy who had been running messages and information between the Church of Money, SHID, Karma Corp, and the terrorists. I wondered how much it had cost him to sell his soul and whether his church had set the price.

Mr. Smiles smirked. "I knew I should have just disappeared. What tipped you off?"

"The missing head," I said, taking a seat across from him. "They're less common now since the Unification War but you can still transplant a brain into a full body prosthetic. I figured whoever was backing you was willing to shell out the ten or twenty million credits for a new body. Not really a good investment in hindsight."

Mr. Smiles chuckled. "Probably not. I wouldn't have paid it. Of course, you know who was responsible. He can afford it."

"You can say the name," I said, staring at him. "He may have played us both but that just means you don't owe him anything."

Mr. Smiles chuckled. "He's obsessed with you. You know that right? That's why he recruited me. You survived his trying to kill you and he's of the mind he can recruit you. Bring you around to his way of thinking. I'd say he loves you but it's more that band of brothers bullshit I used to believe in. Romance dies so much quicker than the honor of two men who fought together. Even when one tries to kill the other."

"Was faking your death really easier than a divorce?" I asked, half-joking. I didn't want to listen to his analysis of mine and Nigel's relationship. I was going to bust his ass and the only thing I wanted out of Steve was the information to do it.

"You don't know my husbands' lawyers," Mr. Smiles replied. "But you're going to find out what I've figured out, what everyone in our profession eventually figures out: that everything we do is meaningless. Fight the good fight, nail the bad guy, save the innocent, or avenge them. It's all just background noise for the universe."

"I'm sure your church was proud," I replied. "Must have made betraying your country a lot easier if God was behind it."

"You want to make a lot of money, start a religion," Mr. Smiles said. "L. Ron Hubbard. As for my country, it's a shithole. A crime ridden disaster that only exists because the Moon is a slightly easier place to launch the thousands of starships necessary to colonize space with. We've discovered life out in space and even transplanted colonies of humans. What are we doing with them? Fighting with them over land."

I didn't disagree with his premise, just his conclusions. If nothing we did mattered, then the only thing that mattered was what we did. My soul wasn't for sale. As stupid as you'd have to be to pay for it. "Testify against Nigel, Hudson. He's the missing piece in all of this. You could live very comfortably, free from all the awful consequences of your poor life decisions. I'm sure I could set you up."

"You have more friends than you know, Neal," Mr. Smiles said, pausing. "It's why I didn't have you killed."

"You tried to," I replied. "You failed. Repeatedly. Because you weren't nearly as smart or talented as you thought you were. You were just the bagman for Nigel and the Albionese he wants to sell Karma Corp too. You've served your purpose for him and are now just a loose end."

Mr. Smiles frowned before recovering. "But I don't think I'll be mentioning any names. Maybe you're right. Maybe we're all just loose ends. I think I'll trust in the billionaires rather than a failed corporate police detective that can't keep it in his pants."

I sighed and got up.

I knew what was going to happen and was proven right. Later, despite trying to get every possible protection for him, he was shot and killed trying to escape. His brain case was destroyed in the process with no chance of revival. This time we confirmed the brain matter just to be sure and there was no mistake it was him. How it had happened with all his cybernetics turned down to minimum and his body mostly made of steel with a thin veneer of grown flesh was anyone's guess.

Mostly because the answer was blindingly obvious.

EPILOGUE

In Times of War, the Law Falls Silent
(A Quote from *Star Trek: Deep Space Nine*)

N ot just the Sons of Mithras but all their financiers, contacts, and suppliers were rounded up in the aftermath of taking Penny Cash prisoner. I'll spare you what her interrogation was like because the woman was a pathological liar and had gone through a dozen stories even as she threw everyone under the bus that she could. I would have recommended tossing her in the deepest hole we could find, and did, but a bunch of very important people dressed like Kate had showed up to take her prisoner. Later, I found her once again doing the talk show circuit.

No one moved to arrest me for the death of Kate or all the AC police at the Grand Dragon Hotel. True to Lady Zero's word, I'd received protection and the case effectively ceased to exist. Lady Zero slipped into Kate's identity as special agent and the dead unit was reported as having all died of the Red fever. Nigel didn't show up to headquarters after that but, lacking evidence, he'd just continued his job at Karma Corp as CSO according to their website. If Penny Cash had been willing to roll on all her cohorts, she hadn't said a thing about him.

After that, Lucy and I had been frozen out from all future decisions and influence. We were left just chasing down vaccine smugglers and doing the paperwork that had piled up in the meantime. I was almost done with it all when the most defining event of the Moon's history since its founding just sort of... ended.

The Community relief fleet arrived after about three months more of the event known as the Outbreak. Yeah, I know, real fucking original. It took a while for us to settle on a name for it but now there are a bunch of infovision shows, movies, and documentaries coming out about it that had all settled on a coherent narrative: evil bad terrorists versus an incompetent government. Which, hey, close enough for government work.

The fleet consisted of about a thousand vessels that treated all existing patients of Red fever for free, vaccinated everyone who wanted one, and provided a bunch of upgrades to our medical equipment that would require the Community to replace if it ever broke down. There was plenty of resistance, vaccine denial, and xenophobic ranting but most of the people fell in line regardless of the Moon's reputation for being a bunch of freedom-obsessed crazy people.

Eight hundred thousand dead will do that to you.

Shinobu pointed out that getting it under a million deaths was fantastic and SHID had done a far better job than could have possibly been believed beforehand. The fact that unreported or misdiagnoses probably tripled those numbers only put a slight damper on her enthusiasm. The Moon was disease-free enough to end the quarantine, open the space ports, and get the economy back to normal.

And wasn't that what was *important* in the end?

I'm being sarcastic by the way. I know you probably get that but there were plenty of people who looked me square in the eye and told me the same thing without irony. Mostly because their view of the Outbreak had been that it had mostly killed old people, poor people, and the ones living in the Deep.

Assholes.

"I really don't know what the man took so personally," Aurelius said, lying in the hospital bed with a bandage on his head. He was presently dressed in some kind of personalized hospital gown that was as bright green as his current hair color. I had no idea how he'd gotten it and wondered if the gift shop sold them at For Profit Hospital.

Lucy, Barksley, and I were visiting the Albionese spy since he didn't exactly have many friends on the planetoid anymore. Having been burned by his own agency, he'd mostly started serving as an informant for Department Four and ended up hanging around with us. The fact he'd been willing to help against Steve and company had allowed him to buy into our social circle. This despite the fact that we didn't much care for the guy and how annoyed he was whenever I pointed out telling everything about your country to foreigners was the definition of treason.

Still, he was an okay guy.

Just really dumb.

"The guy was a member of the Nationalist Moon Front," I replied. "You're Albionese."

"Oh, but he said he wasn't anti-foreigner, just pro-Moon people," Aurelius said.

"Uh huh," Lucy said, sighing. "It says you also were in bed with his wife when he found you."

"I invited him to join in, is that not how things are done on the Moon?" Aurelius asked, honestly confused.

"You're supposed to ask permission *before* sleeping with life partners," Lucy replied.

"Tsk, tsk, tsk. So many rules," Aurelius said. "So, I'm getting out in a couple of days, what fantastic new adventures will we have together!"

I stared at him. "What?"

"I have applied for sanctuary on your world," Aurelius said, pausing. "Mostly because the Albionese government wishes to execute me for espionage. I'd appeal to my father, but he claims I was brainwashed by a heathen Earth religion, so I've been disowned. I talked with your little robot girl, and she has decided to bring me aboard your police unit here. The Cyberlife department."

I blinked. "Little robot girl?"

"I think he means Shinobu," Lucy said.

"That's worth a kick in the nuts," I muttered. "But we're not with Cyberlife anymore."

"I wouldn't be so sure about that," a voice from the door said.

It was Kate.

Well, *a* Kate.

Lady Zero had casually shown up at SHID and claimed the murdered version of herself was just her bioroid duplicate. Which, while true, ignored the fact she was one herself. They probably could have scanned her to determine the truth. However, someone with enough pull made sure that never happened and she effectively just slid into Kate's life without incident. I could have blown the whistle but why would I? Neither of them was the "real" Kate.

Right now, Lady Zero—no, Kate, even if she was a "fake" one— was standing there in the same bland government suit her predecessor had worn. This Kate looked identical in most ways, but the trained eye could still see minor differences. This version of Kate was a lot more tense, like a panther forced to act like a house cat, and I could see she was privately seething at having to play the role of SHID headmistress.

By the way, I was doing my damnedest not to think about the fact the government was employing a bunch of bioroid duplicates of people in what was increasingly looking like an AI-driven conspiracy. Mostly because the AI-driven conspiracy looked and acted a lot more competent than the actual government. It was way too above my paygrade to try to deal with the goddamn robot Illuminati in addition to megacorps, criminal organizations, and crooked info-churches.

"Ah, hello," I said, uncomfortable for reasons of my being a sane person and not a lunatic who could ignore all the crap I'd found out about her.

"Hello, Ms. Roebuck!" Aurelius said. "I fear I must tender my resignation to SHID."

"You were never a member," Kate said, pausing. "However, we're going to honor your plea for political asylum."

"Splendid!" Aurelius said, ignoring just how deep a hole he'd dug himself. He really was the worst spy ever.

"I need to speak with you three, alone," Kate said, gesturing out the door.

"Do we have a choice?" Barksley asked.

"No," Kate said.

I nodded and walked out. The hallway of floor 55 of the For-Profit National Hospital was practically deserted as we were in a blue-tier patient zone where only the super-rich alongside other VIPs were permitted. Most of the nursing was done by bots and the only two organic staff were on the other side of the west wing. The window on the side of the hallway gave us a pretty good look at downtown Luna City with the Karma Corp building dominating the skyline.

Despite everything, Karma Corp had largely weathered the Outbreak intact with only several trillion in losses that they'd inevitably make up in next year's profits. That a huge number of their plans had been thwarted, they hadn't been the ones to cure the plague, and the Slavers Guild members had their numbers halved meant little in the grand scheme of things. Indeed, the digital ink was already drying on the contract between them and the Albion Commerce League. It was, to quote an old saying, "too big to fail."

"So, what's the sitch?" I asked, trying to keep a calm and steady tone while avoiding her gaze. I was just uncomfortable in her presence now. She remembers the time I'd spent with the original Kate, even had her personality, but she wasn't her. She wasn't even the one who'd recruited me into SHID.

"I thought I'd give you some information," Kate replied. "Things you deserve to know."

"Oh, really?" I asked, not believing for a second that we were going to get the truth about any of this. "Because I thought ignorance was bliss."

"I'd like to know what happened, actually," Lucy said. "Who, what, when, where, and how. I'm a masochist that way."

"I have a pretty good idea," Barksley said. "Albion bad, Church of Money and Sons of Mithras badder, and EarthGov let them both run wild to blackmail them but screwed it up in the long run."

"Close enough," Kate said. "Albion's parliament denies all involvement and their Watchers claim that any actions taken were by agents working a rogue operation."

"A million and a half dead Lunes is the result of agents doing a *rogue operation*?" Lucy asked, staring. Her eyes were filled with the fury of someone who was murderously angry but knew the people she wanted dead were probably untouchable.

"Yes," Kate explained, giving what I assumed was just the mutually accepted cover story. "The two senior agents involved hoped to get back one of the planets ceded to Earth for colonization as a way of impressing their bosses but they're both now floating in orbit without spacesuits, so we can safely say they're dealt with. Both expected fat promotions instead of executions."

"Aside from that, they got everything they wanted," I replied. "Charon is going off to a bunch of Albion puppets."

"Not quite," Kate replied. "The original population of Charon has been released from Karma Corp's custody and are disputing control over Karma Corp. Their lawsuit, I have assurances, will be swiftly moved through the courts, and deprive the Church of Money of what it treasures most: its wealth. I expect them to appeal but they'll more than likely be bankrupt in four to five years."

"That's not enough for what they did," Lucy said, her eyes cold and full of murder. If this got out, they'd have riots in the street and people stringing up every member of the church.

"I have a little more good news," Kate said, handing over her infopad. "A gift from Director G, Chief of Department One and co-owner of Atlas Security. He wanted me to deliver you this gift personally."

On the front, it showed a headline reporting a private space shuttle breaking up in the atmosphere. Onboard was the Reverend Cash Junior, Penny Cash, and a selection of their highest-ranking lieutenants. It was a lot harder response than I'd expected from the Reformer government.

"I feel bad for the stewardesses," I said, staring at the date. This was tomorrow's headline and the article described it happening right now.

Spy shit at its finest.

"They're called space attendants," Kate said, making a particularly dark joke. "Also, they were Church of Money members too."

"Oh, then that's different," I muttered.

"Are you being sarcastic?" Kate asked.

"I'm not sure," I muttered. "All I know is there's a lot of innocent blood being spilled for so-called justice."

"And if someone were to tell the truth?" Lucy asked, daring to voice what I was considering. "Blow the whistle on all of this?"

"Then you, your friends, and probably the people involved would all end up dead," Kate said, sounding like she was just describing the natural forces of the universe at work. "Nothing could protect Rashid or your little vigilante squad of anarchists either. Possibly not even your sister and dog."

"Not the dog!" Barksley said, appalled.

My sense of humor was severely impeded by then, though, and I couldn't keep my disgust out of my voice. "Not funny, Barks."

"My circuits are overloading with the banality of evil on display here," Barksley said.

Kate had the good grace to look ashamed. "Even if you did report the truth, nothing of consequence would happen. The truth would be discredited alongside you. A failed actress and a dirty cop with a history of violence. Just one more conspiracy theory to add to the pile. Even if believed, it would also disrupt interstellar relations as the only possible outcome. Right now, the Albion government is embarrassed and trying to make it go away with gifts, We need the medical aid, technology gifts, and outright cash money to continue colonization efforts. They also need to buy out Karma Corp if we're going to dismantle that organization's leadership."

"That's great," Lucy said, shaking her head. "Instead of a bunch of local tyrants, we'll have a bunch of tyrants a million light years away."

"The galaxy is only a hundred thousand light years long," Barksley pointed out,

Lucy glared at him.

"Sorry! I was designed to teach children!" Barksley said, covering his snout with his paws.

"The Albion government denies all official responsibility," Kate said, letting us both know what she thought of that.

Still, Lucy wasn't going to let it go. "Bullshit! Someone high up gave whoever they named as fall guys the okay or turned a blind eye to it or both. There's no way this kind of operation gets pulled off without the very highest people in charge knowing about it."

"And they would have gotten away with it if not for the fact that someone got greedy at a brothel and started to make a side hustle selling men and women as Puppets," Kate replied. "It wasn't spy work that ended up exposing this conspiracy and getting what little justice there is to be had here but ordinary police work. Which is what you should be doing instead of working for Department Four."

"Are you firing us?" I asked.

"Yes," Kate said, not softening the blow in the slightest. "However, you'll find your old jobs waiting for you back at Cyberlife as well as a Public Safety Medal of Valor for what each of you have done. Your newfound friends in the intelligence departments should protect you from any future issues with the civi government."

"Ah, so we're being bribed for our silence," I replied. "The carrot and the stick. So noted."

"Yes," Kate said, at least being honest there.

"I don't need your help or your medals," Lucy said, practically spitting.

"We'll take the jobs," I replied. "As for the medals, you can keep 'em as we'll just be putting them in our desk drawers anyway."

"I'm sure they can go with the others," Kate replied, ignoring my refusal of any commendations. We were going to be heroes for this whether we wanted to be or not.

"Don't speak for me, Neal," Lucy said.

Barksley looked unconvinced.

"Better to be on the inside than the out," I replied, simply. "Sorry we had to meet this way, Kate. Clone or not."

"I'm not a clone but I agree," Kate replied. "Neal—"

"Don't call on me again," I replied. "If you ever need someone else for your tinker, tailor, soldier, spy bullshit, send someone else."

Kate opened her mouth as if to say something then closed it, sighing. "Take care of yourselves. All of you. You may not believe it now but the work you've done saved millions and will guarantee peace and prosperity for Earth's citizens in the long run."

"Sure," I said, watching her walk off. "But not the Moon's today."

Kate walked off.

"I suddenly understand wanting to throw my badge as a shuriken," Lucy said, clenching her teeth. "Except, I would have thrown it at the back of her head."

"You did good," I replied. "Way better than I would have under the circumstances."

"Our circumstances were identical," Lucy said, looking at me. "You accepted her offer."

"Oh, then I'm just a habitual liar," I said, shrugging. "However, you were made to be a cop, Lucy."

"I don't know if I can go back to being a cop after seeing this nightmare," Lucy said, shaking her head. "We should—"

"Go to war with Albion? Which we'd lose?" I asked, getting the depressing reality there wasn't a damn thing we could do against a culture that was part of a vast interstellar empire. "Yeah, scooping up the little fish and leaving the whales alone is something that bothers me all to hell too. Sometimes, though, we get lucky and manage to kill one."

Lucy blinked. "That's a horrifying analogy."

"Okay, maybe it's not the best—"

"I love whales," Lucy said, seemingly distracted from her previous state. "They're some of nature's most beautiful creatures. Why the hell would you talk about killing them?"

I gave her a sideways look. "You're punking me."

"Absolutely," Lucy said, sighing. "But I do reserve the right to be pissed off."

"The best we can do is keep chipping away and hope we can do a little bit of good," I muttered, thinking of our next target. "The other option is quitting and joining Barksley's maple syrup cartel."

"Alas, my criminal empire is no more," Barksley said, sighing. "Governor Hopewood has ended the Food Prohibition Act on a dozen classifications of organic produce as well as decriminalized possession of consumable contraband. It's a last-ditch attempt to keep her job after her utter failure to help the populace during the epidemic."

I gasped in faux horror. "But how will civi cops arrest people if not for ambient cheese smell? If smuggling harmless produce isn't disproportionately punished, then how will we justify all our battalion of new tanks and the plan for SAM rocket launchers on every street corner? That budget isn't going spend itself!"

Lucy gave me a sideways glance. "You are both terrible cops."

"Yes," Barksley said.

"Just a pair of dishonest, honest ones," I replied. "Or maybe an honest dishonest one."

"Yeah, does anyone know where we can dispose of two metric tons of Canadian pure?" Barksley said. "I was planning on cutting it with synth corn syrup to double my profits, but Neal kept saying that it was terrible for the buyers. I'm like, Neal, they're junkies. They wouldn't know the good stuff if it was on pancakes or bacon."

"I don't know what we're going to do next," Lucy said, shaking her head.

"I can make a suggestion," I said, pausing before I shared my decision. "Nigel."

Lucy looked up to me. "Are you ready for that?"

I closed my eyes. "He's been lying to me from the beginning, and I never didn't want to take him down. Still, I was hoping there was something left of the person I knew."

"Is there?" Lucy asked.

"I don't think I ever knew him," I replied. "The question is whether we're able to take him down. He's only grown more powerful since we let him help us against the other Slavers Guild members. We also just alienated our only allies who might be able to match Karma Corp's Chief Security Officer."

"We have other friends," Lucy said, pausing, taking my hand into hers and giving it a squeeze. "Neal, there's something you should know."

I wanted to draw my hand away from hers, try to establish some professional space but couldn't.

"I really don't—" I started to say.

Lucy took a deep breath. "You know the reason I broke up with you. It's not that I don't..."

Oh great, this was going to be a conversation with actual feelings. I wasn't good with those. "Lucy, you don't—"

"I do love you, Neal," Lucy said. "Which is a really complicated and uncomfortable emotion for me to have right now."

Okay, wow.

"I love—" I started to say.

"Don't," Lucy interrupted. "Because you need to know something. The reason I broke up with you was because I realized I love you. It's related to Dick Grayson."

Now I was just confused. Was this one of those soap opera plots? She fell in love with me but couldn't because of her feelings for Dick? "I mean, I suspected but if you need more time—"

Lucy sighed. "That's not what I mean, Neal. What I mean to say is Dick isn't dead."

"What," I said.

"What," Barksley said, simultaneously.

"He faked his death," Lucy said. "He just reached out to me."

That was when I saw the top ten floors of the Karma Corp building explode outside the window. Someone had just launched a terrorist attack against the company.

Dammit.

AFTERWORD

"Down these mean streets a man must go who is not himself mean, who is neither tarnished nor afraid. He is the hero; he is everything. He must be a complete man and a common man and yet an unusual man. He must be, to use a rather weathered phrase, a man of honor—by instinct, by inevitability, without thought of it, and certainly without saying it. He must be the best man in his world and a good enough man for any world." - Raymond Chandler, *The Simple Art of Murder*

"Take a close look at the track record of this company. You'll see that we've gambled in markets usually regarded as nonprofit. Hospitals. Prisons. Space exploration. I say, good business is where you find it." - Dick Jones, *Robocop*

Hey folks,
    I hoped you enjoyed this installment of MOON COPS as it was a bit darker than the previous volume but something that I felt was an even better detective story. Well, detective, cyberpunk, spy, apocalyptic virus, and comedy all wrapped into one. It was influenced by real life events, of course, but also a larger theme that I hope you'll have noted in helplessness.

One of the elements shared by noir detective stories and cyberpunk fiction is the corrupt systems of power are larger than any of our heroes (or antiheroes). Our heroes may be people who might want to do right but they can't fundamentally change the world. The system is corrupt, the police are useless, and nice guys finish last.

The noir hero is someone who might be a good person themselves or they might be a bad person, but he is certainly not an *evil* person. He

247

or she sticks to their own code and attempts to live by it even if the rest of the world says he's a fool for doing so. I feel this is the same for cyberpunk heroes and particularly my protagonists in the FUTUREPUNK setting (Agent G, Cyber Dragons, Space Academy, and *Lucifer's Star*).

Neal doesn't think of himself as a good man but he's practically a saint in the corrupt post-capitalist hellscape of the Moon. Indeed, a genuinely good man probably would be eaten alive by the corruption and brutality of the place. He can't do anything against the megacorporations and is even compromised by them. However, there's lines he won't cross and maybe one or two people he can try to do right by.

For me, the Outbreak is the perfect metaphor for our protagonist's struggle. It is an impersonal, overwhelming, and devastating struggle that our heroes are largely helpless against. However, despite being an impersonal enemy of mankind, there's still plenty of people trying to use it for their own gain. People who will only make the situation worse.

If you've finished the story (and why would you be reading the Afterword if not), then you'll note that there was a lot of stuff going on behind the scenes that our hero just can't deal with. He never gets the full answers as to what's going on and can only come up with a decent approximation of what's going on.

A lot of the conspirators get off scot-free and only a few pay any sort of repercussions. That doesn't mean Neal doesn't try, though, and while he can't defeat the engines of profit that drive the devastation of the moon—well, he can certainly gum up the works.

Readers hoping for resolutions to the plots of Nigel Blackwood, Lucy's fiancé, and Neal's relationships, as well as who, exactly, upgraded Neal into a posthuman will just have to wait. It is my hope this will be a long-running series and a magician never reveals their tricks. These questions will have resolutions but not until the next book.

See you, moonatics!

LEXICON

Action Dan: A popular series of movies starring George Revlok (and his brother Ted briefly) that is currently on its eighth entry. Action Dan is a former special operations soldier turned cop who engages in large amounts of quip-filled violence while bedding a variety of beautiful women. They are poorly written, full of nonsensical twists, and extremely popular.

Advanced Crimes: The name of the Black Briar PMC corporate police division.

AI: Artificial intelligence. Humanity has achieved fully sapient beings that come in a variety of forms ranging from robots to biological constructs to living computer programs. It is a common fear that mankind has lost control over their creations.

Albion Commerce League: A megacorporation in the Community that was created by the off-world Albionese. Megacorps have far less power in the Community than on Earth but are still far richer than any run by Sol humans.

Antarctica: A now-settled population center on Earth that is still considered to be a barren frozen wasteland. Antarctica has a low crime rate and is primarily known as a port for incoming space goods due to the automated port created by the Galactic Community.

Ares Electronics: The world's largest megacorporation that produces most Earth's bots, computers, and starships. It is owned by Patricia "Trish" Ares and is heavily invested in working with the Galactic Community. It is the parent company of Atlas Security after a hostile takeover.

Atlas Security: Formerly the world's largest security company before being bought out by Ares Electronics. It is famous for its professional and technological focus. Most space colonies and orbital habitats contract with it for law enforcement as well as military protection.

Avatar: A human being who serves as a voice and conscience for Cognition AI to relay their will to their fellow humans. They are enhanced in intellect as well as longevity due to their bond.

Big Brother: The internet handle and anonymous news channel of Rashad al-Fariq. He has exposed numerous cases of corporate malfeasance, crooked government activity, and criminal activity with a network of fellow hackers. It has been shut down numerous times but always returns with more revelations.

Biofuel: Artificially created combustible fuel made from a variety of organic materials. It is far more efficient than oil but far less practical than electrical vehicles. Biofuel is one of the products of Karma Corp that was made with large numbers of flying cars being able to run only on it.

Bioroids: Biological constructs with artificial brains and material inside. Some of them are as sentient as humans.

Black Briar PMC: The official security company of Karma Corp and its counterpart to Atlas Security. Black Briar has gone through several rebrandings and even restoration of its old name due to continued scandals and incompetence. It has been sued several times and even brought up for war crimes tribunals due to its support of the Neo-Militarists.

Black Lotus: A genetically engineered plant that provides a mellow and relaxing experience to its users as well as removes physical and emotional pain. The drug's illegality is controversial, and many believe it is solely due to its medicinal properties threatening Karma Corp's pharmaceutical interests.

Bots: Automated machines that are different from bioroids because they have no biological parts.

Chromes: A nickname for cybernetically enhanced criminals.

The Church of Money: The United Prosperity Church that teaches financial success is a sign of righteousness and the former corporate-government-military alliance is the only divinely sanctioned government. The church uses infospace RealDream chair experiences to indoctrinate its followers. Founded by the self-styled Reverend Peter

Cash, his children have since taken it over. It has been resoundingly criticized by Reform Christian movements and atheists alike.

Civi Cop: The term for police officers working for the civilian governments of countries or planets. They are generally paid less and are more corrupt than the corporate versions, as counterintuitive as this may be.

Cognition AI: Unlimited growth AI that are the most powerful forces within Sol system. They are universally "quirky."

Colonial Council: A democratically elected council for Earth colonies. The Moon and Mars both have one of these. They are overseen by the colonial governor who is appointed by Earth.

Community: A pan-species government that has existed for more than ten thousand Earth years. It is generally benevolent and works for the promotion of all its citizens' welfare. The Community is utterly ruthless in the suppression of its enemies, however, and gives its military great latitude in unilaterally dealing with threats. Earth is believed to be working toward membership within the next fifty years. Also known as the Galactic Community.

Corpo Cop: The term for police officers working for the megacorporations or transtellars. They are generally better trained, equipped, and paid than their civilian counterparts.

Crater Town: The underground city below Luna City that is far vaster and more shoddily built. It is where the bulk of the population lives and is the size of a small country. It was primarily built for the Community by its alien engineers but was abandoned and then filled with human buildings of varying quality.

Credits: The official EarthGov currency that is an attempt to stabilize the fluctuating markets under the new government.

Cyberlife: The technology crimes division of the Atlas Security police department. They are handpicked by Armstrong from the best of the Sol system's detectives. They also tend to be among the most eccentric.

Cybernetics: Artificial body parts that replace lost or removed limbs and organs. Many function much better than the real thing.

Cyberpunks: A murderous gang of Moon transhuman petty criminals that recruits primarily from the people living in the Deep.

The Cyberpunks heavily modify their bodies with back-alley cybernetics and deliberately inhuman cyberware.

Dataslicer: A term for a high-end professional hacker.

The Deep: An abandoned project to expand the colonization of the Moon that would have created a community for the overflow of refugees from the Unification Wars. It is still inhabited but illegally and off the grid. Its residents are subject to violence and ruled by the local gangs.

Dummy AI: AI that only simulates free will and intelligence. They are the most common form of AI and have no rights.

Dusting: A infamous method of execution by the Moon's criminal syndicates. It involves forcing Moon dust down the victim's lungs and causing horrible injuries and death.

EarthGov: The post-Neo Militarist government created by the rise of a democratic republic.

Fair Cop: A four movie series (with television spin off) starring Ayanna Breeze. A young street urchin and part-time prostitute is recruited by a secret government organization to go undercover in a crooked corporate police unit. She ends up fighting terrorists, gangsters, and an ancient Egyptian cult while showing copious amounts of skin. The movies are considered trashy fun everywhere but France where they are considered arthouse films.

Fiddler's Green: One of Karma Corp's subsidiaries. It primarily runs prisons and labor camps that are slowly being phased out by the Reformist government.

First Contact: The day that the Community contacted Earth.

The Five: The five most powerful narcotics distributors on the Moon. They are also food barons and smugglers of other black-market goods. The Five exist hand-in-pocket with the corrupt government and megacorporations to keep the Moon functional. Three are Syndicate, one is Trikuza, and the fifth is independent.

Fleur De Lis: A formerly prominent gang that was completely absorbed by the Syndicate but is mostly used as cannon fodder.

Flying Car: A self-explanatory term for cars equipped with gravity manipulators.

Food Prohibition Act: The Food Prohibition Act is a law strictly enforced by STRIKE that prohibits food importation from Earth save through the megacorporations' monopoly. It is a ridiculous and destructive law designed purely to serve Karma Corp.

Fusion Weapons: Weapons that shoot balls of plasma. They are based on alien technology and immensely effective.

Golden Tigers: A Martian gang of Spanish-East Asian bikers. They have chapters on multiple human colonies.

Gravity Manipulators: Alien technology that allows the simulation of Earth-like gravity and essential for colonizing planets versus artificial habitats. It is tremendously useful for space travel and flying cars.

Gray Heaven Riot: A gruesome prison riot that lasted for a month and killed over three hundred people. It was a failed attempt to rescue a mob boss that got way out of hand.

The *Heart of Sorka*: A kilometer-long triangular Sorkanan *Shi'ruuk* cruiser used for patrolling the further reaches of Community space and beyond.

Hollowed: A posthuman who has had their free will stripped away. They can act entirely normal until activated.

Infocom: An infonet-based telecommunications network that can communicate in real time through jumpspace.

Infonet: The replacement for the internet that contains all of Sol's communications and knowledge. The Earth infonet is not yet hooked up to the greater Community's.

Infopad: The equivalent of personal handheld computers and cellphones. They are ubiquitous.

Jumpspace: The dimension used to travel faster than light through.

Karma Corp: Karma Corp is an agricultural, pharmaceutical, and biotechnical firm that also produces bioroid machines. It is based on the Moon and essential to the functioning of that planet. It is heavily involved in the Neo-Militarist government and is the parent company of Black Briar PMC.

Line Marriage: A legally recognized Moon institution of polygamy. Essentially, it is any marriage where both partners are able to marry other people with the consent of the other participants.

Lizards: A slang term for the Sorkanan.

Loop: A highly effective euphoric stimulant that comes in candy or pill form. Variations are known to cause hallucinations or violent behavior. Loop is believed to be a combat drug invented for the Unification Wars that has since spread to the civilian population. Addicts are frequently derided as Loopheads.

Luna City: The most prosperous lunar settlement that exists under an environmental dome. It is the home to most of the city's tourism, businesses, and has an artificial bay.

Lunar Rangers: An elite military unit of zero-gravity trained soldiers of the Moon.

Lunes: The formal term for Moon residents. *Loons* is an alternative spelling.

Mars: Earth's most populated colony with two billion residents. It is mostly terraformed but remains a dry, rocky, and desert-like environment despite attempts to change that. Many of its colonies remain underground despite the surface being habitable.

Megacorporations: The nearly all-powerful corporations that used to rule the world before First Contact. Most of them have combined to become the transtellars.

The Moon: A world colonized by the Community to start treating Earth's collapsed environment and massive inequities. It was eventually abandoned by the Community and recolonized by humanity before becoming its largest shipyard and space port.

Moonatics: The partly derogatory, partly flattering name for the original human settlers of the Moon.

Nationalist Moon Front: An extremist hate group that rejects any Moon citizens who don't fit an arbitrary set of criteria. They are heavily anti-immigration, anti-alien, anti-refugee, anti-Deep, and pro-Neo Militarist. The organization is largely considered to be a joke and more about posturing than a genuine threat. Its victims would disagree.

Neo-Militarists: A collection of militant anti-alien authoritarian parties that rose to power after First Contact. Collectively named the Neo-Militarists, they actually had large numbers of supporters embrace the moniker. The Neo-Militarists held power for almost ten years before being utterly disgraced at a failed economy, uplift of technology, rising crime rate, and numerous civil wars.

Optical Camouflage: A portable holographic projector that effectively renders a subject invisible.

The Outbreak: What the Red fever epidemic on the Moon is eventually referred to.

Posthuman: A group of nanotech-enhanced soldiers who were employed by the Community to help overthrow Earth's isolationist and xenophobic government. Posthumans can either be Hollowed or Willed.

Posthuman Network: A collection of shared consciousness between posthuman soldiers, often the Willed and their Hollowed creations.

Puppets: A loathsome practice where a human being's body is hijacked by programming to serve as prostitutes or voices for another individual. A more primitive version of the Hollowed.

Quantum Bomb: Antimatter bombs lacking any form of fallout and used sporadically during the Unification Wars.

Red Fever: A modified version of smallpox and the common cold that is roughly 50% lethal and was created by Albion scientists from their own diseases. It is very lethal to Sol residents but easily curable in the Community.

RealDream: A form of virtual reality used to replace video games. Your consciousness physically uploads to infospace where all manner of sensations can be experienced. It is also used as an interface by serious dataslicers. Most people use it for porn.

Red Dust: A red powder that has properties like cocaine but is chemically produced rather than grown and refined. Red Dust is often cut with Moon dust and can become genuinely dangerous to individuals who take it.

Reformers: Technically, the United Human Social Reform Party. It is a highly progressive, completely ineffectual, democratically elected government struggling to dismantle the apparatus of the Neo-Militarists. Many in the Sol system believe the Social Reformers are puppets of the Community.

Retros: A slang term for humans or AI who are obsessed with past pop culture and media.

SAW Troopers: Space Assault Warriors are special operations soldiers for the Atlas Corporation.

Shells: Full-body cyborgs that only have the brain and spine of their original subjects within their enhancements.

SHID: The Strategic Homeland Intelligence Department is Department Four of the revitalized EarthGov intelligence apparatus and primarily deals with coordinating responses to natural disasters and terrorist attacks.

Slavers Guild: A nickname for a conspiracy of Karma Corp, street criminals, and crooked police officers designed to sell human beings to alien criminals in exchange for technology.

Smart AI: Sentient AI and self-willed. They are granted the rights of citizens under the Social Reformers. All Cognition AI are Smart AI but not all Smart AI are Cognition AI.

Sorkanan: A race of bipedal lizard men that are the most powerful and populace race in the Community.

STRIKE: A government organization that exists for the purposes of monitoring colonial law, import/export, and anti-terrorism. STRIKE is considered to be an ineffectual and overmilitarized response to space exploration and the presence of aliens. It is often exploited by local government as personal militias.

Syndicate: An alliance of Earth's largest criminal syndicates that were recruited by the Neo-Fascist governments and megacorporations to distribute black market goods, intimidate reformists, as well as provide vice to soothe the masses' discontent. They are responsible for much of the Moon's troubles due to importing millions and trapping them in debt slavery.

Tranquility: A massive state-sized dome with estates for the super-rich, resorts, golf courses, and wildlife preserves. Tranquility is considered to be a waste of resources by most and a sign of the staggering corruption on the Moon.

Transhuman: A human who has been enhanced with cybernetics or gene therapy. It used to have an entire philosophy around it but is now so common (mostly to correct hereditary conditions or the vagaries of old age) that it is considered just an extension of medicine.

Transtellars: Extra-solar corporations that have extended their efforts to humanity's colonies and some alien worlds. It is believed that the transtellars have even made contact with other branches of humanity, as ridiculous as that sounds. EarthGov is unable to rein them in beyond the solar system.

Trikuza: The second largest criminal organization on the Moon after the Syndicate. The Trikuza are an alliance of three Yakuza gangs that spread from Japan to the United States and other countries after opening its membership to more ethnicities. It is considered somewhat kitsch and stereotypical but very loyal.

Upload: A scan of a human being's personality and memories uploaded into a machine. It requires a person's consent to clone them this way and each successive copying must be done from the original brain. These scans cause brain damage and ultimately death if done too many times.

Unification Wars: A series of wars fought after First Contact over whether to preserve autonomy or create a united world government. The Neo-Militarists briefly held power after winning the first conflict and attempted to create an isolationist state. They were then overthrown, and the Social Reformers were elected in their place.

Willed: The posthumans who are still possessed of their own free will.

Xenos: A slang term for aliens.

AUTHOR'S NOTE

I'd like to thank you for reading this book. The publishing industry has been changing dramatically since the advent of eBooks. It is now very difficult to get any book noticed, regardless of quality. If you enjoyed this book, you could do some very simple things to help me attract attention. Word of mouth is the number one source of success for novels, so simply telling family and friends about the book is a great start.

Here are a few other ways of helping out, if you are so inclined:

* Post a rating or review where you purchased the eBook
* Post a rating or review on Goodreads
* Talk about the book or write a review on Facebook
* Tell folks about the book in a blog post.

If you like any of my other books, please feel free to check them out. A lot of my series are interlinked, and you never know when you'll find someone familiar showing up. In this case, *Moon Cops* is set in the future of my Agent G cyberpunk books and the past of my *Space Academy* and *Lucifer's Star* series. Collectively, they make up my Futurepunk setting. Fans will certainly get a kick out of seeing how the galaxy changes in a few centuries either way.

ABOUT THE AUTHOR

C. T. Phipps is a lifelong student of horror, science fiction, and fantasy. An avid tabletop gamer, he discovered this passion led him to write and turned him into a lifelong geek. He is a regular blogger and also a reviewer for The Bookie Monster.

Bibliography

Novels

The Rules of Supervillainy (Supervillainy Saga #1)
The Games of Supervillainy (Supervillainy Saga #2)
The Secrets of Supervillainy (Supervillainy Saga #3)
The Kingdom of Supervillainy (Supervillainy Saga #4)
The Tournament of Supervillainy (Supervillainy Saga #5)
The Future of Supervillainy (Supervillainy Saga #6)
The Horror of Supervillainy (Supervillainy Saga #7)
Tales of Supervillainy: Cindy's Seven (Supervillainy Saga #8)
The Fall of Supervillainy (Supervillainy Saga #9)

I Was a Teenage Weredeer (The Bright Falls Mysteries, Book 1)

An American Weredeer in Michigan (The Bright Falls Mysteries, Book 2)
A Nightmare on Elk Street (The Bright Falls Mysteries, Book 3)

Esoterrorism (Red Room, Vol. 1)
Eldritch Ops (Red Room, Vol. 2)
The Fall of the House (Red Room, Vol. 3)

Agent G: Infiltrator (Agent G, Vol. 1)
Agent G: Saboteur (Agent G, Vol. 2)
Agent G: Assassin (Agent G, Vol. 3)

Cthulhu Armageddon (Cthulhu Armageddon, Vol. 1)
The Tower of Zhaal (Cthulhu Armageddon, Vol. 2)
The Tree of Azathoth (Cthulhu Armageddon, Vol. 3)

Lucifer's Star (Lucifer's Star, Vol. 1)
Lucifer's Nebula (Lucifer's Star, Vol. 2)

Straight Outta Fangton (Straight Outta Fangton, Vol. 1)
100 Miles and Vampin' (Straight Outta Fangton, Vol. 2)
Vampiraz4Life (Straight Outta Fangton, Vol. 3)

Wraith Knight (Wraith Knight, Vol. 1)
Wraith Lord (Wraith Knight, Vol. 2)
Wraith King (Wraith Knight, Vol. 3)

Dark Destiny (Dark Destiny, Vol. 1)
Destiny's Paradox (Dark Destiny, Vol. 2)

Brightblade (The Morgan Detective Agency, Book 1)

Daughter of the Cyber Dragons (The Cyber Dragons Series, Book 1)
Revenge of the Cyber Dragons (The Cyber Dragons Series, Book 2)
End of the Cyber Dragons (The Cyber Dragons Series, Book 3)

Space Academy Dropouts (The Space Academy Series, Book 1)
Space Academy Rejects (The Space Academy Series, Book 2)
Space Academy Washouts (The Space Academy Series, Book 3)

Moon Cops on the Moon (Moon Cops, Book 1)
Moon City Vice (Moon Cops, Book 2)

Psycho Killers in Love

Anthologies (as editor)
Blackest Knights
Blackest Spells
Tales of Capes and Cowls
Tales of the Al-Azif
Tales of Yog-Sothoth

Curious about other Crossroad Press books? Stop by our website:
http://crossroadpress.com
We offer quality writing
in digital, audio, and print formats.

Subscribe to our newsletter on the website homepage and receive a
free eBook.

www.ingramcontent.com/pod-product-compliance
Lightning Source LLC
Chambersburg PA
CBHW030243200626
46816CB00002BA/486